Undercurrents

≈ ≈ ≈

Undercurrents

a novel

Joan Maki

BAOBAB PRESS

First Edition

ISBN-13: 978-1-936097-52-4

Library of Congress Control Number: 2024942505
Baobab Press
316 California Ave, #24
Reno, Nevada 89509
www.baobabpress.com

For Dave, Tess, and Claire

≈ Part One ≈

1. Trees

Patrick pretended to smoke a cigarette. It was November, 1989. *We were ten years old.* The trees were motionless. *And time, momentarily, stopped. Frozen, suspended.* Patrick breathed out the cold like smoke, fingers poised, grinning. His red knit hat was pushed back on his head. And there was the shattering of late fall snow and the white hollowing of the sky, like an upturned bowl. The river glinted black through the trees. The trees stirred. *There was no smoke. There couldn't have been smoke. Why do I remember smoke?*

"Race you, Kitty," he said. He turned suddenly and ran ahead into the leaning cottonwoods. Kit ran after him. The earth crackled beneath their feet, as if it would break open. *And what would be inside? A roaring depth? Lava, rising out?* The sky through the trees was illumined. So bright it almost hurt to look at it. The branches were like graphite sketches. The cottonwoods formed a tunnel. *We found a path and where from?* Out of the depths then came a startling movement. Kit stopped. A bird or cottontail quickened out of the brush, shaking the undergrowth and then gone. And he was far ahead in the trees. A sliver of blue, cutting through the dark places. All sound ceased. The trees were angled above. Towering. Breaking through the sky. He splintered suddenly into the darkness between the cottonwoods. And the space around swallowed him. The knots on the cottonwoods blinked. *What I saw there.*

The sky burned white through the open spaces. *Absolute quiet and all I could hear was my own breath.* She stood on the empty path. *Where from? Had it always been?* The path was worn down although hardly anyone came down there. She did not recognize where she was. *Everything inverted. Topsy-turvy, upside down.* There were places where things get through, Marg used to say. Passages. *You've got to leave passages. Open windows, unlock doors.* Kit ran ahead, calling for him. The trees closed in around her. *I felt them there.* Darker and darker. *And you were gone somewhere and I didn't know where.* The light was wrong. Same as during a solar eclipse. The shadows flung in the opposite direction. Reversed.

Kit ran up the path where he had gone. The path led everywhere and nowhere. She stopped. She could not recollect where she was. *Every direction the same.* She walked slowly backwards, like Marg said to do. *Like on a tightrope.* Her hands out to her sides. The dark spots flickered like they were waking up. A silent, singular breeze passed her, moving the fallen leaves along with it. *An invisible runner.* Something pounded inside her. *The drumming of the earth, we heard it, didn't we? You and me?* The trees felt like they were closing in around her. She closed her eyes, lightly. She sensed them dart past. Vaguely they flitted from tree to tree and then moved along the ground. *Crossing over. Light to dark.* And they were gone. *They run from the light, Marg said.*

The sound came crashing back. The shaking cottonwoods, river, birds. Raucous, immediate. She was right near the river. *Roaring.* Around her the woods were ordinary. And it was growing dark.

Kit ran into the open field, the cold burning her skin. She thought she could hear his breath at first, but then it was her own. Everything was mixed up. She looked back. The trees leaned gray in the dark. *Their eyes and they were watching.* Something nameless and feral stumbled through the brush and loped away. *And here it was up beside me and I thought it was you and it seemed like you were there but it wasn't and their hands like chokecherry branches and you were gone.* The field was empty other than the rows of oats left still standing on the border, luminous in the darkening. They used to leave the grain on the edges of the field, she was told, for the gleaners. *Way back when.* Later she would recognize it in the painting of the women bowed over the fields. *The gleaners. Sometimes someone needs a little help. Nothing to be ashamed about, Marg told you.*

The Canada geese landed in the field. A cacophony. The honking drowned out everything. The porchlight across the field was hazy. It seemed to move, like a lantern carried. *The dead, carrying lanterns.* Kit ran across the frozen earth. So fast she nearly tripped. *The dead, looking for a place to settle down.* She felt them like they were following her. The blood pounded in her head. *Nothing is in plain sight. We don't know nothing, Marg said.* The canyon held the last vestiges of light. *The wilderness right there and we don't even think about it.*

She climbed the barbed wire fence and the wire snatched and the front porch seemed to waver and tilt. The front door opened. She did not remember opening it. She closed the door behind her. Her father sat in the lamplight, reading the farm magazine. A shining combine on the cover.

Nothing is in plain sight.

Hands like chokecherry branches.

The way they folded into shadow.

He lowered the magazine and studied her. His hands were ignited in the light, like they were on fire. *And I heard them scratching there and saw them slipping along the trees. Not for the first time.*

"What's the matter, Kitty?"

The blood pounded. *The river in my head.*

"I can't find him," she said. "We were in the trees and then everything was all wrong like it gets sometimes and he was way ahead and then he was gone." *And we had seen them crouched there and you had wanted to go with them.* "The light was all wrong and switched like afternoon light and the sun going down and the trees like they were bent funny and then it happened. The trees took him. The maahinen. Or he went." The pounding. *The roaring. The river in my head and then it never went away.* She kneaded her hands, aching with cold. Her hands would ache with the cold for the rest of her life. Turn pale and yellow and numb.

Her father stood and the magazine slid to the floor. *The gap between sleeping and awake was what it felt like. Always like that out there. Like being on the brink of something and you can't place it.* He asked her again what had happened, stooping down, and she could smell the wool and earth and tobacco and then he stood again and then went to the landline in the kitchen and called them. The kitchen light flickered. *And nothing would be the same ever again.* And the river in her head. *Like changing elevation.* She rubbed her hands and Paul appeared in the kitchen. He was still browned from the sun.

"Kitty?" Paul asked. "What's wrong?"

Everything shattered, then and there.

Say you were asked to go with them.

A sanctuary, you were told. Nothing could touch you there.

The lights went past that night. The following nights. Lit up fields, trees, logging roads. They dragged the river. A net; a rake. They brought dogs. A helicopter. The cars and pickups gathered along the road. Along the riverbank. They did not find one single thing. *Nothing.*

Those undercurrents. Could sweep you away for miles. Kids got to watch that water, they said.

And then there was Rob. Patrick's father. *With that rusted yellow beater pickup and his eyes like oil spots. You hated him.* They brought him in for questioning. They were only going checking all the boxes, they said. *And the way he looked at you.* He drove slowly alongside and rolled down the window and stopped the pickup. *And the pickup spitting dust and gravel and he called Patrick to come here and greet your old man and his face wolfish and gaunt like the wolf the pack kicked out. He had sharp cheekbones and looked years and years older than he was.* He said he would like to take Patrick fishing and said he had to ask when Carrie was not around because she had said things that weren't true and he wouldn't put anything past her or anyone else from around there.

And Rob flicked his cigarette and the ash burned momentarily on the ground and then went out. Right now, he told Patrick. They could go *right now*. Patrick could come along and they would be back before dinner and Carrie would not even know the difference. He had a pole, he said, jerking his head back a little, indicating somewhere behind him. "Your friend here can come along. She can sit in the middle." The gearshift shook beneath his hand. *Eyes like oil spots.* The pickup spit black smoke.

"I don't think so," Patrick said.

"What?" Rob asked. He leaned out of the window. "I can't hear you," he said. "Speak up. You've got to speak up."

Patrick rubbed his fingers into his palm.

"I don't think I should. I think I should go home."

He stared at Patrick. He seemed to be chewing on something. *Bone marrow, the fatty bits.*

"You afraid of me?"

"No."

"Why don't you come along then? Kids like to fish."

Patrick rubbed his hands.

"I don't think so," Patrick said. He walked away and Kit followed and that was when the pickup veered closer and she felt the heat of it and they jumped into the weeds alongside and Rob laughed and the pickup kicked up dirt and he said he would be back and to ask his mother if that made him feel okay about it. And Patrick stood in that cloud of dust and he seemed to be shaking unless it was only from the dust settling. *Maybe then you decided you wanted out.*

And that first night that Patrick disappeared, Marg's house was like a cave and the overhead kitchen light layered in dust and the floor rattling when you crossed it. "You stay here with Marg," her father said. *And he went to go look with them and Paul kept looking at me like there was something he wanted to say but there was nothing he could.* It was Marg who first got the idea into their heads. The stories her husband, the sawyer, had told her. The creatures underground. *The maahinen. People think they know so much but they don't know nothing, Marg said.* And then the way the trees had thickened around them. *Liminal space*, Kit would hear, years later. *Betwixt, between.* They were older than anything around here, Marg said. In the old country they came up with explanations, the sawyer said. For when you're alone in the woods and you feel like the ground is moving beneath you. And then everything is flipped upside down. *Too much to drink maybe. A problem with your health.* Although the sawyer had seen it happen frequently enough that he knew there was more to it. And you had to be respectful, considerate. They look after things, he said. But they did not want to be insulted. *Because they were here first.* They were not malevolent, but they could really cause problems if they wanted to. And sometimes people went missing, and sometimes children, and sometimes they wanted to go. And when they came back, they hardly recognized the place they knew. *And we knew they were there, but we didn't know how to say we knew.* Why doesn't anyone believe in anything? Patrick once asked. Why's it so hard? He would lean forward when Marg talked about them. *Everything is true, only we've forgotten. They don't get it. They don't see it.* The root you do not see. Like stumbling through the darkness and you know your way but don't know how you know your way. You just remember. *And they've always been here. Keeping things in order. No one to thank them. Reckon with that*, Kit thinks now. *Thousands of years and they've always been and always will be.*

The cuckoo clock whistled. The tiny woodcutter emerged, chopped, and receded.

"The maahinen took him," Kit told Marg. "Or he went with them."

"Don't tell them that," Marg said. "Don't be foolish."

And we ran into the trees you and me and there were the flat stones and we threw the mud and they watched from the trees. Animal eyes but not quite. More obscure. Thousands of years, Marg said. Maybe longer. They never bothered us. They became familiar, like a tree root or boulder.

After a few days passed and he was still missing, the authorities came. Paul stood upstairs in Kit's bedroom. The attic room where the cottonwoods tapped.

"They're here, Kitty," Paul said. "They want to talk to you. You've got to give them something or they'll never leave you alone. They'll want to get your head checked. Careful what you say." He pressed his long hands to his sides. *Our mother's hands.* "They want to know what you saw, Kitty. What you remember."

The path, suddenly unfamiliar. Like it was folding up around us. Kit felt the cold wall. Then followed Paul downstairs. They were at the kitchen table. A man and a woman. They were slouched, like scarecrows. And like scarecrows they were creased and haggard. *They had button eyes.* They wanted to know what she had seen. To the best of her ability. What she remembered. *The compass couldn't find north and it wouldn't stop moving.* Had she seen anyone else around? Was there anything in particular that stood out? Had Patrick said anything out of character? Perhaps he had mentioned his father? Had he mentioned his father? *I'm nothing like him, you said. I don't know why she ever.*

Patrick carved the bark boat and his hands were moving too quickly somehow and he cut himself and pulled back and the river swelled right there. And he went and dove in. *And Rob asked if you'd want to come to Anchorage and shoot a Kodiak. And his face like cement. And your hands kept shaking and you said to come on and we ran down to the river.*

Patrick was faster, she told them. Had always been faster. Got way ahead. She shook her head a little, like water in her ears. The river and I could never kick it. "He ran ahead and I couldn't catch up with him because I didn't know where he went and it was getting dark out and I knew I had to get home." *We were in the trees.* "Be quiet, Kitty," Paul said soon after. "Shut up about it. Or they'll be poking into your head. Shut up."

The man turned the pen in his straw-hand. They pushed their cups around and forced smiles and thanked her father for the coffee and hospitality and zipped their long winter coats. They looked like they were from somewhere else. Somewhere urban and industrious. The snow was coming down harder this time. "If she thinks of anything," the man told her father. "Don't hesitate to contact us. The smallest thing could be very helpful. There's just no telling." They shook her father's hand. The woman put her scarecrow's hand on Kit's shoulder, resting it momentarily. She winked at Kit and something rushed through the room and no one else noticed. Her father walked them out to their car. Through the old window they looked strange, misshapen. The blood thumped again. *Like the river in my head. And even now I can't think straight and so maybe I invented them. I hadn't slept for days.*

That evening Kit lay in bed, her entire body pressed against her bedroom wall until she could feel the cold coming through. *The snow we dug out. The ice caves.* Her father came in and covered her in the wool blanket. "I never should've let you kids run around down there," he said. "I'm so sorry, Kitty." What else could he say? He stood in the doorframe. Quiet. Then his footsteps retreated down the stairs. Weeks passed. Months. Years. They never found Patrick.

2. Gravity

The farm borders wilderness. Miles and miles *and who the hell knows what's out there really, Paul used to say.*

One day, nearly ten years after Patrick disappeared, Kit and Paul's father walked up along the rock fence the same way he always did only he did not come back. When they found him out there, he looked to be napping in the sun. And him, stone quiet in the early mornings and his large hands and hunched shoulders and he never knew what to do without their mother around, he said. He used to walk along the rock fence, smoking, head down, like some sort of contemplative. "All that smoking," they told Kit and Paul. "Catches up with a person." They called it a heart attack. *Gravity*, Kit thought but did not say. *The heft of living. He died of grief and cigarettes.*

The cattle clouded in the kitchen window, the red and black smudges of them like pastel. Paul leaned against the kitchen counter. Kit had received a grant for a college in the northwest. He would be alright, he told her. She needed to go. Get out of here. Broaden her horizons. Things would turn out for the best on all accounts. A *new leaf.* "You'll be fine," her brother told her. "You'll see the ocean. I never have."

"I haven't either," she said.

My mother had wanted to take us. She had only known this place.

The cattle blurred in the window. "You can get perspective, Kitty. It'll be good for you. Can't go backwards."

Paul, the voice of reason. Deciding to stay. I don't remember him ever wanting anything else. Paul had left for college, only to come right back. *Sucked back in, like a vortex.*

He and his wife, Elise, were moving into the farmhouse, planning to fix it up. They had been living in town. They had been met during college. She was from the suburbs of Denver. Another westerner. A like mind, Paul thought. Elise would fix up the old house, she said. Burn some sage, she joked. They would clean the place up, get their bearings. *Elise and her clean, clean hands and she was always washing her hands and the way she pushed the dog away. It should have been a sign.* But he did not see it or maybe did not want to.

Paul rinsed out his coffee cup. Elise was thinking maybe a few lambs too, he said. Suffolk. Maybe quit her teaching job. *The way those kids look at you, like they're looking right through you, she would say. Lost causes.* Those kids knew they weren't going anywhere, she would say.

Kit left for the coast the following day. Away from the heaving consciousness of the land where they were raised.

3. Glaciers

The glaciers carved out the canyons on the west side of the valley, millions of years ago. Cut through the earth and dragged the rock and good soil along with it. And would Paul even be here otherwise? Likely not.

The sun collapses into the canyon now and he thinks *God, what have I amounted to?* The room dampens around him. "You've got to be present, Paul," Elise said before she had left. *Who could blame her for going?* And now he is alone. The empty kitchen, hollow room. The kitchen floor is bowed with time. "I've got to fix this," Paul says, to no one. The peeling linoleum. *Everything falling apart*, he thinks. *Right from the start. That's what you get when you stick around and try to make it work. Elise was right to get the hell out.* When she moved to California, he was already drowning. *Or at least wading in. Dog-paddling, maybe. Who could blame her?*

"You're tied to it," she told him that last day. "This place isn't everything."

The larger mountain range looms directly above the farm. The canyons are sheer, nearly vertical. *Millions of years. How do you contend with that?* The peaks are still jagged, having existed above the ice. A *glacial moraine, the valley floor.* And what was underwater. At one time. *Pleistocene, a moving mountain range. Talk about moving mountains. I just need to get things done. Day to day.* At times Paul thinks he hears it, that initial glacier, slicing through. *Everything is happening all the time and nothing is finished and everything that happened is still happening.* In the spring Paul clears stones from the field and adds them to the rock fence, the way they had always done. The rock fence has been here as long as he can remember. The river runs alongside the farm, through the cottonwoods. There is a convergence point where the river runs nearly parallel with the rock fence, the fence curving downward alongside the farm. Like a boundary. Then the rock fence ends. The fence changes to barbed wire. Worn out, sagging. *Another thing needing fixed.*

Paul stacks the rocks in his sleep. The rocks never quit. There are always more, pushed up somehow. *Nothing ever changes*, he thinks. *The rocks, days, the way the light falls. At some point you start to give up or give in or forget why you began in the first place.* The mountains seem closer lately. *I don't know how else it could be. My entire life wasted.*

The light on the wall shifts around him. Sometimes he hears someone walking around the old house. He is alone too much, he figures. And now the same kitchen he has always known. Same wallpaper for decades. Orange flowers and vines. *Work until you die.* What does he have to show for anything? *Already drowning.* He can hardly see straight. Cannot think clearly. Every day a diminishing. *Like being sucked straight down into the canyon until you're smaller and smaller but then the next day same thing all over again.* He rarely answers the door when anyone stops by. Although they hardly ever do. Other than the occasional Jehovah's witnesses, Mormon missionaries, Schwann's man. He sees their silhouettes appear, hesitate, and walk away. *They must really need customers to drive clear out here*, he thinks. He has nothing to say to anyone.

A few weeks last summer those kids came by and changed water for him. He thought maybe the help would be good. They stopped at the house on that first day and he had not known what to do with them and so asked them inside and offered them coffee and they seemed to search his face for some kind of meaning or something to adhere to but he had nothing to say. They sat awkwardly at the kitchen table while he looked for something to give them and he poured them percolator coffee and the coffee was boiled and full of grounds which never bothered him but they swirled the grounds around with their silver spoons and pretended to drink it. They were clean-cut kids from out of state and their parents had moved out here to get away from the crime or pollution or who knows what and they drove their fathers' new pickups and they did not know how to do much of anything and they were lazy and by the time he showed them how to do anything it was already not worth the effort and they wore puffy jackets and drank energy drinks and took pictures with their smartphones of the fields and the canyon and the old barn and the mountains and him too maybe who knows and he never knew where the pictures ended up. They stared past him at the dismal room. He thanked them, paid them for the work they did not do, offered them more burnt coffee, and when they said no thanks, he closed the door behind them. After a few weeks they quit showing up and he was relieved. He would not have known what to do if they had continued coming by. After this he quit talking to anyone. Other than when he went for groceries or a drink. He no longer saw the point.

More and more he let things slip. *It'll get done. Eventually.* Anymore when he looks in the mirror, he sees he is graying, same as that old dog. *At least I have Queenie,* he reminds himself. *She sticks around. Loyal or stupid. Whichever. Anyway, I can't go back and do things different.* This is what he always wanted anyway. To stay here and farm.

Every day he crosses the fields, as if on repeat. Goes out to change water, hay, check calves. The mountain range like a film reel. The wilderness right there and when he was six or seven maybe he heard a cougar screaming and it sounded like someone being murdered and he pushed down into the bedcovers until it stopped. He never heard another one until after Elise had moved in. And they found the prints. Then the calf carcass. Half-buried. A few mornings passed and Elise swore she saw the cougar slinking past the bedroom window. The sun just barely up. He took the rifle down from the wall and shot out at the pink sky. The cougar was already gone. Elise started locking doors. *Because lions use door knobs?* She did not think this was funny.

Months later she would send the papers.

And a sticky note: *So sorry, Paul.*

≈ ≈ ≈

It starts to be more frequent. A knocking sound beneath the floorboards. The door wide open in the morning. *I don't remember leaving it.* The shadows playing on the rock fence. *Like kids out there.* He is alone too much, he decides. Starting to see things. *Got to get my head checked,* he thinks.

He opens the door now and looks out into the pitch black. Queenie comes inside, pushing past him. *Maybe she's going blind.* He has not seen a cougar ever again. Or any sign of one.

He did not want to experience anything, Elise said. To be part of anything. *The center of the universe. Where did I hear it?* A public television program, years ago. He had seen the program before the television went digital and he did not bother to upgrade. The program discussed time. It depicted people in various locations around the world. Standing in random places, waving at the camera. "The center of the universe," the narrator said, "is wherever you are." *Axis mundi.* Somewhere he had heard it. Some college class elective. *Perspective.*

In the morning he feels good. The light is on everything. Then the day passes. And the disquiet tracks him like the cougar. *You don't even know it's out there.* The stars appear over the eastern mountains. Venus. He hardly notices.

4. Compass

The room undulates like pool water. "Now I don't remember the whole thing and I don't know what to believe," Kit tells Nancy.

"No one does, Katherine. Our childhood memories are so complex. We have to be at ease, at times, with uncertainty."

Without the medication Kit is able, now, to see a blurry contour to things. Like through snow. Hints. "This is uncharted territory for you," Nancy says. "Let me know if you change your mind." *Uncharted*, Kit thinks. *A compass, pointing nowhere.* "We can try a different combination. See if it helps. I'm concerned about a sudden break." Nancy pauses. "It can be a difficult adjustment. The withdrawal. I want you to be absolutely sure."

It's like seeing someone out of the corner of your eye. But they're gone when you look. And there are places where the light can't reach. Like a black hole. And time could change. Switch up or not exist the way we know it. Topsy-turvy, Marg used to say. We don't know the half of it. They live upside down, she said. Backwards. Night is day. Day is night. They live beneath the earth. They come out once in a while, play jokes, look after things.

The wall behind Nancy shimmers. "Our minds play tricks on us. We need to be able to differentiate. And sometimes there's an imbalance. There's nothing wrong with needing a little help."

"I just want a clear head," Kit says. The sky is sheet metal. She hears it creaking. "I'd rather feel something than nothing."

"It's a balancing act," Nancy says, leaning forward. *Her woven blazer. Tapestry.*

"I want to at least try."

"That's commendable," Nancy says. "Just realize there will be rough patches. Where that line gets blurry."

It's only in your head.

Shut up about it, Kitty.

Nancy jots on her tablet. The room wavers. *Vertigo*, Kit thinks. *That must be it. Like climbing a steep mountain and you look down and you don't think you'll make it. And this is only temporary.*

They set the compass on the ground and watched the arrow spin. "It doesn't work," Patrick said. They brought the compass to Marg and placed it on the kitchen floor. Same thing. Marg wasn't surprised, she said. The magpie tapped on the screen door then, wanting cake. "Magpies can recognize themselves in mirrors," Patrick said, opening the door and tossing cake. The magpie bounced toward him. Gleaming blue on black. "Smart as a whip," Marg said.

She goes over it again and again in her head. *And maybe it's somewhere deep inside us, Paul thought, only we don't know it's there and it runs through us like a current and eddies here and there and passes through generations before it resurfaces. And Paul alone now.* "You can only do so much," he said. *To salvage anything.*

Patrick handed her a smooth, polished stone and the stone was the weight of the world. He had thin hands and eyes the color of the blue clay marbles they found in the dirt outside his house. *And when did they stop looking for him? And the way Rob looked at Patrick.* His gaunt face. Rob had been working in Alaska, on a fishing boat. Thought he would stick around a bit. Get to know his kid. *Wonder what she ever saw in him?* "Me and Patty are fine on our own," Carrie told him. And her bracing the chair there and the muscles in her neck like twine. And his mouth like something burnt inside it. *It was his turn, Rob told Carrie. He wanted to see his kid, was all. What's with the religious garbage? Why's he like that? Why'd you fill his head with that crap?* And her face darkened.

He wouldn't leave, you said. Came right into the house and stomped around and demanded things. Like he was owed something. Ice water, something to eat. He would be back, he said when he found us walking out there. It wasn't up to Carrie, Rob said. And he didn't want nothing to do with Carrie. Only wanted to see his kid. Which he had a right to do, he said. Without her interfering. Making him look like some kind of monster. Bet they'd see a Kodiak, he told Patrick. He didn't want to shoot anything, Patrick told him. *And you walked away and I followed, feeling sickish. Your skinny shoulder blades sticking through your t-shirt. Throw the comb down and a forest will appear and block him out and throw the ribbon down and a river will divide and keep him out.* And Carrie had one hand on her face and past the patch of grass the magpies collected there. Marg had tamed the boldest magpie, which she named Pie, and Pie would sit in the windowsill, waiting for handouts.

And Carrie. Venus de Milo. *Some museum we would never see.* National Geographic, Smithsonian. Then, the geraniums. The produce guy, Sean, brought. His hound dog's face. Apron, plump hands. He loved her or close to it. *You could see it in the way he looked at her.* He had set aside the hot pink geraniums for her. They were always the first to go. *And his soft hands and sagging eyes and something about him made you embarrassed so you didn't want to look.* Carrie had started to see more of him, she confided to Kit.

Kit goes to the parking lot, outside the mini mall where she meets weekly with Nancy. The sky unfolds around her.

She needs to go home, maybe. Lie down. *Get through these next few weeks and it'll be okay. First trimester is the hardest, they say.*

5. Gatherings

In the evening everything glows. Jason holds the balcony door open. Kit cannot distinguish his features. His face, eclipsed. *I never know what you're thinking anymore. You never say. Something's off-kilter and I can't place it.*

"Come inside, Katherine," Jason says. "They're asking for you." The waves beneath the balcony break. Smashing. He takes her elbow. Hardly touching her. The people inside are like marionettes. *How did I end up here? With him? With any of them?* The door slams shut behind her and the ocean is quelled. *Nothing makes any sense.*

The townhouses are identical. Same layout, vaulted ceilings, open floor plan. *You could get lost*, Kit thinks, *trying to find your way home. Opening doors on rooms that look exactly like yours.* Something moves past. *I don't want to be here. Why don't I want to be here? It would take some time, Nancy said, to adapt.* They clutch their phones, wineglasses, tiny plates. *They are vapid. Offering nothing.* Kit feels heavy. Substantial. The ocean is blocked out. *We hardly even notice it.*

When she first told Jason, days ago, his expression fell flat. He looked skeptically at her and turned his waxen hand on the doorknob, as if wanting to escape. He was already late, he said. Something felt urgent. "Are you sure about this, Katherine? I wasn't prepared for this. I thought maybe we would wait and see. There are options, you know." The ocean smashed in her mind. *You never really know anyone.*

Now she can see the objects getting through. The shadowed places. And Jason laughs with them. *I don't know how I ended up here.* The windows are closed and the doors. *And the ocean smashing out there only we forget. And you have to leave them open, unlocked.* The ocean does not say a thing. *He said he wanted this.* Months ago, on the pier. Granted, they had been drinking. And his face was red and flushed and he was jovial. "A little family," he said. "Think about it. Three or four, maybe." He laughs now and glances at her and the laughter ceases. *Well.* His face wrenches. Then softens. *It's your decision, Katherine. Just think about it, okay?*

Jason designs the programs. The internal infrastructures. Computer programming, coding. She imagines his mind as a kind of motherboard. Sensors, simulators, flashing lights. He helped her learn how to be in their world. Participate. "Just play along," he told her. And now the blood drums in her head.

We're mostly water, Patrick said. Nine months. Options. She turns toward the window. The ocean is silent. Forgotten.

Stephanie is tall, lithe. Perfectly proportioned. She takes Kit's wrist now, gently, and leads her to the hors d'oeuvres table. "You look pale," she tells Kit. "Like you could use a bite." There are tiered plates stacked with an assortment of cheese, crackers, pear slices, chocolates, condiments. Above is a chandelier shaped like a tumbleweed. Airy and light, like it would blow away. *Wild West*, Kit thinks. *Lariats, cowboy songs. The Oregon Trail.* Stephanie hands Kit a shining plate. *We pretended we were cowboys and we pretended to build a fire and the birds came smashing down into the brush and you thought they were something else.* "What would you like?" Stephanie asks. "A glass of wine? What can I get for you? You look sad." She frowns at Kit now and Kit can see her face is like a child's drawing. Asymmetrical and with too many empty places. The features slightly wrong, adrift.

"What's wrong? Cat got your tongue? Weird saying." Stephanie laughs and pops a stuffed fig. *Something isn't right and I can't pin it down.*

"I'm okay," Kit tells her. Stephanie smiles with her bleached teeth.

"Okay. I'll take your word for it. I'm going to make the rounds. Then I'll come back and check on you. You've got something on your mind." She walks away. Kit stares at the tiered things. *Not one bite.* She sets down her empty plate. *Not one bite or they'll never let you leave. I'm trapped. For God's sake.* She touches her own arm and her arm is fleshy and hot. The room feels sterile.

And we found it in the woods, like a banquet, only not, bread on rocks, and something like wine, and we tore the bread and the bread tasted like air and felt like cattail fluff and we ate it anyway and we ate the smashed berries or whatever they were and things were altered.

Not one bite, Marg told us later. And we tried to stop but it had already occurred. And you did, and then I did. Same way we touched the electric fence, just to see. You, then me. Well. I made that story up, I told Marg later. And other ones too. She did not look convinced. The things we came up with, me and you.

Carrie taped magazine pictures to her kitchen walls from old National Geographics. She filled jars with bachelor's buttons. *She was so pretty. I remember thinking she was so pretty and the hollyhocks that grew out there and you could see them through the window and the house was always cold but she never said anything about it. It used to be a bunkhouse, they said. She heard ghosts sometimes, she said, and we believed her. You and me believed her. Because we believed everything. And then he came back. He comes anywhere near you, she said, and you let me know.* The school called her. He said he was there to pick up his son. *Only begotten. And you said maybe Jesus walked on this same water. And you started across the slipping rocks and then I did too.*

Stephanie and Josh have two boys and Stephanie invites the grandparents and the grandparents take the boys down to the shore. The sun hovers over the horizon now, a red marble shot across the water. *Keepsies.* She only wanted a clear head, she told Nancy. Nancy said it would be safe for the baby. To continue. If she happened to change her mind. "Even so," Kit said. "You never know until after the fact. You can't be too sure." And Nancy nodded and said she respected her resolve. *Regardless.*

Through the enormous window the sun is going down. A red smudge. Kit can vaguely see the grandparents on the shore. They are elegant and they glide behind the boys and the boys run along the shore and the automatic lights come on and the boys disappear momentarily beneath the townhouses. They are both in Montessori. "Absolutely thriving," Stephanie said. "Everyone should consider it when they have children. The public school system is a mess. Too much red tape." The window seems to shudder now. The sun is gone. *We knew the names of the birds and plants and constellations and we were worlds apart from everyone else. I'm starting to recall and I don't know what's true and what's not.*

A man in horn-rimmed glasses hovers nearby. The light disfigures his face. He comments on the sun going down. So fast, crazy. He introduces himself. He is new here, he tells her. He thought he recognized her from the main hub. He wants to know what she does for a living. *What do you do? What's your net worth? Are you worth my time?* She feels something inside her like it is unfurling. She tells him about the gray corner where she works. Where sometimes, if she leans back far enough, she can see a strand of gray coastal sky. A tuft of clouds, at times, between identical gray buildings, like a memory held. Or a warning. He stares at her, mouth widening like he is trying to smile but does not remember how. "Sounds like burnout," he says. He takes his phone out and scans.

Carrie had these bachelor's buttons and asters and cosmos. Hollyhocks. Things that grew easily. Came along on their own, wild and random.

Her legs are heavy. She feels gargantuan. Like a monster in the townhouse. Sasquatch. *When did this happen?* She suddenly feels like she is on the outside, looking in. The thing unfurls inside her, like a plant reaching for air. She looks around for an exit strategy.

Tiger's eyes, aggies, steelies.

He drew a circle in the dirt.

My only friend. He ran ahead. He always ran ahead.

Jason waves from across the room. Out the window the boys are on the shore again and she can see them with the lights coming on and they are throwing something into the air and catching it.

She feels too large. Like she will crash into things. *Bull in a China shop. Boondocks. Sounds like you're from.*

And my mother held the shell to my ear and I could hear the ocean through it and she said maybe we'd go someday and she'd never seen the ocean and wouldn't that be fun and so maybe we would. The thought of the ocean back then was something elusive and make-believe. They did not have the time or money. Although they had it better than a lot of people. *And Patrick showing up early to school for the free breakfast and I watched him wolf it down.* He never left a crumb. And he stashed the extra butters and jams in his backpack. *And we got off the bus and ran out there directly and the dark spaces moved and murmured and we saw and heard them but that can't be right and give it time. Adjustment period.*

The thing, unfurling.

And you held my hand and your hand was wet with the terror of it. Old wives' tales, they said. There's something very much the matter and I can't get it straight. She used to wake with the memory of it like something jarring her awake and she would push the blankets away and her father would bring her a glass of milk. *And the milk like grass the taste of it.* And he would stand in her bedroom door like some kind of watchman. "I don't know what to do for Kitty," he would say. "She never asked for any of this." *Rob would keep coming back, Patrick said. He was never going to leave them alone. And he didn't want nothing to do with Carrie, he told Patrick. Only wanted to spend time with his son. They shouldn't get it into their heads they could just dismiss him. And your hands were thin and the sun burned through the trees and you said he would never stop.*

But you got out of this, she thinks now. *Will never have to suffer the bright fluorescent lights or stagnant hours. And the water seemed to lift the closer we got to it. We're mostly water and maybe that's why we always want to be close to it.* The ocean. River. The river flowing ultimately into the ocean. Everything connected. Tributaries.

The boys run up the outside steps from the shore. The grandparents follow, slowly, carrying found things. *And they think they have it down but the water will rise and that's why the houses are built so high above the rocks.* Rising tides. Tsunami warnings. At times it gets so windy it shakes the thin townhouse walls. They're made of nothing. Paper and particle board. *Something isn't right.* Kit hardly recognizes her reflection in the big window.

The boys come bursting into the house, carrying sea-air. The grandparents follow, moments later. The ocean roars behind them and is quickly shut out again. *The moon pulls the tide. Changes the depths of things.* She cannot remember quite how it goes. *You said we're mostly water.* The moon could make you act strange, Marg used to say. Animals and people. The boys wear matching striped polo shirts and their clothes are muddy and dank and they bolt toward the hors d'oeuvres table and cram their faces. The grandmother tells them to please slow down, adjusting a pearled sweater. She is overly animated when she says it, as if she does not quite mean it. *Amused.* The boys snort and punch each other. *Bull calves.* The grandmother shepherds the boys away. The room goes still again. Quiet. Mundane.

Hardly anyone uses the outside stairs. They spend their days indoors, the ocean shut out flat. *It's enough that the ocean is right there,* she thinks, *that they can say it's there.* They paid for a backdrop. Scenery. They didn't really care. When she told Jason this, he told her she was not being fair. *Ambience isn't free, Katherine.*

The thing, unfurling. Trumpet vine.

The sun hardly shines.

She first met Jason at a housewarming. He was mellow, cordial. His eyes flashed like obsidian. "You find it sometimes," they said. "The obsidian. On the flat, open spaces. You can take it."

"Can you take too much?" she asked. "Will it run out?"

"No idea," they said. They only knew you could *take* it.

Jason invited her onto the balcony. Gathered the wine bottle, glasses. *Obsidian and the way he held the door.* They could actually talk out there, he said. Away from all the commotion. He poured her a glass. The ocean was metallic and flat. What had brought her out here? he wanted to know. She seemed set apart. The moment he saw her he knew he had to get her alone, he said. The way she carried herself. She was different. In a good way, he hastened to add. *You know.* She was *earthy*. He did not know how else to put it. He refilled their glasses. She was terrible in social situations, she confided. She was not sure why she had come. "You've got to play along," he told her. "Let them think you care." His teeth sparked. Things blurred, rearranged. He watched her. They drank another glass and another. They sat together on the top step. The tide was going out. They finished the bottle and he leaned against the banister and looked at her. They talked for hours. He retrieved another bottle. People came and went, interrupting them and then leaving. Then started to go home. "Guess we should wrap it up," he finally said. He held the glasses and his hands were very white. He would like to see her again, he said. He looked not at her but at the ocean when he said it. Dinner, maybe? Did she like seafood? He would take her out to dinner. All right? He held the door for her. *Everything lightened and I thought I had a place at the table or at least could play the part of having.*

At his townhouse, newly constructed, he talked the light and music into being. There was a faux-fire on the wall. The ocean was silent in the window. He had no books, superfluous things. He had the minimalist mindset, he told her. He poured her a glass of wine. She studied a framed print he had on the wall. Geometric patterns. He had ordered it from RealArt.com, he told her. Did she think it was any good? He was not very good at these things, but had needed something on the wall. He appreciated the symmetry, he said. It was comforting. The precision.

With Jason she had felt reassured. He was considerate. There was a mellowness about him, a warmth. She had one brother, she told him. She should bring him out here, Jason said. He would love to meet him. Kit laughed. "He doesn't leave," she said. "He abides." He paused, turning his glass. "Okay," he laughed. "Anyway, I'm glad you're here." *Another prescription, another night out. Whatever gets you through.* "You kind of lived in the boonies, sounds like," he said. *Without meaning.* "Wasn't what I meant," he said. *Boondocks.* He tapped her knee. "Hey." She looked at the fire image on the wall. "I just mean you have no idea what it's like to be around a human being for once. They're all on autopilot. They could be robots for all I know. You're the real deal. A breath of fresh air." He propped his head on one hand in the deep cushions. The wine warmed her. She opened up to him. *Doesn't matter where you're from. You can start over.* She sat up taller. Cleared her throat.

"There were unexplainable things we thought we saw when we were kids," she confessed. *Enough to drink.* He was scarlet from the wine. She felt the heat from him or maybe from her own skin. He looked strangely older. *Too old.* She pushed the thought away.

He leaned his head on the microfiber.

His eyes were black. *Obsidian.* She told him there were things she remembered but was not sure she remembered correctly. She thought maybe she had invented things. *Like dreaming awake.* She was not sure what was what. He leaned back, holding his wine glass. When she was a kid, she said, some strange things happened. She could not explain them. *I had this friend and he was my only friend and they never found him.*

Kids come up with all kinds of things, Jason told her. Everything could be explained eventually. He did not believe in any god, had zero spiritual inclinations. You are born, you die. That was what he knew. What he could see. *So. Carpe diem.*

Jason turned the empty glass in his hands. Everything could be quantified, he said. She felt her skin heat. The wine, the anxiety. She was probably tired, she told him. Long day. He said he understood.

Faster and faster, into the trees.

He gripped her knee *and his hand was like alabaster.*

They sat in the lit room with the faux-fire crackling. Her head felt full of down. *Cattail fuzz.* She shook her head a little, as if to clear things out. *Paul wouldn't like him,* she thought. The meticulous room. The trick of fire. The soft hands. *But Paul doesn't like anyone.* At least she could breathe. He smiled warmly and watched her. She did not know what to say. *Just go along with it.* He was attentive, it seemed. She felt she was lingering outside of herself. It was only the medication or wine, she thought, distorting things.

I don't remember who I am. She was someone different, new. Temporarily. The truth cracked open but she did not see it.

Eventually she moved in with him. Away from the gray asphalt and adjacent to the ocean, resounding. A beach house, townhouse. She was not sure how these things worked, how long he intended her to stay. Soon there was always somewhere to be. An obligation. A meeting, party, event. They were married. She floated along, cloudy-headed. The ocean seemed synthetic or phony. She ignored it. She went to the gatherings. Played along. And it worked. No one should live in the past, Jason would remind her. You can only go forward.

I don't belong anywhere, she thinks now. *I'm getting sick or going to be sick maybe.*

The boys return a second time, carrying shells. She had not seen them leave again. The grandmother is no longer with them. They appear to be on their own. "Drop those," Stephanie says, charging across the room. She leads them onto the balcony and they drop the shells into the rocks beneath. Lost. The outside lights are ghostly. The sun having depleted. *It's never dark here,* Kit thinks. *It was always dark back home. We knew every stump and roots and curve of ground and could walk it with our eyes closed and never trip we knew it so well. Or thought we did.* She feels weighted to the floor. *They don't want it dark for some reason. Something they don't trust. And we walked on the ice, the water. I no longer live, but Christ lives in me. A deep kid, Carrie said, real spiritual.* Carrie thought maybe he would be a priest. She wouldn't have any problem with that, she said.

Stephanie brings the boys into the bathroom and washes their hands, flipping their hands over and over again as if she would find some secret they were withholding. "They creep me out," she once confessed to Kit. "The way they look at me. It's like they're plotting something. Sometimes I don't even like them."

The boys double in the spotless mirror. The smaller one arches back, crying. "You lost them to us," he says, almost shouting.

"God, Blake," Stephanie says. "That doesn't even make any sense." The older one is quiet, subdued. They turn and flee the room.

Out the window the ocean is a backdrop. Could be a screensaver. The guests hold their wineglasses and bob their doll heads. *Hard, plastic parts. To be sorted out and put together again. She took me to Ben Franklin's and there were bins of them.* Heads, legs, torsos. They had scared her. One could easily be switched out for another. Swapped around. Legs and arms shoved on backwards. Eyes popped out. *Hodge-podge.*

"I'll be honest," Jason said. "I thought we were on the same page. There are options. Just something to think about. I support you in your decision. You know. It's just up to you to decide." He squeezed her hand. Tried to smile.

He said he wanted this that's what he said he wanted. Everything is suddenly too bright. The room is too bright. All pretense and she does not know what to say to anyone.

Stephanie touches her as she passes. "Katherine? What's the matter?"

Something's the matter with Kitty. The way they looked at her. Concerned.

She opens the sliding door and closes it behind her and descends the stairs and the stairs collapse like quicksand. She is lightheaded. Things are spinning. *Whatever's wrong with me I'll pass along*, she thinks. *Corner of your eye. Quicksand.* Her mother and the seashell. *You can hear the ocean, Kitty. Listen. I'm not okay.* The rocks are jagged. They rise sharply into the sky. The tide is coming in. *Another trial, she said. Another combination. Won't hurt the baby. Don't worry so much.* Above her, when she turns back, they are gliding throughout the yellow room, like some tedious purgatory. *The dark we had.* She has the sudden inclination to leave, to quit, run away somewhere. *They need the dark*, Marg said. *They're scared of the light. They look for shadows.* The food upstairs will dry out, go stale. They will throw it away. They will waste it the same way they waste everything. *I'm not being fair. And something isn't right. Listen, Kitty. You've got to pay attention.*

Farther down the shore a woman walks toward the caves. She is nearly phosphorescent. She momentarily disappears behind the largest rock and then reappears. She slides into the water. Comes up and goes beneath again. Walks back up to the shore. *Freezing cold and what's she thinking?* Kit laughs to herself, despite everything. *Polar bear club.*

"I see things that aren't there," she confessed to Marg. *Same as my mother.*

"Hogwash," said Marg.

The pressure could cause, they told us, hallucinations. The morphine. All kinds of reasons why. *Other than.* Auditory and visual. *The shadows like hands and faces. She saw. Bloodswell like water to my head. The swallows came down and they must have been catching things because they were flying so erratically and swooping.* Her mother went inside to lie down and Kit drew the cherry trees. And brought the cherry trees to her. *Look at that, she said. You've got an eye, Kitty.* And the following day they took her to the hospital.

≈ ≈ ≈

When Jason comes down to the shore, he looks awkward. Out of place. "If this is what you want," he tells her. "I was watching those kids tonight. What's one kid? We can handle one kid. It'll be good for us." He gives her his hand, smooth as a fish belly, and they head back toward the townhouses. The solar lights come on and his hand is cool, clammy. "I'm here, Katherine. I'm not going anywhere. Don't worry. We'll be fine. Time to make some plans."

And Carrie, her saints and geraniums and she had nothing to prove. She seemed to have a belief in a world apart from this one, the one they could see.

Jesus fed the five thousand, you said, and turned water into wine and stilled the raging waters and cured the lepers and brought his friend Lazurus back from the dead and walked on water. A crosser of boundaries. And we saw them splitting into the trees and they were contorted and they carried clods of mud.

"And what if he came walking, right now, across the river?" Patrick asked Kitty. And he almost seemed to expect it, the way he stood there.

The stories Marg told he held in much the same manner.

I suppose you believed them.

6. Earth

"What do you think happened, Katherine?" Nancy asks. "People don't just evaporate."

"I don't know anymore."

"And your mother?"

"I was seven."

"Do you remember her?"

"A few things. I don't know."

"Do you have a spiritual life?"

"That's a loaded question."

"It's a valid question."

"I suppose."

You went to mass that morning and your hair was combed and neat and you wore a polo shirt and pressed dark blue Levi's that woman Maureen from social services gave to you and we saw them from out of the ground and their black loam eyes and we left them a steelie. Set it on the rock fence for them to find and the next morning it was gone.

The watercolor on the wall depicts a washed-out gazebo. An abundance of milky pink flowers. *People resonate with paintings like those,* Kit thinks. *And you would be alone in the gazebo with the azaleas and everything candy-pink and the stone bridge and the blue water and lanterns everywhere even in the middle of the afternoon.* Perpetual springtime. *That would get old.*

They came out of the dark places and they receded with the sun. Everything was opposite where they lived, Marg said. *Beneath and beneath.*

"I used to think he would come back. Patrick, I mean. I was eleven when Paul left for college. My dad went through the motions. Fed, changed water, hayed. That was it. And he wanted me home. He worried if I was out very late or if I walked home from the bus stop. He started to meet me there. We would walk back together. Not saying anything. I used to go and look for him and Paul or Dad would come get me. He rarely had anything to say."

"Sounds like he was depressed," Nancy says.

"Certainly."

A few of them had hands like twigs and they pushed down fast into the earth and you said you heard one of them laughing and we waited but they didn't come back that day. Got to go in the evening, you said. Or early morning. When there's places for them to hide out. And you were like them. Hiding out.

"The farm was less than a mile from the river."

"And you were down there quite a lot?"

"Yeah. It wasn't far. We crossed the road, the rock fence. And we were there." *Could hear the river when it was higher. River access, the water coming up onto the bank. Mud. And beneath there are aquifers and natural springs and you don't know how they go. We practically lived out there.*

"And Marg?"

"She lived alone."

The smoke in rings, whisked above.

"She never discounted our stories. What we had seen." *Or when you ran into the trees and dissolved like some magic act.* "Marg never said she was going to help out as much as she did. That was where we went after school, first thing. She used to tell these stories. Patrick used to come with me when Paul got older and was helping dad. Carrie was always working. Marg would give him cake and sandwiches and apples. Carrie took extra hours whenever she could. Overtime, you know. Anyway, Marg would give us these big slices of cake." *The smoke would hover there like a cloak and she waved it away and it didn't matter anyway because the cake was so good.* "You couldn't stop. Once you'd tasted it."

Nancy sniffs.

The faster you ran and I could not catch up with you and that afternoon we went to Marg's and Marg gave us cake and the cake was thick with icing. Patrick was in the window and when she looked at him, he seemed odd. There was something in him wider, more expansive.

"You never can tell," Marg said. She waved the smoke away and the cottonwoods clattered and she cut extra slices. She garnished the cakes with candy she bought from the bulk bin at Safeway. Gumdrops, licorice. Huge slices with fresh, whole milk. She still had the Jersey cow then. *Dottie.* Black-eyed, docile. *A magic cow, she used to say. And why wouldn't she say that?*

They had seen Marg once after she had cut her hair. She lit a cigarette and her hair was hacked and all over the place and she never thought much about it, she said. Just got tired of it and so chopped it off.

"You could have it done," Patrick said. "Mom knows someone who will cut it for free. A friend of hers."

"Why bother?" Marg asked. She did not want to waste time on silly things that don't matter, she said. The magpies came down and Marg tossed them cake.

When we told her what we'd seen, her eyes gleamed like mud then and she seemed to smile but she was not smiling. She dropped the cake and brushed her hands together and gestured for them to come outside. She meant it. Her face, brimming over with meaning. "You have to be careful," she said. "You could get lost out there." *Right in the place you think you know.* There were creatures down beneath the earth, she said. They were quick-tempered, mischievous. They had a hand in everything. They could lure you in. They weren't bad, she said. It was just their nature. Same as a coyote or a hawk or anything else. She lit another cigarette and seemed to forget what she had said. "You have to take care of things," she said. "The woods, the animals. Or they may notice. The maahinen, my husband called them. That's what he knew them as. You have to ask their permission." *For what? We forgot to ask.*

They were like people, she said, but not. Impossible to explain. It was like passing an invisible threshold, like some forgotten wisdom. Something you had always known. "No one can explain these things," Marg said.

Patrick looked at the trees. *Credulous.*

"The wilderness was right there," Kit tells Nancy now. "And we took it for granted. I mean, I don't think we considered what it meant. The weight it carried." *We took all kinds of things for granted.*

Patrick crawled up onto the rock fence. Lifted his arms. They scooted back into the recessed places and the sun shook. *And they had always been there in some way. We instinctively knew it. Like the back of your hand.* Patrick shouted at them. The trees shook and closed.

It was most likely a narrative Kit had constructed, the school counselor would tell her father, in order to deal with her grief and confusion. Trauma. Anyone else might do the same. She only needed time to sift through it all. The counselor had turned to Kit and smiled. Offered a chocolate kiss, the foil shining in her delicate palm. *Not one bite.*

The space around you could crack open any time. They kicked up clods of mud and Marg swept the clods up again and again. We saw them and they were crooked and they were slipping up and down the trees and they had these pointed things and their feet some of them were switched on backwards like they were decided absentmindedly. An *afterthought.* "God doesn't make mistakes," Patrick said, chiseling. "They're supposed to be that way." *They were like mounds of earth and tree roots.* She did not know how else to think about them. *Like they were part of the earth. It was very early and the light was wrong and so maybe we couldn't see them right.* He had not wanted to go. She yanked at him finally and he jolted like he was startled into awareness and he blinked fast and followed her through the trees. Early morning.

And after he disappeared, she couldn't think right. The scarecrow woman smelled like rain. "It's okay, it's okay," she told Kit. "They're doing what they can. Checking every nook and cranny."

Nancy opens the blinds.

"Did you have a religious upbringing? You never told me."

"Somewhat. When I was younger. Carrie was pretty devout, I think. I think Patrick picked up on that. Maybe it helped her. We only went a few times after we lost my mother. I never knew why we went when we did. We always got out of there quick."

The light in the old church was an amber-light and Kit felt momentarily that time had slowed, or that she had entered some other dimension. *You can only see through the forest, find your way out, with magical help. Bread and ritual.*

They sat a few rows behind Patrick and Carrie. And the way Patrick bowed, genuflected. *I no longer live, but Christ lives in me.* He was the first to rise for communion. And when he returned to the pew, his face was lit, and he looked ageless. There was a certainty in him Kit envied. He held the sacred reverently, like a quail egg. He knelt and the amber-light caught up in his hair, on his neck. *The kingdom is within you.* He was absolutely still. *You believed all that. And the traipsing things, the stories. Come to life.* The church was a sanctuary, Carrie used to say. Like the trees were a sanctuary. *Nothing could touch you there.*

On the way out of the church Kit dipped her fingers in the holy water and the water was cool. *It was Easter maybe or why would we have come? And we drank right out of the falls and we ate the bread and drank the wine and the trees around altered. You cannot unsee what you have seen.*

"Hurry up," her father said. "We have things to do. We need to get home." *Why had we come?*

And Patrick back there, in the sunshine. He was looking up a little, at the window or maybe at the sky. His hands were in his pockets and his face held a strange depth. *Like a child-mystic. He was different. But then, we remember wrong. We romanticize things. I've put you on a pedestal. We embellish, invent. You were just a kid. We both were.*

"Some people just feel things so strongly," Kit tells Nancy now.

"Yes," Nancy says. She seems distracted.

Maybe I want it to be a certain way. For it to go the way I would have wanted it to go.

Nancy's phone buzzes. She glides a small, manicured hand to the phone and touches the screen and smiles. She looks at Kit and the smile collapses. *Practiced solemnity.* "You know, you could try something else. There are a few new things on the market that seem to be working for people." *Blot it out.*

7. Hands

She needed air, Kit told Jason. They sat on the back swing and his hands were smooth. *Alabaster.* Like those old Greek statues. *What happened to their arms? Where'd they end up? Maybe there's a stash somewhere.*

A few people walked along the beach. They were dark smudges and they leaned down and the smaller one ran and then tucked back behind the big rock. Jason rocked the swing.

Her mother had always wanted to see the ocean, Kit said. She never had. *These things take time.* "We had this shell from somewhere and we used to listen to the ocean through it. There were only a few places she said she'd like to see. The ocean. The redwoods. She never did any of it."

Jason leaned back and took her hand in his and his hand was smooth as plaster and warmed her and she felt the pulsing there. *Then she was gone. That fast. And everything flipped upside down, backwards.* She looked at the water there. The figures had vanished. *They skirted around me. Like I knew something I wasn't saying.* Problem was she had said something to a few of them. Those girls had dragged it out of her. She was not sure why she had told them. They had offered her zebra cake. A place at their table. *Come sit with us, Kitty.* She had believed, momentarily, in their generosity. They wore bangles and designer denim and they were from southern California, newly arrived. They asked her what she knew. *He was your neighbor, wasn't he? They asked me and I told them and why'd I tell them? What did I expect?*

"That isn't funny," the lead one said, her mouth turned down, snapping. "He was probably murdered and it isn't funny to make up stories." *He was probably murdered.* The blood pounded in her head. It was all she could hear. That blood.

And now, the medication helped.

The fall after Patrick disappeared, Kit left the school carnival. She couldn't breathe in there, she told Paul when he came looking for her. He tried to make her laugh. They had set up a jail, he said, and he was going to arrest his girlfriend, Gretchen, and keep her in there overnight maybe and he brought out the cake walk cake he had won and he tore a piece and handed it to her. *His hands were like our mother's.* She could see them milling around in there. She was on the periphery. *Her hawk eyes.* Kit had not known what to say. *I never know if I'm dreaming or awake.*

Paul leaned against the brick. "You're not missing nothing," he said. And Gretchen came out and the three of them leaned against the brick, sharing the cake. The stars were sharp. *And it's like we were from some other time. Some other place in time. One hundred years behind everyone else.* Gretchen draped her sweater around Kit's shoulders. "That's Venus," Gretchen said, smacking her gum, one arm around Kit. "That real bright one."

She was learning to meld in at the gatherings, Kit told Jason. The wine helped. She carried a glass wherever she went. A prop. He laughed. Said he understood. She mingled, she told him. She figured out how to move from pod to pod. To ease into conversations. Nod and appear interested. She networked. She became a cog in the wheel. For a moment Jason seemed reflective. Then he stood.

"Let's go," he said, the wine spilling onto his immaculate sleeve. He did not seem to notice. He took her hand. Curled his fingers around hers. Smooth as wax.

They walked down to the shore and to the largest rock where the inky figures had been and scooped up sand and found the starfish and they peeked into the caves and she said she thought she'd lost her mind and he said where do you think it is? Here? Over here? How about over here? He burrowed his hands in the sand and laughed and the sand was on his pantlegs and in his hair even and in his sleeves and he shook his sleeves and the rocks were black and smooth on the sand and they collected the smooth, black rocks and he put the rocks in his pockets and they walked down the shore until they hardly knew where they were and they were both slightly drunk or maybe very drunk who knows and nothing seemed so daunting anymore and they went up to the town and ordered chai tea and sat together and watched the people going by and guessed their stories. The tea sobered them up and he glimmered there. She felt good. Only months later she would call Paul to tell him. Was she sure? he asked. How long had she even known him? You just know, she said. And he did not argue the point. "Guess you're doing okay, Kitty," he said. And she turned back to Jason and she watched the muscle twitch near his mouth the way it sometimes did and he straightened there. And the sand was in the folds of his clothes and beneath his perfect fingernails and he grinned.

8. Cougar

A year into their marriage, Paul and Elise went to Seattle. They stayed in a hotel with red printed carpet and every night they met Jennifer and Jennifer's boyfriend and Elise wore silky things and heels and Paul hardly recognized her and he did not want to be there. She thought it would be fun. They needed to reorient, she said. *Get out of Dodge, she said. Take a break.* And she knew he did not want to be there but she only asked that he at least pretend to have a good time. *The traffic, noise.* "I can't hear myself think," Paul said.

"Maybe that's a good thing," she said. "You're too introspective. Open up, live a little."

She was joyful out there. She belonged. They could visit, she figured. Now and then.

When they returned home, Elise invited people over. They stood around in the drafty rental, drinking box wine. She was lonely. He saw it then. *Out of place.* And he was sorry. "I thought you'd wanted this," he said. "To be out here."

The cougar showed up shortly after they moved into the old house. *Nail in the coffin.* He had not heard one since he was a kid, he told her. They didn't usually come down this far. She was not convinced. *They see you and you don't see them, she said.*

A few days after the cougar, she brought up California. She needed a break, she said. A vacation. She would teach at a private school. One year, maybe two. Enough to get her mind right. Figure out what she wanted. It was fine, Paul told her. She owed him nothing. She got tired of it out here was all, she said. She got tired of him going out, night after night in the winter when he was calving. Or the need to get home early enough to change water or feed. They never went out and did anything, she said. She needed momentum, color. And all winter she had moved aside the fencer and cans of nails and bags of ear tags when she rode with him. She only wanted one nice dinner, once in a while, she said. She had waited and waited while he pulled the calf and the calf died anyway and she was all dressed up when he returned and he was covered in blood and shit and she hardly batted an eye when he said he'd lost the calf. She was done, she said. She was just done. This was not what she wanted. Well, what did she want? he asked her. She blinked at the dark window. "I don't know, Paul. Other people, maybe. Experiences."

The mountains shift. Closer. And now he is drinking too much maybe. Seeing things. He has the notion he is forgetting something that has been entrusted to him. He knocks the mud from his boots. *Another year.*

9. Milk

The sun went down fast and red. "Finally, someone gets it," Jason said. There was a depth to her, he said. He had noticed it right away. Like she was years older than she was. Or held some kind of secret. He felt she knew more than she was letting on. About everything. *An old soul, Kitty.*

"She grew up on a farm," Jason told them. He put his arm around her. "She's the real deal." The lights spun above them. Jason pulled her against him. "Oh, my God," a woman in orange, Stacey, said. "Did you have a milk cow?"

Jason swirled his glass and grinned at her, waiting. The red light cast over them. When she was little, Kit said, they did. She felt herself warming. Jason held her shoulder with one wide hand. *If you sit straight enough and nod like this then maybe they won't notice it or see it because otherwise they would know right away. If you open your mouth. Don't open your mouth. Hick. Redneck.* "That's awesome," Stacey said. Jason gripped her shoulder. "See?" *Grinning ear to ear.* She felt her body loosen. "They love you," he said on the walk back. And she believed him.

10. Artifacts

In the evenings it begins. A stirring and he has to stop it from coming on. Things are done, Paul figures. There is the slant of evening light and the slant of light aches inside him. *Get it together,* he tells himself. And then. *One more.* Only one more to ease the aching inside him. He goes to bed. *You've got to get out of your head.* Only a habit, he tells himself. There are times he feels like something is around the corner about to jump out at him and then he has to have one more and one more and one more and he wakes later and later but still he gets things done. *Jumpy and I can't get out of my own head. Not that it matters. Things are getting done.*

It began weeks ago, when he found the bones in the riverbank. A knife inside him when he saw. He has to ease it some which way.

He had gone into the trees to get the cows out. They were always getting through. *I'm always having to fix that fence and they always find another way through.* The cows had wandered out and his horse, Rusty, had not wanted to go near the trees and finally he dismounted and tied Rusty to a post and walked out into the trees. *Because the whites of his eyes and he obviously didn't want to go.* Rusty stomped there, trying to turn back. Finally, Paul went into the trees on foot to get the cows out and Rusty stood back there watching. Eyes still big like that and rolling and him trying to turn around and eager to run home again. Paul ushered the cows along the broken fence and walked down to get the last one and it was near the river and the river so low already and that was when he saw them in the muddy bank. The faded pieces. The last cow ran up through the broken fence, awkwardly, kicking. Wanting through. Paul returned and crouched on the bank. Part of the bank had slid away, revealing bones. *Smooth and chalky and I thought maybe but it wasn't.*

The horse wanted to run home and so Paul ran him home. He would return later on foot to fix the fence. He called and they came out and they put tiny flags everywhere and yellow tape and it was weeks before he heard anything. He considered calling Kitty but what would he say? *I thought at least it would settle things. At least we'd have some kind of conclusion. Closure, they call it.* He would have to tell Kitty. After they called to verify. He would have to tell her. *Kitty, we found him. I'm sorry but at least we know. At least now we know.*

They sent the bones in for analysis. *I thought they were rocks at first but then the smoothness, the texture or shape. I thought it had to be him.*

And the terror of not knowing. Nightmare-like. *Gray like rock in the mud. And I touched what I thought was maybe his skull I don't know.* And he woke up soaking wet and turned on the light and wandered downstairs and poured a drink and then another and sat in the absolute dark.

Hours pass now and he sees Orion through the trees and it is like Orion is trying to warn Paul of something. *Orion tilting his bow.* Forever and always. *And he doesn't have a choice. Stuck in the sky like that.* Held fast.

They called him days later on his landline. *Centuries, they said.* He had found something much older. Ancient. It would take some time to know what's what, they said. *Ages, they said.* They were not sure if the bones were even human, they said. *Was what they said. What I thought they said. Maybe I heard wrong. I can't hear anymore. I probably heard wrong.* "What does that mean?" he asked them. They did not seem to hear his question. They were going to try the nearest archaeology department, they said. They would need expert analysis. "What do you mean?" he asked. "I don't understand." *I'm surrounded by God knows what.* They were still not sure *what* they belonged to, he thought he heard through the crackling. The call dropped. He placed the receiver on the wall. He was shaking. *Something older than.* Not Patrick. *Thank God. Then, what?* Paul sat alone in the empty room. He poured another drink. He had touched the smooth, hollowed roundedness, freeing it from the bank, before he realized it was not stone or wood. *Of what, exactly?* He washed his hands again. *The size of a kid.* And he woke that night hot and wet, the dark like a fist around him.

11. Pier

They drove south. It was warmer there. The seals barked and fell from the pier and the tourists laughed and adjusted their shopping bags and cameras around. Jason held her arm and his hand was warm and firm and he opened car doors and pulled out chairs and looked straight at her when she spoke. "I haven't ever felt this way," he told her. She helped him see things clearly, he said. She grounded him. He tilted the viewfinder toward her and they took turns looking at the water and seals and distant hills.

At the nearby eclectic shop there were crystals, stones. Kit felt something open inside her, like an oyster shell. *Rattlesnake rattle, horseshoe, quartz. Patrick found it there near the rock fence and the space around opened and we saw the figures dropping down.* The woman in the shop explained ions, energies.

"A racket," Jason muttered. Kit bought a piece of quartz anyway. Outside the boats clanked along the pier. The water lapped beneath. "You're always surprising me," he said. They leaned on the railing. She looked at the water. *We saw them early morning. Slouched in the dark places. But then you see things when you're a kid and I don't know what to think anymore.*

He looked at her, rubbing his hands together like he was trying out some amateur magic trick.

"You're always in your head," he said.

The pier swayed a little.

"Where else would I be?"

"Here."

He smiled.

And you said maybe you'd go if you were asked. Carrie never said but I could see it in the way she waited. She couldn't say anything to any of them. And her glancing at the door like he would walk right in. Patrick collected stones, wasp paper. "He wants to sleep outside," Carrie said. "Can't get him to come in hardly." *I can still see her standing there.* It was nice to have another girl around, she told Kit. *She braided my hair. Just us girls, she said. And those kids gave us grief, me and you. Those other kids on the bus and the playground. Got even worse after you left. And I loved you and yes. And you burned red when they said. When they. And you hardly spoke to me until we were safely on the dirt road and it was only us and the bus had lurched away and then we ran together past the burning bush. And you would stop and listen, at times. And swear you'd heard God. And the light fell through the trees and we held the light burning in our palms. Like holy bread. On you my favor rests.*

Kit sat evenings by the rock fence until her father came out and said it was time to come in and she should not be out there. "There's more to things," Patrick said. "Jesus saw it but no one believed him. He tried to tell them." *Other than the women. The women stuck around. And Veronica gave him something to drink. No one else even offered. And Patrick believed Jesus came back the same way he believed in the creatures in the woods.* He had felt it, he told Kit. Inside him. Maybe he would never be hungry again. But he was. They knew he was. They gave him eggs and bread and meat. He took them home to Carrie. *We ate the bread out there or pretended we did. What we saw were only shadows and trees, for God's sake.* And it was only bread. And only wine. And nothing transforms, only remains matter and substance. *Grow up.*

"Anyway, you should be careful with that crystal," Jason continued. "Might attract some things." She shoved him and laughed. *Sun on rocks.* The way he looked at her. "You're one of a kind, kiddo," he said, tipping an invisible hat. "Witchy woman." The pier rocked beneath them. It was just for fun, she said. She felt the quartz weighted there in the plastic shop bag. *Why not?*

12. Riverfront

A fly-fisherman walks into the bar. Fancy vest, hiking boots. Alert, happy. *A fly-fisherman walks into a bar and the bartender says.*

Gretchen pours Paul a drink. They are making the bar trendy now, Gretchen says. There are western paintings for sale. Wildlife scenes and cowboys in yellow rainslickers. Horseshoe decorations, antler lights. You can order wine, cheese boards. "They're trying to *rebrand*," Gretchen says. "This guy came in yesterday. Was going to start some flyfishing outfit. He bought one of the paintings. Buffalo in the mist or some damn thing."

Gretchen recently moved back. Flying solo, she tells Paul. Well, other than the kid. She has a son. Thirteen. He keeps her on her toes. "Thinks he knows everything," she says.

"I suppose we all do," Paul says.

She runs a rag across the bar. "True enough," she says, disappearing momentarily into the back room. They have installed swinging doors, like an old western. The light slips past the window and the bar darkens.

Kit looked right at me when she said it, he thinks. He ran ahead, she told them. He was always faster. They recommended therapy or maybe something spiritual and their father said he would call the priest but then he never did because how in the hell would that help? Somewhere along the way he quit caring about all that. *Carrie and her saints and medals and candles she lit after he disappeared.* They thought they would find him after the thaw. *Jesus.* Paul watches the swinging door. The light moving. *Why am I thinking of this now?* Spring came and they never found him. *I saw them, Kitty said. They had both seen them, she said. They were like mud and twigs, she said, and their eyes like stones and they were part of the dark spaces or coming out of them.* "Quite the imagination," the school counselor told their father. And they had blamed it on her grief. *First your mother, then Patrick.* Seeing things. At some point his mother quit telling Paul about them. She was only being silly, she had said. And he could see she wanted to spare him of something and he saw it again later with Kit. Kit had looked past him the same way their mother had. *The way she saw things or said she saw things and I was the only one who could make sense of anything.* They're coming through the window, their mother told him, that summer afternoon. She believed they would watch over things. *You and Kitty and your father.* The morphine, they said. *Can cause, can create.* Visions, maybe. Hallucinations. And he had only imagined the rest.

Maybe we all have it, Paul thinks. *Somewhere deep inside us only it chooses when to make its presence known.* It was, he figured, some kind of mental disorder that had never been diagnosed. Running through their veins. Generational. *That doesn't explain Marg.* Anyway, he had seen Rob hanging around that same week Patrick went missing. *The rings beneath his eyes like he hadn't slept for months.* They had nothing to go on, they would say. Kids shouldn't be out there. Simple as that.

Gretchen reappears, pours another.

"Things okay, Paul?" she asks.

"Why do you ask?

She shrugs.

"The look on your face is all."

They jotted down notes. Recommended a professional for Kit. Or a counselor, at least. The school provided one. *Spring came and they never found him like they thought they would and they questioned Rob again and again and there was nothing to pinpoint and they had nothing to go on and when did they quit looking?*

The bottom out from under me.

Gretchen looks at him.

"Some night, stick around," she says. "We'll catch up."

"We can catch up now."

She considers the empty bar.

"I suppose."

Gretchen, skating across the grange in her socks. She had this quickness in her eye and he would follow her around. The next summer their mother died. *It's in her bones. Was what they said.* She was thirty-five. She used to watch the sun going down. *Like it was being pulled into the canyon, she said.*

Gretchen picks up the bar rag. Crumples it in her hand.

Lately Paul had started to see things like in a distorted lens. Nebulous, odd. *They're coming through the window, she said. They're climbing through.* At times it jolts him awake. A stone, a face. He is not thinking right. Too much to drink. *No self-control.* Sometimes he thinks he is losing it.

You know how things are around here, his father said once, after Patrick had been missing for months. How are they? Explain, please? He never answered. It was like he hardly had known he had spoken.

We brought Carol coffee and she invited us in and asked how Kitty was doing. She could not have been very old, looking back. *They were down there,* Paul thought. *I saw them down there. Him and Kit and they were throwing rocks.* He hollered at them to cut it out and get away from the water and Kit came up and he stayed behind throwing rocks. *Carrie was shaking and winding the cloth and her face was terrifying.* He was never hers to begin with, she said. Anyway, he was never hers. Where had he come from? she had asked. *She's lost it, they would say later.*

"I thought I found that kid," he tells Gretchen now.

"What kid?"

"The Miller kid. Kitty's friend. Out in the trees."

Patrick.

"Carrie Miller. God," Gretchen says, folding the bar rag. "What some people go through."

He and his father had brought her coffee, he tells Gretchen, while they were searching. Her house was always so cold.

And the bones in the mud. He tells Gretchen what he found. Yellowed, broken.

"When was this?" she asks.

"A few months ago. They sent them away for analysis. Called me later. They were centuries older, they said. I don't know." *Centuries.* "I'm not sure what they were getting at."

"No kidding," she says.

She does not look surprised.

"You know, there were those little people they found," Gretchen says now. "Maybe it was one of them."

He looks at her.

"No, really. They were *small of stature*, I mean. I took an anthropology class in college and they mentioned it in passing. They had sent this relic or mummy somewhere and it never was returned. I don't think they took it seriously though. I mean." She shrugs. "South of here. But there are native stories about them too, you know. These little people. Seems uncanny."

She suddenly seems youthful, vibrant.

"Anyway," Gretchen says. "You know they talk about outer space or the deep sea. The wilderness is the same way. Who knows what's lurking around in there? We don't know anything. Why do we think we know everything? We're vain, that's what it is. Think we're so smart. People are so disconnected. I think that's what's wrong. We miss everything."

Well.

She is glowing.

There was a fire and we ran through it.

"And we aren't the only place with stories like those. Every place has them. Why does every place have them? Seems pretty coincidental." *Carrie was still in her work clothes with the black apron and starched shirt and nametag and she was just a kid and I never thought about it but Jesus she was just a kid. And she wound the dishcloth and stared at the door like he would suddenly appear and the whole thing would be a farce.* That afternoon the snow collected on the pickup windshield and Paul could see the frosty mountains vaguely through the trees and his father leaned his head on the steering wheel and broke down and Paul only stared ahead at the darkening trees.

They're coming out of the trees, their mother had said.

They made her laugh. That little one, especially. With the chokecherry hands.

Somewhere deep inside us only it doesn't always surface and maybe we all have it there, swimming around inside us only it was never diagnosed. And it could show up anytime.

Gretchen taps him on the hand. "It's so good to see you, Paul."

"Don't act like you've never seen nothing," Marg said to him, the smoke snaking above her and her eyes flashing like nickels. *I was the only rational one,* he thought. *I've had too much to drink and what time is it? How long have I been here?*

Gretchen disappears through the swinging doors and he edges past the yawning fisherman, and the door opens wide and wider and the moon wanes through the trees. Outside his shadow stretches up behind him. Stalking him, catlike. *Why can't I get it together?* He sits in the pickup. The streetlamp arches across the parking lot. *You're going to drown.* He turns north. *You can always find your way back. Say you ever got lost.* At home Queenie is waiting for him.

13. Bark Boats

At the river they threw stones. "Maybe Jesus drank this same water," Patrick said. Tiger shirt, blue jeans. The darker spots on his knees where she had mended them. *And when we got back Rob stood there in the front yard and he was smoking and Carrie was with him and had one hand on her face and she was rigid.* Rob turned his head a little and grinned at them. *And his teeth were black.* And Patrick in his patched highwater jeans and t-shirt too big for him. "Quite a kid," he said. "Could use a sandwich maybe," he said. He flicked the cigarette and eyed Patrick. "He's awful skinny," Rob said. "Don't you feed him? Doesn't she feed you?" *You said nothing but your hands were shaking and you held the bark there.* He would chisel it out. "Nothing's wrong with him," Carrie said. "He's just a kid." *And his eyes were like oil spots and his teeth were black.* He squeezed Patrick's shoulder. Her face cemented. She did not want to take a dime from him, she said. *"Take a dime from him and he'll think you owe him and we don't owe him nothing, Patty. He tries to give you anything you say no thank you and just keep walking, okay?"* Undercurrents, they said, could sweep you away for miles. *Or fathers, slighted, plastered, lurking in rusted pickups.* "It wasn't him," she would say. She had seen the trees take him. And it wasn't him. *And we ran along the bank and we watched the boat twirling down and they wouldn't get it back and it didn't matter because he could carve another one.* He would carve another one. "Air moves like water," he said. *Air eddies and swirls and ebbs and flows just like water and just like water there are deeper parts, condensed parts, faster, dangerous. Only we don't see it. Just like we think the river is safe because it looks slow. Only underneath it goes faster and faster and pulls you under and does not care one bit.*

She had a brother, Carrie did. He had moved to Michigan or Minnesota. Something like that. He never bothered returning after their father died. *Why would he? Why does anyone?* Maybe they could go stay with him out there. And if he didn't look a lot like Danny then, Carrie used to say. The same ice-blue eyes. They even said so. Those who remembered Danny as a kid. Looks a lot like Danny, they said. She gave Patrick Danny's name belt and Danny's marbles and Danny's

Burlington Northern set. Sent her brother a card now and then but never heard much back.

"There are air currents the same way there are water currents," Patrick said that afternoon.

Sometimes you could see it there, she thought later. The way a bird caught on the air funny and looked like it was being pulled along. Or the way the leaves lifted. As if some invisible person was on the path. *And we ran back toward the trees and you were already leaving.*

He turned the bark in his hand. Carved out a hollowing. There were all kinds of things they could not see, Marg said. A thin veil. Only sometimes things get through. The cuckoo clock, the opened window. *And he was so close to the water and I called him back and he only laughed and his face shone like he had just seen God and him shining like Moses on whatever mountain and when we came back the pickup was gone and Carrie stood there with her arms folded and her face like I'd never seen.*

And the following afternoon Carrie picked him up and drove him to Marg's before she returned to work.

Like a piece of you torn straight out, she told Paul when you disappeared. She couldn't hardly breathe she said and she thought she'd maybe stop breathing altogether. It was like being held underwater. I wish they'd just keep me down there. Keep holding me down there. Until I was dead. I wish someone would drown me. Was what she said. And Paul said he hadn't known what to say.

And she and Patrick sat on the sagging couch together and they ate the day-old donuts she brought home and he showed her the pictures he had drawn at school and she taped them up all over the house and she said someday she'd get a better job or go back to school and they could go out to where Danny lived. There was a zoo there, she said. *Right up your alley.*

≈ ≈ ≈

Sometimes, Marg said, it was a good thing. Sometimes they helped. A hiding place. There are variables. Sometimes it was a refuge. *A sanctuary, you said. You'd run to the church or at least into the trees.* You just never can tell.

14. Cubicle

It is raining in the suburbs again. It is always raining and Kit has filed things away and made coffee for them in their shining silver suits and they are like schooling fish. They do not look at her when they take the coffee or paperwork. The blinds are partly down and the lines between are gray.

Lately she can hardly eat. She only wants bread. Cake.

And Patrick reached for her hand *and his boy's grin, tiger shirt. Come on, Kitty, you said. Guess what I saw down there and there's a whole den of them and we went down and they were gray and yawning there. Your hair was combed back for mass. Carrie and her white legs and bachelor's buttons. I almost forgot.* It was so hot that summer and no one could sleep hardly and the ground dried up and webbed.

Something isn't right.

Creamer. Someone wants creamer. *Vanilla latte hazelnut peppermint mocha pumpkin and you've got to play along.* She brings in the tray. They still do not look at her. Their hands are delicate. Like they would snap apart.

Patrick got off the bus with her on that first day. First, he only walked beside her without saying anything. Then just started jabbering.

And you were alongside the water and running toward the water and I said to slow down and then you sank beneath the ice crashed there and it was a hard January and you were so cold and could not quit shaking and you probably have hypothermia I said and you did not say anything but smashed your teeth and Paul came when he heard me and there was your wet knit hat and your coat and I brought your mittens back she had made.

"I feel like I swallowed the earth," Kit tells Stephanie now and Stephanie says she understands. *And also. Everything around like it is closing in.* She does not say. *Without the medication.* They have what they think they need. *They think they can block things out and return to their cavernous homes and send one another meaningless messages and remain on the surface with their organic cotton mocha skinny almond milk and I'm not being fair just like Jason says.*

Kit stands in the breakroom. The coffee is tepid. She feels heavy. They would have a little family, he said. What's one kid?

Said he.

Play along.

Kit looks out the window at the density of rhododendrons, heavy with rain. The size of your head, some of them. They still astonish her. They could never have flowers like that at home. *High mountain desert, they always called it. So dry sometimes the land puffed up ahead of you. Like a spirit there. A tiny tornado. We loved those.*

She suddenly craves the sunlight. The dry air. The river so black and he crossed over and back again. "It's easy," he said. "Right across like Jesus did." And people used to believe in things or at least try to.

≈ ≈ ≈

In the evening the kids play video games on the gigantic television screen. The characters leap into oblivion. "Die and reboot is all it takes," Bethany says. "I'm so glad you could make it." Her hand, a dry leaf. She is in the middle of a divorce. "Rocky," she says. "Anyway. Got to live your best life. That's how it goes. What would you like to drink? Seltzer? I'll take your coats."

Jason holds her arm the entire time. Looks at her while she speaks. As if she will say something wrong and he will maybe need to intervene. *To err is human.* He was worried, he told her on the drive here. She had not seemed like herself lately. She was tired, she said. He stared forward at the road. He was not convinced, he said. All the lights, she said then. She never saw the stars anymore. He glanced at her and back at the wet road. She felt stuck. They were quiet on the rest of the drive.

15. Charcoal

Very early morning and the sky is charcoal-gray. At first Kit thinks the woman on the beach is waving at someone else. *Who else? No one else around.* The sun is hardly up. She realizes she has not been down on the shore for months. Maybe even longer. She had practically forgotten it was there. The wind is steady.

The seagrass bends.

The woman walks toward her and extends a hand. "Muriel," she says.

She says she had seen Kit out on her balcony. Wondered if she lived alone. "There's Jason," Kit says. "At work. And now I'm home. Waiting for the baby."

Muriel looks steadily at her. *Ageless.*

"Cold out. Why don't you come over? You don't look like an axe murderer. I'll make tea."

She and Jason had passed the old blue house their first week out here. "Yikes," he had said. A large, rundown porch. Chipped periwinkle blue paint. He did not know anyone could possibly live there, he said. Although he was told someone did. Some loner lady. *And this is her.*

The house is weathered. It seems boggy. "They can't stand the sight of it," Muriel says, kicking her flats across the room. "Want it torn down. Pushed to have it torn down. I had to fight tooth and nail. Said it was in their district." She mostly ignores them, she says. She is grandfathered in and there is not a damn thing any of them can do about it. They offered to buy the house on more than one occasion. They want to tear it down and put in townhouses. "No offense," she says, glancing at Kit. "Obviously you live there." Muriel fills the tea kettle with tap water. The windows are wide open. The house is drafty, cluttered. The couch sags. There are shelves crowded with knick-knacks. Old, threadbare chairs. Junk she had since art school, Muriel says. You never know when you might need something, you know? There are charcoal drawings on the walls and partially complete on the kitchen table. There are fingerprints on the walls and light switches. Side tables covered in bits of plastic junk and shells. Things she found washed up on the beach. She goes out early every morning, she tells Kit. Sketches what she finds. The objects become something broader. Something with a story. Flotsam, jetsam. Which was which? She can never remember and she does not care. She sets her wool hat on the radiator. She likes the clicking, she says. To hear the water moving through the walls. Like the ocean is in the walls. She is slightly older than Kit. Or much older, maybe. It is hard to tell.

Muriel clears a wicker chair for Kit. The room is full of vintage figurines, ocean guides, maps, charts, dusty lamps, bowls full of sand and stones. She hands Kit a porcelain cup, covered in intricately detailed pastoral images. A tiny horse and buggy, trees. She fills the cup with peppermint tea and drops down into the sagging couch. The images on the cup seem to move, the tiny carriage rolling. The couch is faded in places. It looks wet. Everything here looks wet. *Like she brought it all up from the bottom of the sea.* The room is freezing. The wind through the open window flutters the drawings on the kitchen table but the drawings are held down with stones and glass bottles and do not blow away.

The house had been her father's, Muriel says. She was afforded time and space to draw. She sells a few pieces here and there. She cannot go long without drawing. She becomes bored. She feels pulled, obligated even, to illustrate the shape and contour of things. "Every object has a story," she says, settling on the couch. "Same as this house has a story. And they can't see it. It's like they're all walking around with blinders on. Spending all their time earning status or money. Turns out, contrary to popular opinion," Muriel says, "you don't need much."

"Some people think they do," Kit says.

"Undoubtedly."

The house smells like an antique shop or like the mud beneath a stone, which somehow makes Kit feel comforted.

"People think they need all kinds of things," Muriel says. "They're never satiated. You can't satiate them. They're pigs." She looks at Kit. "When are you due?"

"A few weeks."

"That may change your whole world," Muriel says. "One way or another." The water in the wall clicks.

"I keep having these dreams," Kit says now. "Or memories maybe. I'm not sure what they are. Things from a long time ago or like someone else's memories. Sometimes I don't even know if they're mine or where I'm remembering them from." *I don't know why I'm telling her this.*

"It's probably the pregnancy," Kit adds.

"Maybe," Muriel says. She looks straight at Kit. "You just never know."

For a long while they are silent. Kit feels funny. Like she has been here before. *Some previous existence.* Like she has known this woman all her life. *I know her or have known her and she was pulled up out of the sea and all this junk with her.* Kit stands. "I feel funny. I should probably go home."

"I'll walk you," Muriel says. She hands Kit a cardigan. "Keep it," she says. "I already have everything I need. More than enough. And stop by anytime. Or come right in if you need to make a break for it. Which I think you will. I can see it in your eyes."

I don't even know you and I have always known you.

They walk up the shore without saying anything. When Kit looks back, Muriel is a wavy line growing smaller. The ocean is blotted out by the fog.

16. Venus

The bar is mostly empty when Paul arrives.

"Doing okay?" Gretchen asks.

"Right as rain."

Those are just stories, Kitty. Christ. Give it a rest. And the look on her face like she could've killed me. Then spring came and went and they never found him. She said she saw them. That she and Patrick had seen them. Left them stuff. And they were like the mud and twigs, she said. And they came out of the dark spaces and they kicked up the dirt.

"With everything she's been through. It's no wonder. Her mother, then Patrick. She has to sort it out," the counselor said. "And kids say all kinds of things."

They were in the trees, Kitty said. Hands like twigs. Like little people, but not quite. They dove right down, she said. And we looked again, me and him, and there was nothing. You don't believe me, Paul.

"I'm losing it," he tells Gretchen.

"Oh, Paul. We all are."

Years ago. The yellow Datsun. Paul was fixing fence and he heard them through the trees. Rob shouting loudly enough that Paul went to see what was wrong and Rob saw Paul there and then peeled out and she was standing in her work clothes and one hand was on her face and she didn't think he'd bother coming back, she said. She offered Paul coffee. Patrick, she told Paul, was the point of everything. She looked at the trees in the window, one hand still on her face. Maybe they should call someone, he offered. They could call someone. He was only blowing smoke, she said. Trying to make her mad. It wasn't going to happen.

They had nothing to go on and finally he went away somewhere and when did they quit looking? At some point they just quit.

"That kid has an answer to everything," Gretchen says now. "Comes home every day with his big ideas. Were we that way?"

"You were," he says, trying to smile.

I'm drowning.

"When did we get so old, Paul?"

"Speak for yourself."

She swats him with the rag.

She sits beside him.

You see them, Paul?

Him and Kitty threw rocks and I yelled at them to get away from the river. And Carrie was shaking and I never told her. Him down by Conoco. Someone should say something to Carrie, they said. It should've been me. And the way she stood in the doorway and one hand on her face again and she was so cold and she could not get warm and they gave her the blanket and poured her coffee and they said God, what some people endure. Was what they said, eyeing the magazine pictures she stuck around. The plastic on the windows. *The trees through the plastic how they bent and moved with the space heater and how it was only warm in that one spot and as soon as you left that spot you were cold again.*

And those girls after Kit told them. *Why did she?* "Don't listen to them," Gretchen had said. She had taken Kit by the elbow and they walked to the pickup together. "We all grew up here, Kitty. They don't know anything about it." *Now Gretchen with her new age garbage and her going on about how the moon is in Jupiter or some other junk. Although who am I to judge? They're coming through the window, Paul. And it was only the pressure in her head, her heart, and now I'm drunk.*

Marg had given Carrie advice. Because you never can tell. And apparently it had not worked. *We do what we can.*

"Thing is," Gretchen says now, "I thought I had it made. Things were going okay. Things going along like they're supposed to. And I end up right back where I started. And I don't even know these people. I look around and I don't know anyone. It's like everything is upside down and I'm in some stupid sequel."

It was like they lived in the trees, those two. Kitty was just like our mother. Seeing things.

17. Loam

"I had this friend when I was a kid," Kit tells Muriel. "My only friend. He ran ahead and I couldn't find him. They never found him. They thought maybe it was his dad." *Out of the trees. Their loam eyes. I didn't trust what I saw.* Muriel's oxford shirt is white there in the gray.

"They dragged the river, looking for him. Never found anything. His dad, Rob, had this rusty yellow pickup and he used to show up now and then. I remember him following us down the road. They thought maybe it was him. But they never had anything to go on. It's hard to know what you remember. Or if you remember right. There were these stories. You know. Old places have these stories."

Memory fails me.

Muriel pours a cup of Earl Grey. The windows are open and the house is freezing cold. Kit keeps her coat on. The cold does not seem to bother Muriel. *Perhaps she's immune.*

The dark trees and something wandered out. And she stopped to see what it was and he was already running and there was the shattering of blue and he had that blue jacket with the piping and the tiger polo shirt he used to wear. "She made sure they always went to mass. Then she started leaving windows open, because that's what Marg said you should do. I think she was trying every magic in the book. It's like she sensed something. Then Rob shows up. Says he wants to teach Patrick to hunt or fish. Maybe take him on back to Alaska."

"What do you think happened?"

"I don't know anymore. I don't know what's real."

"And this concerns you?"

"Shouldn't it?"

Muriel leans forward and lights a candle. The flame wavers. Past her, on the wall, is a charcoal boat she drew, a storm. The papers on the wall flutter. "We can interpret things in all kinds of ways," Muriel says. "Only sometimes we forget. We don't trust ourselves."

"I was just a kid," Kit says.

"All the more reason to trust it."

Muriel is vivid there in the graying. She has one foot tucked beneath her. There is a certain rawness about her. A blunt edge. She is like one of her drawings. Shades and tints and lacking precision.

"What were they like? Like a tomten?"

"Sort of, only wilder. They lived underground, or in the trees."

"You saw what you saw," Muriel says. "That's your reality." And she is just this silvery figure speaking. A ghost or figment of the imagination. *Like anything.* The townhouse lights come on through the opened window. They seem light-years away.

18. Coffee

Paul does not remember arriving at Marg's house. Marg pours him coffee. *She can see it*, he thinks. *Christ. My only friend. This old woman.* She has always been here, it seems. Since the beginning of time. Windows and doors always open. "You're so thin," she says now. "Aren't you eating?"

"Sure," he says. *Microwave dinners, freezer burnt. Coffee. Cigarettes.* He gets what he needs, he says. "I can't see straight," he tells her. "Things are blurry. I'm seeing things that aren't there. I'm losing it."

He adds sugar to his coffee. *How did I end up here?* He does not remember showing up. She pads across the linoleum in her dirty wool socks. *Ancient.* "There's a lot more going on than you see," Marg says. She pours more coffee. *How long's she been here? How's it possible she's still here?* "Just where, exactly, do you think everything ends up? The abyss? Nothing disappears. It only changes. Think you'd know that by now."

She sits down, puffing.

She has this rag rug, flung over the vinyl chair. She wastes nothing.

"You're still working on that," he says. "When it's finished, then what?"

"Simple," she says, flicking her cigarette. "The world stops."

"Maybe finish it then."

Her eyes spark at him.

You're drunk.

There is the dusty fedora in the entryway. She has never moved it, as far as he can tell. They married very young, she said. "Appendicitis," she had told Paul. "I'd never felt more alone." *He was the only one she could ever talk to, she used to say. Without having to say a word.*

A flapping now, like a wing inside him.

19. Plastic

Her last day. The human resource woman, what's her name, stops by her door. "God, are you okay?" she asks Kit. She brings water in a plastic cup from out of the blue machine in the hallway. *We can't drink the water here.* "What's wrong? I'm here if you need to talk." None of us are talkers. Not Paul, not my father.

≈ ≈ ≈

Later they serve her Perrier with lemon. A phone buzzes and someone has to go into work. Already. Someone she has only just met. And already forgotten. The door opens up and swallows him. "You can't get away," Stephanie says. "We're all connected now."

"You'd have to go off the grid," Josh says. "And I might. I've about had it."

"You wouldn't last a week," Stacey says. "No electricity or running water. No internet. Way off in the wilds. Water filters, generators."

"Sounds fantastic," Josh says. He laughs. *His teeth are too white.* "We'd haul our water from the nearby stream," he says. "With buckets. Everyday."

"You'd have to boil it," Stephanie says, gleaming. "But I'm game. Way out in the hills. We'd have chickens. A homestead. We'd forage."

Amy pipes in. "I've always wanted to forage," she says. "I *love* foraging." She is radiant in her bird dress. *The swallows all came down and they were haphazard and startling.*

"Homemade jam," Stephanie adds, cutting a slice of brie.

Kit adjusts her crepe dress. *What is it? Viscose? What is viscose? Silk, rayon, polyester.* She feels removed. *The swallows came and you said maybe it's something wrong with us and Kitty has it too and something is the matter with her because she keeps saying things.*

"We'd help save the earth," Josh says. "With our jam and creek water."

"We could get a milk cow," Stephanie says.

"Oh my God, a cow," Amy barks.

They used to milk her every morning and every evening and the cream settled on top and we climbed the rafters and found the swallow nest there and the dust settled on everything and nothing has tasted like that milk ever since and they're good luck, you said, swallows. And I wasn't sure that was right, I said. It might be the other way around. And the milk tasted like grass and the sun came in so bright we could hardly see each other or anything around.

Josh pats Amy on the arm. "Old Bessie," he says. They all laugh and pour and drink. Toast to the wild places.

"I'm just so tired," she says. Jason helps her with her sweater. He says of course she is. On the walk home she sees Muriel's house is mostly dark. One smoldering light and Muriel moves through it. She is drawing. One arm up toward the ceiling. Gauging.

20. Razor Clams

They wandered near the fishing boats and read the boat names and Jason squeezed her hand and said maybe they should make things permanent. The boats clinked. She felt impulsive. "I'm all in," she said. *And there you have it.* The seals popped their heads out of the water. "Nothing big," she said. And he agreed. "My wish is your command," he said, bowing. The buoys bounced on the water, like children's toys. She had cracked his hard exterior, he joked. *Like a crab.*

Then. Several weeks later. Flowers. Stephanie and Josh as witnesses. Done. Check, check. They walked out together, laughing. "They're like middle-schoolers," Stephanie told Josh. "Kidding around."

"And now it's official," Jason said that night, wine glass in hand. "Court papers to prove it. Legally binding. You're trapped, honey. With this old man." He laughed and the wine sloshed on him and he did not notice. His glass caught the light and the light was in the glass and he drank the light. *Justice of the peace. Any ordinary day.*

"You're not that old," she said.

He winked.

He never told me.

They opened the wedding packages and drank gobs of wine and laughed and he stood and closed the window and turned on the faux-fire and the ocean was obliterated.

21. Rhombus

Kit feels enormous. *Mammoth*, she thinks.

"We don't go down to the shore anymore," she tells Stephanie. "We hardly even talk. "

"You don't need to worry about Jason," Stephanie says. "The way he talks about you. And the baby. Constant."

The women gift her plush blankets and board books and mobiles and diapers and lotion and small mechanical things. Pastel-colored stuffed animals. They all sign the card. They pour champagne for themselves and sparkling water for her. "What I wouldn't give," Stacey says, adding orange juice. "Whoops, tipsy," she says, bracing herself on the granite countertop. The gray afternoon light falls inward. Makes rhombuses. *The sun used to be so bright.*

Pink and blue. Guess the gender. Fuzzy navels, mimosas. "A boy," Stephanie says. "The way you're carrying. See? You can't tell if you turn around. Vanished." She tips her glass. A toast. A little mermaid. Merman. Hooray. Another mimosa. It is as if Kit is watching them from another sphere. *I am not a part of this.* She is so far away. *Eons.* The women dress up. Games. Tiny clothespins. Gifts. Tissue paper.

Nothing feels right.

They pour her seltzer.

"Sorry you can't partake."

Mirth.

They wander around, clipping the tiny pink and blue clothespins on one another. *Listen and you'll hear them. Caught up. I wouldn't mind,* Kit thinks now. *Inhabiting a cottonwood. At least you would know what you were or how you had gotten there. At least there would be something tangible. The seasons, the sunlight warming.* The great blue heron. They thought it was a dinosaur, the way it sounded. Flew up from out of the bank there and astonished them. *I saw him going. Vanished.* If she ever needed to talk, the school counselor said, she only had to knock. *Knock, and the door shall be answered.* Blue carpet. The yellow bus. *I sat alone and the trees going by and they were all blurred together and that was all I could see or think about were the trees.* Bluebird. *And before that we sat together and you made trees on the window and the real trees filled in the temporary ones.* And with the wilderness right there and he said he would someday live out in it and never have to be around anyone, ever. *Other than you, Kitty.* At recess the kids chased after the magpies, wielding sticks, and the magpies flew away, undeterred. "They'll attack you," those kids said. "Peck out your eyes." And why couldn't anyone leave anything alone? he asked. "People have to wreck everything," Patrick said, his hand on the foggy glass. *And the clay marbles we found in the earth outside his house. The quartz and copper pennies. And his eyes held some truth impossible to impart. He did not know how to, maybe. Maybe none of us know how.*

The ocean goes on and on and sometimes it looks like someone is out there swimming. Only driftwood. They used to put messages in bottles and maybe they still do. *And now there are microplastics and the fish and seabirds are eating them and we are eating the fish and everything is disrupted. And it's never dark here.* The light pollution. And the litter ends up in the ocean no matter how hard they try. Stephanie makes the rounds with the tiny, colored cakes. *We don't belong so close to the shore. I wonder if the light confuses the fish. Or do they care? What are we leaving the next generation? An old soul, Kitty. Always worried. I'm not thinking right.* Stephanie chortles and brays. This is where she lives. *Inebriation.*

Wooden hangers. Hardwood floor. They tried on flowing pieces. Organic cotton, muslin, linen. Earth-tones, natural fibers. Hand-milled soap. *You can afford it now.* Carrie and her scraps. Patched jeans. The falling apart places. *Your house was always so cold.* Paul brought her a cord of wood. Never said anything about it. Stacked it at the back-door while she was at work. Angels, I guess, she said. Shrugged it away. Was maybe used to things like that. *So cold and the water freezing, too.*

"Katherine," Stephanie says now. "Get some rest. You look beat."

They hug her. Barely touching. *Pretense.* Their arms are like sapling branches. Jason is gone. The room is so quiet she can hear her own breath.

22. River

The river flooded and they could see it on the bank and it caught fragments of the moon and they stepped out onto the water. Hopped across the lit parts. Or that was what she remembered.

And Patrick's picture, again and again. They were in the trees. The snow, starting. The black water. *We looked again but that was the last time.* Weeks later he vanished. *Hands like twigs and they pushed fast down into the ground. The sun changed direction. And they were crooked and slipping up and down the trees and maybe I dreamt them or maybe I dreamt the entire thing and their feet were like they were stitched on backwards.* And they were natural, like roots exposed.

You came over very early that last time and the light was wrong or maybe I was sleeping and you came through the front door slamming and never knocking we never knocked and we ran out into the trees and the sun was just coming up. A pink thread on the mountains.

Carrie wanted to leave, Patrick said. Find her brother, figure something out.

And Patrick cut the bark, the knife steady in his hand.

To leave the place you love most, belong. And he looked up and the sun was on him and he squinted at her or at the sun, she could not tell.

They don't like the sun, Marg said. They want the dark.

Later they went out again and the shadows split and the sky drowned in the darkness and the swallows darted across the last smudge of violet sky and the trees and river and everything was lit with gold. Haloed. The light came through the rock fence and they found the light and captured the light and the last light vanquished and then dissolved into the canyon and everything paused and the last birds skimmed the dark water. And she left him there to stand on the edge of the trees and she went home and the windows were open the same way they always were. *So maybe we followed the rules without thinking we were following the rules. As it is written.*

23. Detritus

Marg tossed the cake and Pie hopped around the porch. *Blue-black shining and his steady eyes watching and it was like he was listening in and maybe he was. Always looked like he knew something he wasn't letting on.* "Not so sure he didn't used to be human, the way he acts," Marg said. "Can't discount anything. People think they know so much."

"Corvidae," Muriel says. "Very smart."

"And the trees," Kit says. "You could hear the trees, if you listened, she said. Souls caught up in the trees. And we believed her."

"I don't know why you wouldn't."

Muriel sharpens a pencil.

Adjusts her easel.

And the smoke used to circle around. *The trees were right there like they were in the room with us and you could hear them shaking.* "She always left windows open. Same as you."

"Smart woman," Muriel says.

She begins a rocky horizon.

"With the forest right there, you could get lost," Kit says. "For years, she said. Maybe even longer. Lost in a place you thought you knew."

"We think we know places," Muriel says. "We think we know everything. We don't even know ourselves."

The baby turns suddenly. As if offering insight.

Kit adjusts her weight.

"Liminal space," Muriel says. "The space between. You've had that feeling, obviously. Like you're about to pass into some other realm. Hard to explain."

You understand this, don't you? Tiger shirt, blue jeans. *Hurry, Patty, or we'll be late for mass. Your mother was trying to save you. Any magic she could get her hands on.* They lit candles every week. *You just never know. Hurry, hurry. They snatched our heels.* A sanctuary. Hideout. *You never can tell.*

Carrie thought you would maybe be a priest. You were so devout, for just a kid. You loved the stories, especially. Hung on every word, she said.

"There were these creatures beneath the earth, the sawyer told her. Beneath the roots and detritus."

"I love that word."

"Quick-tempered and mischievous. They could lure you away. Or make you lose your way. They weren't being malicious. It was just what they did. Same as anything. And if you paid attention, you would maybe notice them. Or they'd let you see them. They'd lure children in. Animals too. That kind of thing. You'd find footprints. We thought we did. Footpaths. Trampled down places. Where they're still walking and walking and can't find their way out. Unless you wanted to go. You could want to go maybe. Say you had a good reason."

The room wobbles. "Sometimes you forget who you are. Where you are. Time stops."

You stood by the rock fence. Your face shining. And my bones were your bones and your face a likeness of my own.

Muriel leans back, assessing. Rubs a rocky bluff with the heel of her hand, smudging the edges.

"Everything is opposite," Kit says. "Day is night, night is day. And so on. There are ways to get out," Kit continues. "You can inside-out your clothes, walk backwards with your eyes closed. You have to be very deliberate. And if you're trying to find someone who is lost, you can fill their tracks with water."

Muriel turns and looks at Kit.

"Do you think that's what happened to him?"

Her eyes are black.

"Of course not."

"I don't believe you for one second."

Kit feels something like throbbing. The baby kicks hard.

"Which part?"

Muriel only turns back to the easel.

He tried to hit us. He did not tell her. I think he tried to hit us. Run us over. Or at least scare us enough to get some kind of rush.

"Was he kidding?" Kit asked Patrick, after the pickup rushed away.

"How would I know?" he asked.

His face was red from anger and he was walking fast and kicking the rocks in the road.

How would I know?

Then Rob showed up at the school. Said he wanted to take Patrick out and they told him he needed to have a form and he said he didn't have a form and he didn't need a form because he was Patrick's father and that should be enough for them and they had to escort him out.

“And he goes out when it’s raining,” Carrie said. “Goes out and gets drenched.” And she towel-dried his hair and laughed when his hair went staticky and awry and they sat on the sagging sofa together and they ate the day-old donuts and she said someday she’d go to school. “But right now, this is enough. This, being here with you, is enough.”

24. Trapezoids

The night like it was furry. Her mother stood in the doorframe. *The attic room, and I used to hear things knocking around in there and I'd wake her up and she'd come in and she'd always come in when I hollered and she'd knock and ask them to please be quiet.* And she'd nestle in beside Kit. *And she smelled like loam.*

"Trauma," the school counselor told their father. "First her mother, now Patrick."

Her father turned his wool hat in his hands. It was early spring, still cold, the sun throwing trapezoids across the drab schoolroom carpet. Her father turned the hat. He wore heavy boots. His hair was pressed flat. He looked out of place. Like he was too big for the room. Or had teleported from some other century. *He looked like the woodcutter.* Kit sat outside in the hall. They had not bothered closing the door. The bulletin board was lined with hearts. *The hearts we cut and I gave one to you and the mud and the bus window open and the trees smashing through the slush.* He crammed it in his pocket so they would not see. Stones, mud, the red willow. *The burning bush, he called it. "Quick, Kitty. Faster."* Maybe extracurriculars, the counselor told her father. What was Kitty interested in? Her father glanced at her in the hall. *We ran and the twigs snatched and I don't know what's what anymore and I don't know what happened. And they were all along the fence and they were in the dark spaces beneath the rock fence and it was like they were waiting and you said what else is there?* An understanding she saw then. He turned the hat. Looked back at the counselor and said she had lots of interests and she seemed just fine, fine. And he thought she was improving. And it would only take time. *Things take time, he said.*

That night Kit could see Orion, angled in the sky. Her father sat alone in the darkening kitchen. He could not sleep either, he said. *That same recognition.* She went out with him to the kitchen and sat with him and he rotated the saltshaker in his hand. "I've seen things too, Kitty," he said. He did not look at her when he said it. His face was a mask in the dark. *And you think you're alone and you're never ever alone. Atoms. Nothing goes away. It only changes, she said. And he never left, and she never left either, don't you worry* Kitty, *and that's why the room always felt so charged with life like she was still there and the land too maybe and you ran faster and faster and we felt them at our heels and it was like a game.* Anything she needed, he said. He would be right here.

25. Off-shore

In the waiting room there is a photo in a glossy magazine of a child by an easel and the child wears a clean smock and holds a paint pallet of untouched colors in a vacant, gray room. A *tabula rasa*, Kit thinks. The child in the photo gleams, otherworldly, androgynous. Serene. They call her name. The magazine slides beneath the chair. "Very close," they tell her. "Any day now. Get some rest while you can." A pat on the shoulder. *Get some rest.*

Jason is not home. She walks down to the shore alone. *Like I swallowed the earth.* She has cravings. Cake, chocolate, peppermint. The ocean blocks everything out. The townhouse is too bright. Deflating. She walks down to the blue house but Muriel is not home. She goes inside and sits alone in the house a bit and then leaves again. Walks farther down. She is not sure what she is looking for. *Nothing disappears, turn a stone, look again.*

26. Kaleidoscope

The images flickered like cut stars, around and around. Clear, fractured glass. Kit held the kaleidoscope over Queenie. Versions of the black dog. And Patrick crossing the barbed-wire fence and running toward the trees until she could not see him anymore for the sunlight. *You got enough to eat? You and your mother? Marg asked him. And we sent him home with sandwiches and roast and whatever else.* And then the cars parked alongside the river. Like they had been dropped there. Willy-nilly. *Take Kitty back to Marg's, would you? Won't do her any good being out here.*

"He was faster than me," Kit told them. And Paul nodded from behind them, slightly. What did they think they'd find? *An ally, Paul. Always.* Just keep your head, Paul told her. They questioned Rob. *And if you ever see him again you just keep going, Carrie told him, and you go into the trees. She must have known.* And Rob kicked the geraniums when he showed up that day. The wind picked up. *And you and me, he told you, we'll go see those Kodiaks. Shoot one.* The wind eddied around. And he could not get through. *I saw it myself. He could not get through.* He tried to follow them into the trees but the trees shut him out. Like Marg said they would. Shook and thickened. Quickly. *And we could see him through the trees and hear him cussing and shouting at first and then he was completely blocked out. Throw a comb, a forest will appear.* He had not needed to throw anything. The forest closed up around them. Like a wall. The cottonwood eyes. Kit could hear him breathing. "Oh, my God," he said. "Kitty." And he turned to her. *A sanctuary. And your eyes like those clay marbles and you seemed infinite. How else to put it? And you think you're alone but you're never alone out there.* In his countenance was a knowledge that she could not interpret. *And you moved so fast through the trees and maybe that was it and I couldn't see where you went and you found the quartz that day and it looked like it had been dropped by someone and it was funny how it appeared there like that and we wondered who would have dropped it.* And he held the quartz in his hand and he was by the rock fence and the dark spots hurried back into the trees. *Queenie with them.* And Queenie used to disappear for weeks and they would think she was gone for good. Until she returned and she always returned. "Someone must be feeding her," Paul would say. "Fat as a hog." *Not one bite or you're one of them.* And he had slipped like the dog had maybe slipped. And things were topsy-turvy like Marg said and he wanted to go back again.

And Paul took her to Marg's then and people started picking their kids up at bus stops, at school. You never really know, they said. Things are changing and more people moving here and a who knows. You hardly know anyone anymore. The way things are going. Aloof. Things aren't what they used to be, they said. And they put his photograph on television. Tiger shirt, boy's smile. The blue background, like he was floating on water. *And I loved you I loved you I loved you.*

Offerings we made. The thin veil. The trees. Kit threw her jelly shoe into the river. Asked the river to help find him. *Only those were just stories and this was not a story.* He ran into the trees. *And I asked the river for help but the river never said a thing the same way the burning bush never said anything but some things did. The cottonwoods and the dark spaces and the night and the magpie laughing like a child.*

"Things know more than they let on," Muriel supposes.

27. Votives

She would like a stonger prescription, Kit told Nancy. Things were trying to get through, she said. Nancy complied and the world eased. It was just a matter of finding the right balance, Nancy told her. The antidote.

She hardly noticed when the shadows had completely gone. Vanished without a trace. There was only the subdued light. "It's simply allowing you to be who you were meant to be," Nancy told her. "Breaks down barriers so you can live effortlessly. Fully. People weren't meant to be isolated, afraid. Reserved."

≈ ≈ ≈

They had been married for several weeks. "And this is what it is to lead a normal life," Kit joked. *Did you ever think any of this would be yours or that you would even want it?* She could hardly get enough, she told Jason. She was adjusting quite well, actually, she said.

She went to the boutiques with Stephanie and there was the dressing room with its flattering lights and plush, chaise lounge. "You can afford it now," Stephanie said. "Treat yourself." They wore heels. The boutique served chilled wine. She felt buoyant. *Vintage, turquoise. What was it I thought I needed?* The woman with the platinum bob adjusted the blouse Kit was trying on with her quick, cool hands. She offered them more wine and Kit felt lighter and lighter and she bought more and the platinum woman handed out chocolates and complimented them. *And she was like a nymph.*

"No woman is an island," Stephanie said, accepting another glass. She was not supposed to drink, Kit told her. The medication. "Bah," Stephanie said, waving her hand like she was swatting a mosquito. They all ignored the rules, she said. They were all trying to tame the demons, as Stephanie put it. And they were all one hundred percent perfectly okay fine. "About time you chilled out," she said.

28. Kelp

They drove south, to the sea lion caves. Down the elevator into the rocks. There were postcards and popcorn available. Right in their natural habitat, the narrator proclaimed. Someone threw popcorn. The sea lions appeared ambivalent. "I don't think they care, do you?" Jason asked. She was not sure. She felt fuzzy. He took her hand. "Got my fill," she said. They squeezed into the elevator. *Bizarre.* They drove to the nearest tourist town. The baskets were full of geraniums. *Hot pink.*

On the street he had a call he had to take. "So sorry," he said. They could meet back at the hotel. She wandered alone through the tourist town where the old houses were weathered, shingled. A woman in a plaid bathrobe was spraying the salt from her pickup. "Careful," she warned Kit. "Tide's coming in. Sneaker waves." She dug in the pocket of her bathrobe, removed a tide book, and handed it to Kit. "Keep it," she said. "The ocean could yank you straight out," the kelp woman said, practically hollering. "Sneaker waves, they're called. Come up like a big old hand and snatch you." She reached out a hand to demonstrate, clamping it down in midair. The kelp woman observed a couple walking toward the shore. They had plastic bags from one of the boutiques. *Just like us,* Kit thought. "They'd better get back here quick," the kelp woman said. She removed a strand of seaweed from her bathrobe. "Idiots." She looked back at Kit. She appeared to be cut from rock. "Never turn your back on the ocean," the kelp woman said. She had grown up here, she told Kit. Before the boutiques. All that garbage. "People don't respect it anymore," she said. "They can put out all the damn flower baskets they want. That doesn't make the ocean any less a fact." She shrugged and turned off the spigot and went up the stairs then, as if she had forgotten Kit entirely.

Kit found Jason behind the hotel, on his phone. There were no flower baskets back there, only pavement and garbage bins. He gestured, two fingers, and turned back. She waited for him. They would have to go, he said. There was a meeting tomorrow. Stakeholders. He was sorry but he could not miss it.

They went down to the point of interest that evening. A viewfinder on the dock. She captured the ocean, sunset, cave, lighthouse. *Someone out there drowning.* She wondered what the kelp woman was doing.

Eventually there was an obligation nearly every weekend and many evenings and Jason checked up on her once in a while and she drank the wine she was not supposed to drink and quit going down to the shore.

29. Driftwood

Thirty-eight weeks. *We used to walk down to the shore together.* The last night they walked down he had been in a hurry. When had he quit wanting to go? Maybe he had never wanted to go in the first place. Maybe he thought she would forget.

And the way they look at her now. She had never noticed. Their faces scrunched, bunched, knit, screwed up. *I can't think straight.* "You need rest," Jason says. "Any day now and you need to rest while you can." She sits in the corner. They scan, pour, repeat. At some point she leaves the room and she does not remember leaving. Only finds herself down on the shore and the townhouses back up there lit *and they won't notice anyway.*

She sat on the rock wall and Queenie was out in the tall grass. What had she seen? they asked. *Stick figures, scarecrows. Their creased faces.* She could not say. "Who were those people?" she asked her father. "Someone from the police department," he said. *The way she touched my shoulder.* Queenie ran back.

Something's wrong with Kitty and she needs help, Paul said. He didn't see me there.

≈ ≈ ≈

At the shore Muriel wears a frothy cardigan and a dress that looks vaguely like calico. Her legs, Kit sees when she comes closer, are bare and mud-splattered. She is barefoot. Muriel leans down and picks up a crab leg and puts it in her pocket. Kit is comfortable around her. *Like I've always known her.*

Inside the blue house Muriel turns on the oil lamp. *Like stepping back in time.* Muriel sprawls on the couch with her mud-splattered bare legs. She holds the crab leg, moving the joint as the kettle starts to boil. The objects in the room shift and alter, like they are coming to life. Kit rests in the wicker chair. The charcoal drawings on the wall tremble a little. "I feel strange," she tells Muriel. "I had to leave. I don't know why." Muriel nods and hops up and holds the crab claw as the pours the kettle water. Adds tea bags. Rapt. She has not been able to sleep lately, she tells Muriel. Things are distorted. "Maybe your unconscious is trying to tell you something," Muriel says. "You should pay attention." She brings out the cookie tin. "Stay awhile," she says.

The bus puffed out gray and we waited in the snow and then passed the burning bush and God never spoke but what was there to say anyway?

They were still bothering her, Muriel says. They are determined she should want to be part of Stone Harbor. She would rather rot. "I can't figure them out," she says. "I could make a fortune selling this, they say. And what would that do for me? Got to dig a little deeper." She pours more tea.

30. Cherries

Late summer and her mother and Marg were in the yard and they were pitting cherries and Paul was roaring with laughter and what was he laughing about? *I can't remember Paul hardly ever laughing. Or maybe that was after the fact. Our mother dying. And he closed up.* Marg pitted the cherries and the cherries fell and the sun was going down then and their mother stood there in the blotched light. Everything was off-kilter, she said. Like a fever-dream.

And she sat on the edge of my bed with a glass of milk and the milk tasted like grass. Night terrors, she said. Like having a nightmare when you're awake. "It's just a dream," she said. "A kind of weird dream. You can wake yourself up, you know." The attic room boxed them in. Like the dioramas they made in school. Messy and glued and nothing aligning quite right.

And we walked up into the canyon and the bear-grass was blooming and Marg showed me how to pit the cherries faster and she had her hand on her head then and she went in the house and Marg said let's go get your mother. Everything was haloed in red with the sun going down. She couldn't see straight, she said. Things were fuzzy. Her bowl of cherries spilled. She knocked them over and never noticed. The crickets were going. And it was so dry. "My head," she said. "Like water on my head." *Her with one arm on her face. Her mouth I still remember. Her mouth looked wrong.*

"Get her water, Paul," Marg said. *And it was always so dry and the crickets already going and the dust on everything no matter how hard you tried.* They opened the window for her and the curtains were motionless. The red was on everything and then gone. Sucked up.

≈ ≈ ≈

After she died, Paul walked along the rock fence and the earth was scorched then and it was late August and he twisted the quack grass in his hand. And the food people brought over. *Who were they?* Their father went out to irrigate in the evenings and mornings. *And everything about him was heavy and gray and we never knew what to say and so we said nothing.*

The milky way, Marg said. The path of birds. And Paul stared out at the black like he was waiting for some kind of answer. And there was none. Nothing disappears, Marg said. No one dies, only looks like it. And Paul got mad and walked out the door. And Kit found him twisting the grass around and he was looking at the canyon. "You can see where the ice came through," he told her. He had not spoken for days. "Carved that canyon right out. Pushed through it like nothing. You can see it in the rock," he said. "A record."

And those smoky figures gathered on the rock fence out there, like they were listening in. And she almost mentioned this but then decided not to. *You don't always remember right.* They had their heads down. And they made her think of despair. *She'd seen them too. A few times. And never hesitated saying when she had.* Until right then. And Paul said nothing else.

The baby flips and kicks now. "Like a pouncing cat," she tells Muriel and Muriel laughs.

"Rob used to drown them down there," Patrick told her. "I never saw him do it but that's what he said. I could never do that," he said. "I could never go and do anything like that." He notched the wood.

31. Acedia

"They're building another trophy home up there," Gretchen tells Paul. She is stacking the pint glasses, the bar gloomy behind her. The first house is massive in the trees. She has no idea who these people are.

He is lucky to live out here, the fisherman-lawyer tells Paul. The fisherman-lawyer has obviously had a few. In California the lawyer has to commute. It takes most of the day. "Everyone down there hates their lives," he says. "Gets you down. Which is why I'm here. Getting my mind right."

The silt. Paul can already taste the silt. *Quit feeling sorry for yourself.* The river roars in his head. Already. It is a possibility he entertains now and then. When he gets so tired that he can hardly function. *Falling in and it would happen so fast.* A way out. An escape. Quick. *The possibilities are endless.*

"Acedia," the lawyer says. "Indifference." So dark it pulls you right down into it. "You have to fight it," he tells Paul. "The mind can make a hell of heaven or a heaven of hell. It's all up here." He points to his head. "It's about presence." *Real quick*, Paul thinks. *And it would be over.* Someone would find him eventually. Or not. Although he cannot go. There are cattle to feed. *I can't even opt out*, he thinks. The lawyer checks his watch and leaves. Wool jacket, elk shirt. *I hate everyone.* Gretchen sidles up. *Not everyone.*

"Are the stars aligned tonight?" he asks.

"No idea," she says.

She pats him on the hand.

32. Roots

A deep searing pain courses through her, like electricity. *We grabbed the fence at the same time and it charged through us and you said you felt it long after.* Heart rate, they said. An emergency cesarian. The lights flash overhead *and the lights are wings* and they hurry her through the automatic doors. The lights chopping past. *You said you saw them and there were wings.* They lift her. The blue cloth like water. *Wings and they rose and were gone and they were like the swallows and then like the shadows and nothing makes any sense and it never has.* A stabbing then. Through and through. They hold her down. *Your mother is in the stars, she said. Watching over you. And then the nurse and the birds on her shirt and the empty hallway and there was no going back. They had already taken her away. Your mother is watching out over you, she said. Honey. Quiet, honey.* A wailing now and they hold up the baby, red and screaming, above the blue curtain. *What is this you're telling me? And the curtain a wave and the wings closing and the child screaming and the child is my child and the red and mottled and blue and how did I get here from there?* "That's what you want," the woman in blue says. "Girl's got pipes." They cross the room with the baby and weigh her and wrap her in swaddling clothes and the woman in blue puts a cold hand on Kit's forehead. *You sit here with me, honey, the nurse said. And she rocked me there like a baby and the hallway narrowed and narrowed and I could see the black end of it and the black end of it was a vanishing point and it's all perspective, she said.* "They'll only be a moment," the woman in blue says. *And my mother in the sky and the path of birds and his hand on my shoulder then and he lifted me and let's go home Kitty and now there's nothing else and no reason to be here anymore and I don't know what to do without her, he told Marg.* They bring Lucy around and her eyes are wide open already and red like that from the crying. And she is searching around. Her hands and mouth searching around. *The roots in the bank were like bones and I thought they were your bones and they were only roots but maybe you became them because nothing disappears.* She holds Lucy awkwardly on her chest and Lucy is feeling around, searching.

Another dose they give her, another round. *A perfect skipping rock, Patrick said. Across the river and in the dark places they laughed and waved their weird hands and we weren't scared anymore.* A hand on her arm. *Time to go. The nurse and her bird shirt.* The little golden cross was twisted up there and she had freckles on her chest. She had been there all night. Graveyard shift, she said. The hospital hallway was vacant. *I didn't know where she had gone. Spirit. Spiritus. She's with Jesus now, honey, she said.* She was fine and then she was not. Just like that. Snap of fingers, closing of door. Vanished. And then a few years later Patrick arrived. He could call things toward him. And he walked across the water only he didn't. The stones chopping across the river. Gone with God, honey, said the nurse. Her birds moved slightly when she rocked. *One for sorrow, two for joy. And we were in the river and the water carried us down and we never said.*

She wakes in the glacial room. A fabricated sky. Orienting. "They took him," she says. The woman in blue peers down. "*Her*, honey," she says. "*Her*. She's doing just fine, sweetie. They've got her under some lights. To give her a little boost." She leaves the room and returns shortly after with Lucy and Jason and Jason is carrying Lucy and his face is wide open ear to ear and he brings Lucy around. *Lucy, light-bearer.*

The courtyard lights seep through the blinds. *It used to be so dark*, she thinks. Jason is asleep in the hard chair. Lucy in the bassinet near the bed. *Like water on my head, she said. We were in the river. And her hands were in the water and we caught the minnows and let them go and weeks afterward she was gone.* An hour passes and the lactation consultant comes around and Jason leaves to find coffee. She tumbles in and out of sleep and Lucy cries like a banshee and the woman comes around to help her and the light changes in the window and the shadows merge and split. And she is so tired. Like she is being buried in sand. An oppressive fatigue she cannot define. A weight. *I can't hardly.* Lucy wakes again and again with her crying mews. *Muse.*

And they were very, very old and they crouched in the trees with their chokecherry hands and their wiry limbs. Lucy wakes and Jason brings Lucy around to her and asks her what does she need. Coffee? A bite? He puts a hand on Kit's head. *Chivalrous.* Then grins and pushes back the baby blanket. Adjusts the knit hat they gave her. *She smells like earth and like beneath stones or wet sand or pine bark.* "She's so tiny," he says. "Look at that. Crazy." He crosses the room and closes the window. Goes out to look for food.

At night Kit walks the hall because that is what they tell her to do. A tight aching in her core. Late at night the hall is mostly empty and dark and she wanders past the partially opened rooms and the last room holds a glowing blue television screen and a vacant face looks out at her and says nothing. Only watches her with glossy eyes. She says hello and the face only looks at her. The light moves across the deep sockets, bare head. She looks down the hall. Feels the empty eyes on her. Lit. An end. She walks slowly back. Feels the eyes still on her. Rolls the IV beside her down the hall. She feels a grasping there behind her. She wants to get back to Lucy. Has the sudden feeling that Lucy has been swiped away. The hall grows smaller and smaller until she finally finds her room. Liminal space. Jason has returned. He holds Lucy in one arm. Balanced there. And she is fast asleep.

"Let me have her," Kit says.

And we ran ahead and they were moving back into the trees and then your dad there with his hard hands and eyes like oil spots and we ran into the trees and he at first paced out on the road there and then finally drove away and we were in the bowed brush and your breath was quickened and I held your hand hot in mine and you were shaking. Long as we stay in here, you said. The pickup returned a few times and then no one saw him around for weeks.

Thresholds. The space between. Dawn and dusk, Muriel said. And he was like the Christ he always spoke of, ever-present and moving through. Quick in the darkening. And nothing leaves or disappears. He used to come by so early in the morning. Everything pink.

They bundle Lucy and go out to the car. The gray sky lifts. "I hope you're ready for this," Jason says. The sky crumples.

33. Treading Water

At the townhouse the hours pass like water. Kit hardly sleeps. She wakes to Lucy crying and she stumbles through the muted house. Three, four in the morning. She brings Lucy into the living room. She familiarizes herself with the shadows throughout the day. Their shapes, routines. They swish across the floor and she can hear them. Crouched, nibbling. Lucy sleeps against her, hot and sticking, fists curled like seashells.

They would drive out to the ocean, her mother used to say. She had never been. She only knew the mountains, the canyon. *And you don't know how close you've got to it. How it's a part of everything you say and do and how you see everything. Like looking through glass.* "Still," she said. "It might be fun to see the ocean. Go beachcombing. Swim."

An eight-inch gaze, they said. Was as far as Lucy could see before things got blurred. *Maybe we all have that.* Kit leaves the windows open throughout the day. The sliding door. The cold ocean air blows in every night and the lights come on automatically. The ocean absorbs what little dark there is. *And we don't even know what's down there.* The realization is like a gear turning inside her. *There's more than we can ever pretend to know.* Jason closes the windows when he comes home. Holds Lucy while Kit showers or goes for a walk. *The dark we had.* Lucy curls her hands, kneading. It is getting colder. *And the dark puts you in your place. Same way the ocean does. We belonged to it. It did not belong to us. And you remember how insignificant you are. A dust mote. A speck.* "Hubris," she says out loud to Jason.

"What?"

We'll have nothing left.

"Please can you open the windows."

"It's freezing out," he says. The shadows hobble in the corners. Form appendages. Then appear to be playing a game or passing around a pipe. *God, I'm tired.*

"The light keeps getting in," she says. I feel like I was dropped down a well.

"You need a break," Jason says. "Stephanie knows a good nanny. You could get some rest. She'd clean up around here. Help out." He surveys the room. "It's a mess in here. It's depressing. It probably isn't helping you any." *Flotsam, jetsam.* Things just appear. "Anyway, you could at least get out and see people." He rocks Lucy there and then checks his phone.

"I'm not going to leave her with a stranger," Kit says.

He groans. Tells her she is stubborn.

The sky churns behind him. She can hear the ocean through the walls. Like it is inside her. He crosses the room and hands Lucy back to her and she rests Lucy on her shoulder. Her milky breath right there. *I don't want anything else. Anything besides.* "I'm fine," she says.

"Suit yourself," he says.

He jiggles his keys. He has to go out, he says. Does she want anything while he's gone? A bite to eat?

"I don't need a thing," she says.

"If you change your mind," he says.

The bottom of a well and he's up there and walking away.

≈ ≈ ≈

He returns that afternoon with a new cell phone. Thought he may as well, he says. He was in the area and they had a special. After she had *idly* dropped hers in the sink. The sink right there and Lucy in one arm and the phone in the other and Stephanie kept calling and calling until finally Kit added more soap and then dropped the phone into the sink and wandered back to the couch to take a nap with Lucy.

"The newest model," he says. "The world in your palm."

She looks at him.

"Try it," he says.

The shadows pause. She needs interaction, he says. He is concerned. As is Stephanie. His own phone pings now and he wanders toward the kitchen island. She flips through the kelp woman's tide book. *No longer relevant but was it ever?*

He has a meeting, he says, shortly. A discussion about industry standards. He feigns annoyance. "Text me if you need anything," he says. "It's all set up." He won't be long, he says. The hall opens ahead of him. Another world. The light changes, a cloud moving past. She does not remember what they had talked about or even if they had. What would they have talked about? The thought gives her pause. *Where am I? The bottom of a well. No rope, no bucket.* She does not even know him.

She does not know anyone. The fatigue creeps slowly up into her temples. The new phone pulses beside her. She shoves it beneath the couch cushion and goes out to the balcony with Lucy.

A hard wind comes up. Lucy looks toward the water. *How far can you see?* "There are entire mountain ranges beneath the ocean," she tells Lucy. "Creatures we don't even know exist. The kraken. Mer-people." She hears the front door click. Muriel appears in the kitchen. "You should lock your door," Muriel says. "You're not in Kansas anymore." *She's one to talk.* Muriel sets a grocery bag on the counter. "Donuts, coffee, milk," she says definitively. She steps onto the balcony and leans. "So, how are we doing these days?" she asks.

"I don't feel right," Kit says. "It's like I'm dreaming awake. I keep seeing things. Things feel wrong. Like I'm stuck in someone else's world."

Don't know how I got here.

"And this bothers you."

"Maybe."

The wind comes up suddenly, blowing Muriel's shirt into a pink balloon behind her. She turns, smiling, and drops backwards into the rocks beneath. Two stories. Kit looks down and she cannot see her. The sun is on the rocks like snow. Muriel is gone. *I'm so tired and I can't think straight.* She bundles Lucy and goes down to the shore. There is no one out there. She goes to the blue house but Muriel is not home. The doors all open. *She's one to talk about locked doors.* Kit walks back up the shore. *She must have gone down the stairs only I missed it. I'm not feeling right.* She walks until she comes to a church on the sand. *Why don't I remember seeing it there before?* She checks the door. *How come I don't remember?* The door is locked. She returns to the townhouse. "All the doors were open," Jason says when she returns. "I was worried." He holds back, assessing her. *Something's the matter with Kitty.*

"Did you know there was a church down there?" she asks him.

"That deserted one. Yes. Is that where you were? Why are you still in your pajamas? Did you go to the store in your pajamas? Geez, Katherine."

The fatigue is like water in her head. She cannot think straight.

"I don't know," she says.

I don't know where I've been.

"You're not sleeping," he says. He takes Lucy from her. *Something's off-kilter.* "Maybe you should talk to someone," he says, tearing a jelly donut.

The lights come on again. "Someone should be looking into it," she tells Jason. "All the light pollution."

"It's a safety issue," he says. "It's not safe to be wandering around in the dark."

"It's a real problem," she says.

"It's only light," he says. "It's not like smog."

"It disrupts the order of things."

She is being overly sensitive, he tells her. Spending too much time with that hippie artist lady. He checks his smartwatch. "It's called progress," he tells her.

He fades in and out.

A hologram.

Lucy starts to cry.

I don't know who I am anymore or how I got here.

"She needs air," Kit says.

"Are you kidding? It's freezing out," he says.

"I'll bundle her."

"I'm honestly concerned, Katherine. You seem out of sync."

We walked down to the shore together. We quit walking down to the shore together. Lucy came along. The world split apart.

Jason kisses her on the temple and heads out. She and Lucy are alone again in the window-room. *The glass room and they can see me and I can see them.* The windows like you could walk right through them. And the other townhouses there too and the balconies. The sparkling wine glasses, glistening. Lights beneath cupboards, on the ceiling. *Blot it out.*

Yet the ocean is still there. The moon pulling the water. Gravitational pull. Tides. The townhouses are built high above the rocks. *You've got to watch that water.*

Lucy's hand is cupped as if waiting for a trinket to be placed there.

≈ ≈ ≈

The townhouse is sinking. Kit pulls apart the bedsheets in the vast and hollow bedroom. *Can't get my bearings.* She treads water. *Sneaker waves, river currents. Currents and you don't see them.* Undercurrents, undertow. *You think it's innocuous but it is never.*

"I can't find her."

His hands.

His hands holding.

"I've got her," he says.

He rises from the murk. His eyes are blacked out. Sharpie, jack-o-lanterns. *Someone pulled him up from the bottom of the sea.* She wants Lucy back. The water-light moves across him and he rises and places Lucy gently in her arms. *She's breathing and I can hear her breathing and feel her.* He has seaweed dangling from him. *Where from?*

Very early morning he makes breakfast. He has not done this for months. Frozen waffles, grape jelly. He is usually gone before she knows it. They need him there. His expertise. Starched collar, insight.

Entire mountain ranges and we don't know what's there. He came out of the dark last night and he looked like a drowned man. This morning he is cheerful. He means to buoy her out of her depression, as he labels it.

She sits with Lucy and unbuttons her pajama top. Lucy latches on. Wide awake. Kit is suddenly thirsty. He pours her orange juice. "We drank right out of the waterfall, me and Paul," she tells him now.

"What?"

"Years ago. Me and Paul."

"Doesn't sound like a good idea," he says, his back to her.

"It tasted so good. There was nothing like it."

I don't know what I believe in anymore.

Lucy kneads Kit's chest, scratching with her tiny fingernails.

≈ ≈ ≈

Months pass like the river and she renews her prescription. She feels the world around her now, slowly warming. Making space for her. He presses her hand. He knew she would be back, he says. *Whatever that means.* He pours her a glass of wine. "Time to celebrate," he says. "A little more sleep. Formula, thank God. Back to semi-normal."

34. Firs

Stephanie decorated the upstairs tree in blue and silver, her theme this year. “The boys decorate the downstairs tree,” Stephanie says. “Out of sight, out of mind. Homemade things go down there. Things they bring home from school. It’s not like you can just throw that stuff out.” She takes Kit by the arm and leads her into the living room.

We made salt dough ornaments and she helped paint them and they weighed down the branches and outside the snow kept coming. And she and Paul sledded down the mountain road. There was no one else up there. *Got it made and you don’t even know it.*

“It comes in a set,” Stephanie says. “You just pop in the branches. Super simple.” She yanks a branch out and replaces it to demonstrate. Her face is patchy, red. She has been drinking for hours, she confesses. Holiday stress. This time of year, you know. The boys come through, hitting.

The evergreen boughs and the depth of pine and the forest went higher and higher. Bet you could walk for days and not see another living soul, Paul used to say. Bet you still could, she thinks now. *And later we found the ornaments. Her glass birds. Paul’s school ornaments. And the ones I’d made. She had wrapped them all in newspaper. She kept every single one.*

Jason wanders around with Lucy and everyone touches Lucy and comments on how observant she is. Kit feels as though the walls are shifting. Adjusting. They stand by the plastic tree with their tiny plates and they pour eggnog and laugh and everything swims. Her adjustment period, Nancy calls it. *I’m slipping.*

35. Ice Floes

They rode the bus home. Patrick drew trees on the foggy window. A forest. Same way he always did. The bus stopped and outside Queenie waited by the red willow in the snow. *The red willow we dubbed the burning bush. Every day I listened and I never heard a word.* There were tracks in the snow. The pleats of blue winter shadow. *The still spaces.* The bus having driven away into the trees. *Our own separate world.* The sun was already going down. Hours later he would knock and they would run into the dark. *You two watch yourselves.*

They waited for meteors, owls. What might escape from out of the depth of night, like out of an opened fist. Patrick howled then and she howled too and they waited for a reply. *And what we got was laughter, wasn't it? I need to get my head checked.* The mountains were so close they could feel their chill and the halo was soft around the moon. "A moon dog," he said. He threw the snow into the air and the crystals fell, chiming. The crystals in the air caused it, he said. They caught up the air and froze there. He had read about it. *And we dug holes in the snowdrifts. It kept snowing and snowing and soon we were snowed in and school was canceled and we spent the days tunneling and falling backwards into the snow and the pines cut through the winter sky.* It might be the end of the world, they decided. Or the very beginning. *And those pines the way they seemed to poke right through the sky when you were on your back in the snow and the birds and sounds were gone and there was only the winter hush.* Maybe they could climb one, Patrick considered. All the way through the sky and find the moon dogs there and tame them and take them home. And they would be glowing and no one else would know how come. He sat up and chipped the hard snow with his pocketknife. *And at Marg's we had yellow cake and played rummy by the woodstove and there was the absence of sound then. A hesitation. And Carrie called to say she was home. She didn't want you home alone when she wasn't there.* And they ran through the dark and their own shadows raced up alongside them and behind them with the moon so full you could see nearly everything. *They skipped alongside. They laughed and ran alongside and you said hold my hand and stay holding my hand so you don't get pulled out. And I waited while you opened the front door and you turned and waved and I ran home the same way and the moon on the snow was lit and with them traipsing alongside me.* "You never can tell," Marg would say. "There's a reason for stories like these ones."

≈ ≈ ≈

The next day the cattle snapped in the creek water and earlier her father had pulled a calf and she could see the calf and cow pair across the field and the calf blended into her blackness and Paul was feeding and the old pickup crept along the horizon and into the field and the cows moved toward it and she went with Paul to feed that day and the pickup tossed her around and there were no seatbelts or they did not bother or they were frayed and broken and the air came through in gusts where the floor was rusted out in spots and there were cans of nails and wire exposed and trampled leather work gloves stained and the snow-packed earth and the tracks where the tires had been and the cattle congregated around the pickup, lowing, and Paul stopped to let the bale roll down and the cattle came pushing toward the pickup and Patrick was at the fence line then. He waved over at her. The red knit hat like a beacon there. *You're so skinny why don't you eat? Rob asked. And you went cold.*

She dropped from the pickup and ran across the field and they raced together toward the iced river and they could see the water already through the trees and they could hear the ice breaking free and then Patrick went farther down and she said the water's too fast you shouldn't be down there and he ignored her or maybe did not want to hear her with the water moving and the ice cracking and groaning and then breaking free and he smashed the ice with his heel on the bank where the current was faster and he kicked the ice apart and picked up the broken segments and threw them spinning into the black water.

She went down and stood beside him. They watched the pieces moving downstream. Quick.

He knocked on the ice and then walked out toward the stones sticking out of the water and she called him back and he turned toward her and scrunched his nose and then turned back to the water and went from stone to stone and the current right there black and moving faster and she called him again and he knocked again on the ice. Then suddenly the ice broke and he slipped and fell and the water rushed over him. And he thrashed in the shallow part of the iced river and he swam to shore and he was drenched and the ice already forming in his hair and everywhere and the water dripping. *Why didn't you listen?* And it was shallow there where he had fallen, otherwise who knows? *And thank God he didn't go farther down than he already had.* That was the only reason he did not drown right then and there. *I told you not to and you never listen.* And she shouted at him and she felt the hot tears and he squeezed out his sleeves. The ice would have broken through there and the current pulled him under and he would have drowned. *Any farther out I would have watched you drown.* One hand she would dream for years. One white hand in the black water.

Then Paul came charging through the trees, as if on cue. "Get back," he shouted. "Get back, Kitty." *And you were shaking so hard by then and the water dripping down and the black water was moving so fast and carrying the ice and you were so cold and you were like the ice.* The ice knocked around in the black water and Patrick was soaked to the bone and his mittens were in the rocks. And Paul peeled away the coat and gave his own coat to Patrick, wrapping him up in it, and they jogged through the trees, stumbling, toward the pickup in the field and Paul told them to hurry the hell up. He turned briefly toward Patrick and looked at him shaking there and running alongside to keep up. "Put something on your head," Paul said. "Jesus." And he removed his big, wool hat with the earflaps and pressed it down on Patrick's head and she had the mittens sopping and iced and Paul with his own hair pressed down flat and him burning up with fear. He opened the creaking door and hurried Patrick inside and started the engine and Patrick sat between them and Paul started up the heater blaring and pointed all the vents toward Patrick and the cab smelled like winter and oil and hay all mixed up together and Patrick shook and rubbed his hands together and Paul asked them what the hell they were thinking. Going down there and getting so close to the water. And Patrick rubbed his hands and shook there with his teeth knocking like the ice breaking and he was damn lucky, Paul said. They bounced across the field. Kit held the wet mittens. "Lucky you didn't drown," Paul said, reproachfully. "Anyway, Kitty should know better." And the rutted road knocked them around.

And the mittens in the dirty snow and I thought you were drowned and then you came up with your quick white hand open and grabbed and you wore that old coat from the feed store she used to work at before the feed store closed and she got the job at Safeway.

At his house he tipped the geranium pot to find the key. Carrie was not home yet. Kit stood in the empty kitchen, holding the mittens. She waited with Paul while Patrick changed into dry clothes. The magazine pictures were curled on the walls. Garden paths, cottages. Paul looked at the pictures on the wall and bounced on his toes a little. The room rattled. "Colder than a witch's tit in here," he said. Kit suppressed a laugh. She felt she would lose it suddenly, crack up, and she did not know why. *Not funny with you almost drowning.* The terror of it. And yet. She held it within and did not laugh but turned away, toward the dirty coffee pot. "I shouldn't have to babysit you both," Paul said. "If I hadn't heard you yelling. You should know better. You both should know better." He looked at the ceiling, his fingers in his pockets, rocking. "Man, it's cold." She turned the mittens over in her hands. She did not remember picking them up.

That river's not a joke.

When Carrie finally came home, she pulled Patrick toward her and pressed his head and asked what he was doing out there. Patrick wore an enormous t-shirt and his arms were so skinny and Kit suddenly felt very small and stupid. Carrie kept pressing his head with her hand and smoothing back his hair and asked Paul did he want a cup of coffee and he said he did not want anything and he hit Kit lightly on the shoulder and said they should go. She didn't know how to thank him, she told Paul. It was nothing to worry about, Paul said. Kids just being kids.

Outside the hoar frost was on everything. The magpie was the only thing in the empty sky. *One for sorrow.* The magpie cut the blankness.

≈ ≈ ≈

She followed Patrick down in her sleep. *Look how thick it is, Kit.* The ice shot out fast and she could not see the other side. "Frozen solid," he said. "We could walk across, like Jesus did." And he was lit there and she could not look straight at him. Then the groaning of the river and she could see him like from some other vantage point. The river opened like a mouth and she was down on the bank and the bank was steeper and she could not get down and she held one mitten and he was going after the other one and the river was too loud and the water was above them and they were inside it and she could not hear what he said. And the sun started through the water and the sun was papery and thin and insubstantial and she was again on the shore and the ice crystals were on the knit and she heard the ice groan and then snap and hasten away. And he had fallen through. She saw him beneath the ice. Inside the riverbed. Like the stones. *Lift a stone and you'll find me there.* She scraped away the snow. And he looked right up at her through the ice and the rocks were like flowers and she tried to pry him up but she could not and she could hear him breathing but then it was her own breath and the ice kept knocking.

She scraped away the snow. *And him looking right up through the ice and the rocks like flowers there and I tried to pry him up but couldn't get to him and I could hear him breathing and then it was my own breath and there was the knocking from under the ice.*

She woke and went out onto the cold linoleum. Her father had brought a calf in, the same calf she had seen earlier, and she rubbed it with a towel. The cold was wet and burning. A bad dream, she told him. He pressed her head, the percolator rattling on the stovetop. There was the earthy animal depth smell of the calf on the floor and the legs there bent beneath on the newspapers and towels and she felt the calf breathing there. Could see it struggling to breathe. The river could knock you out flat, they had said. Kids shouldn't be down there. The undercurrents. *The following winter you would be gone. And the sparrow skull you placed in my hand and I felt it jolting there and what was it we shared? Childhood imagination? Mental illness? What? Probably there was lead or arsenic in the water. Because we were all that way. Seeing things that weren't there.*

"I don't know what to do for Kitty," she overhead her father tell Marg after Patrick disappeared. *Corner of your eye.* There were feathers on the glass. Kit melted them with her warm hands. *You made trees and you quit making trees.* "One day at a time," Marg told him. *Nothing disappears, only changes.* And the crabapples, frozen beneath the ice. *Look, Kitty.* "She would have known what to do for Kitty," he said. The snow outside had turned to slush. Everything wet and chilly and dirty. "Nevertheless," Marg told him. "You're what she's got."

36. Offerings

Kit can see the triangle of ocean between the newest townhouses. They are building more of them. There are more lights. She can hardly see a single star. Lucy is asleep, her hands curled at her head. *What did I forget?*

Jason turns on the living room lights. Locks the doors and windows. Plugs in his device. "Things won't stay charged," he tells her. "Garbage." He will have to get another one. *And the garbage is an island in the ocean and the fish eat the garbage and we keep throwing everything away and what did I forget?*

She found Patrick in the snow. He was beneath the cottonwoods and the snow was heavy and wet and it was February. *Valentine's Day and the paper hearts and handmade envelopes and we ate the candy on the bus ride home and I drew hearts on the foggy bus window and he rubbed them out.* They ran out into the field and made angels.

She turns to Lucy. Eighteen months old. She murmurs in her sleep. Sighs and opens her hands. *What do you want? A precious stone? A good luck charm?*

A fire is in the trees. Fire but not fire. Dreaming awake. *There wouldn't be a soul for miles. Bet you could ride clear across those mountains and not see a living soul, Paul said. He loved talking about that. About the possibility. All the way across, nobody, no one, nil.* And Kit is alone in the trees. She wakes up. The light gets in and she cannot block it. *They want to be in the dark places. They go running back into the trees when the sun comes.*

"I don't know how you can be alone all the time," Stephanie said.

"I'm not alone. There's Lucy."

"She's a *baby*."

"Even so."

It was so dark then. They could hardly see each other. He held her hand too tightly. The pulsing there. Your blood. They were going up and down the trees and down into the ground. *And your blood was my blood and our hearts caught up on the barbed wire fence and we had lost them on the way there and they pulsed, beating, and that's what I dreamed, I told you, and you thought that was amusing. And to look at you was looking at myself. In some ways we were both so old. And where did that darkness come? That somberness?*

And Marg tamed that first magpie and she would return, come to the sill. Tap. And Marg gave Patrick more and more. Homemade jam, bread, milk. *And we did too. Take this on home, Patrick, our father would say. We don't need all that. And we ran through the trees and they snatched. We got used to them. They knew us maybe. Or we knew them. If you were embarrassed by it, you never said. And neither did Carrie say anything.*

I've seen things too, Kitty, my father said. What things? Why wouldn't you say?

He turned his empty coffee cup. Grounds. Can you read my fortune? And then he stood and put on his hat and boots and coat and went outside to check the heifers in the pitch black. So dark you could almost grab hold of it. The dark like a living thing. *We did once, remember? Once we held the dark, trembling and vast. Remember? And you couldn't stay here, you said. You had to go with them. You weren't meant to be here. Carrie would get it, you said. She would know. But she never seemed to, from what we could tell.*

≈ ≈ ≈

Jason is gone. Weeks now. She does not remember where. The itinerary is on the refrigerator but she has not bothered to check. He is rarely around anyway so what does it matter? She goes down to the shore with Lucy. The wind knocks Lucy over and Lucy laughs and gets up again and toddles into the wind and falls and laughs and begins again. "Tenacious child," Muriel says, holding her hat on her head. As usual, the beach is mostly empty. The rock cliffs are black in the distance. Like they were drawn there. *They say there are other dimensions. Things we don't even know are right there, existing right alongside us.*

Muriel scoops Lucy up and points out the caves and gulls. Later Kit will find charcoal prints on Lucy's jacket and hands.

And the first time he took communion, he knew, Patrick told Kit. Tasted the thin wafer *that was not.* Like the forest was not. The earth was not. It was more. *You felt you were falling, you said. That the earth or world was expanding around you. Tree roots and boulders and nothing goes away, you said. It's all in your head, that anything goes away. Nothing does. The kingdom is here. And perhaps you misunderstood.* The observable world became much smaller, it seemed. And his world much larger. Or maybe more ethereal, holy even. It was like he knew how to tap into it. Just because you don't see it or taste it, doesn't mean it's not there, he said. And he believed. His conviction was unwavering. He just *knew*. There was an essence about him, a primordial nature, a profundity, that she could not realize. And then just as quickly he would look at her and grin or punch her lightly and she was reminded that he was only a kid, like her, and they would run home. And she would think she had only contrived it.

She does not know what to do, she tells Muriel. At the gatherings it is so loud anymore and she cannot hear her own thoughts and it is like being underwater where things echo and blend and cannot be deciphered.

"Garbled, you mean," Muriel says, setting Lucy on the sand.

"Exactly."

Lucy finds the water where it bubbles up. She shrieks and laughs and hits the water. "Ocean games," Muriel says.

"Something has changed," Kit says now. "And I can't place it."

The three of them walk along the sand, in a chain. "I don't know how to be in the world," Kit says.

"Why do you think I live alone?" Muriel asks. "Why do you think I hardly talk to anyone?" She laughs. And then her face goes flat. "How do you think I ended up like this?"

"That woman has a chip on her shoulder," Stephanie said. "With how attached she is to that derelict old house. It's depressing."

Kit and Lucy wave from the shore as Muriel goes inside the blue house.

"We hardly talk anymore," Kit tells Jason when he finally comes home. He is jetlagged, bleary-eyed. *You need to address this.*

"What do you want to talk about?" he asks. He yawns, leaning back into his folded arms. He settles Lucy on his lap for a short time and then sets her down again. The room feels stagnant. She wants to open the windows but the way he looks at her brings her pause. *He's not sharing whatever it is.* Would she even want to know?

"You should maybe get out a bit," he says now. "Go do something fun. Call Stephanie. Lucy and I can hang out. It would be good for you." He scrutinizes her. "I wish you would call someone now and then," he says. "You're forgetting yourself. You need to get out and see people. It's not healthy to be alone all the time."

"I'm not alone. There's Lucy. And Muriel."

He squints at her. "Honestly, Katherine. I hardly recognize you anymore."

The shapeless night. Furry and what it held. It pushed away and we couldn't call it back.

No one believed me.

She dreams Queenie and Queenie is leading the way and Queenie scratches up the earth until she finds the quartz. And then she unearths the rock fence. And they are pushing beneath. Patrick is down there. They piece together the puzzle bark. Put it back together. *An entire tree.* Ponderosa. "Pinus Ponderosa," he says. "The state tree."

"I know. Everyone knows that." He shrugs. Pieces them together. *The shapeless night.*

"You get to where you don't want to be a part of anything or see or talk to anyone and I don't know," she tells Muriel the following morning. "It's getting worse. I'm getting worse."

"Or are you getting better?"

The dark we had.

The litter is everywhere. In the seagrass and tidepools and the ocean is constantly spitting it back. Junk. Kit takes a bag down with her and collects it. She recognizes some of it. Conveniences. *I don't want what they want. I don't belong here but where would I go?*

37. Geraniums

Patrick labeled the trees, mushrooms, wildflowers. Blue camas. Notebooks, Patrick kept. And Carrie poured coffee for them and then Rob showed up and spat and kicked the geraniums the produce guy, Sean, had brought.

"You want to go fishing, don't you? She can come too."

And his eyes were bullets.

His hollow cheekbones and him chewing on grass or maybe iron shards. Pie was over there squawking. Rob hated birds. The way they stared at him. He threw a rock at Pie and Pie flew up into the cottonwoods and chattered at him. And then he noticed Sean there. *Enough is enough.* Rob ground his teeth. *Funny how one person can be so different, Carrie once said. Like Jekyll and Hyde. You think you know someone.*

Rob looked at Sean and then at her. "Well, I guess it didn't take you long did it, Carrie," he said. "Anyway," he said, "doesn't matter to me. I only wanted to check up on my kid here." He turned toward Patrick. "Thought I could take him fishing. We could spend some time together."

"He doesn't want to," Carrie said.

"I think he can speak for himself," Rob said. He looked directly at Patrick and Patrick folded and unfolded his pocketknife and stared at the ground. Pie squawked from the cottonwood. "Shut up," Rob shouted at the magpie. He turned back to Patrick and Patrick clicked the pocketknife and his face was red and he shook his head. "What did you tell him?" Rob asked, turning toward Carrie. "What did you tell him so he doesn't want to be around me?"

"I didn't have to tell him a thing," Carrie said. "You're making the case right here."

He ground his teeth. Kicked the stones beneath him.

Sean took a step forward.

Tree trunk arms. Wouldn't think.

"Maybe there's a way to sort this out," Sean said then. "We're all adults here."

Rob squinted at him. "Stay out of this. This isn't your business." He turned then and loped back to the yellow pickup. They could all piss off, he said. Sean only stood there with his big, red hands. *Maybe didn't realize his own strength or didn't want to go there.*

38. Riverfront

Vicki parks the suburban in the dirt road and rolls down the window and waits for him. *Just like them not to pave this*, she thinks. *Junks up everything. Your car, clothes. Everything.*

Vicki shakes his hand. His hand is hard and dirty. He is tall, relatively attractive in a Marlboro man kind of way. *Ears like saucers though.* And then, the stains all over his clothes. Cow manure. She can already see he is stuck in his ways. *Obstinate. Runs inside them like blood.* "Some people just get set in their ways," Barry had told her. "They need a bit of encouragement. But if you're patient enough, you can usually break through to them. If you're nice enough. It's only a matter of time. It's like taking a horse and buggy down the highway. Give them a car for a day. Let them see for themselves."

Vicki is worried about Margaret, she tells Paul. She should not be alone. She is at least ninety, perhaps older.

"She's fine on her own," Paul says. "She's always been."

She wonders what he knows about this sort of thing. Is he some kind of specialist? *He's jaded*, Vicki thinks.

"She's like family," Paul says. "She's always been here."

"They're building houses west of here," she tells Paul. "Along the river. Perhaps you've noticed."

"I've noticed," he says.

"They're going for a mint," she says. "This is what people want. Right along the river, the wilderness." She hands him her card. She knows how it is, she tells him. How hard this all is. Farming out here and hardly anyone around anymore and you're getting older and you're the only one left and who will take care of you, Paul? And everything getting harder the way it does these days and price gouging and inflation and what have you and so on. She knows. He turns the card in his hand. "For instance," she says, "you could go do things. Go on a trip or buy a nice house. Go to Seattle now and then. Maybe even Europe. See the sights." She feels him looking at her. *Hot pokers.* "Life is short, Paul. We all know how hard you've worked." *Just be empathetic, Barry said. He's kind of a lone wolf. Show him you're in his tribe. That you're his cheerleader!*

"You must have noticed, anyway, how much Margaret is declining," she says. Vicki has been to visit her several times now. They've become friends, she tells Paul. "I tell her the same thing I'm telling you. She could be a millionaire. You both could." *Why would you squander that for this?* She looks around. It is muddy out. She hates this time of year. "Anyway, Margaret sees things that aren't there. Thinks she owns a bunch of cats. Looks like dementia. She needs assistance. And that place would cover the cost. We can get her in a care facility. She'd have everything she needed. She leaves cigarettes burning," Vicki says. "She could set fire to something one of these days."

He turns the card over. He goes over there most days, he tells Vicki. She can make her own decisions about things. She's always done alright.

"That age," Vicki says. "They start to imagine things. Hallucinate. It isn't safe for her to be alone. You know that. Are you her primary caregiver?"

He laughs then, like a snapping. She rubs her fingers together. *God, this mud.* He takes out a cigarette and lights it. Where from? She surveys his face. "You can call me with any questions," she says. "I understand this isn't a simple decision."

He does not say anything. Just stares at the mountains. Flicks the cigarette and grinds it out in the mud.

She pulls out into the road. When she looks in the rearview, he is still standing there smoking. Maybe he's entertaining the idea. The black dog is beside him and she had not noticed the black dog before, *weird*, and he is patting the dog and watching the trees.

39. Mud

I need to lighten up, Paul thinks. "You're too introspective," Gretchen tells him. "Thinking too hard. Got to cut that out," she says, and she laughs and grabs his arm. She is surprisingly strong. Maybe stronger than him. "Glad you came by, Paul," she says. "Always glad to see you, my friend."

Riverfront, she said. You could be a millionaire. And what good would that do me?

"Maybe you should have someone here to help out once in a while," he told Marg shortly after the realtor came by. And the way Marg glared at him, coring him out. *Just who in the hell do you think you are?*

≈ ≈ ≈

It is already getting dark out. Paul stops the pickup and walks through the muddy field, tagging the new calves. He writes their numbers down in a notebook he keeps in his shirt pocket, leaning into the pickup cab for light. The cab light throws a sheen on everything. *This feels like yesterday and the day before that.* He gets up every few hours to check on the cows throughout the night. Occasionally he brings one in to the small barn in the field and pulls a calf. There are a few times, too many, when he misses one entirely. Finds the cow or calf dead and cold out in the field. *How did I miss it? What was I doing that was so important I let it slip by? I wasn't out there soon enough.* Then with the rain starting and the cow standing near the frozen calf and bawling. The guilt. *Should have seen her out there. Should've been out here earlier. Need a better alarm. I'm just so tired.*

He clears out places best he can. Puts down straw. And he still finds the calves soaking wet and tries to get them dry. *Shouldn't be this rainy.* He hauls them out of puddles, ditches. The rain will not let up. He puts them in the calf warmer. Gets them sucking. *You're on your own. There's no one around to help you. No one to shoulder any burden.* He is trapped.

He goes out to the newest calf. Catches it up and tags it and jots down the number and leaves it with its mother. The cow standing above. Checking it over. The rain blots out everything. *Maybe the world ended years ago and I never noticed because why would I? Tired is all.* He is always tired. *What would it matter?* The empty fields. The frozen furrows. Sure, he told his father. He wanted to stay. *All I ever wanted, wasn't that it?*

Soon after he finds the cow far out in the field and he gets her into the barn and tries to turn the breech calf and he cannot get it turned and he finally calls the vet bu there is no answer. He is one of the only vets who works with large animals anymore. And he is ready to retire. Was hoping to find some kind of apprentice, but you know how these things go, he told Paul.

The cow makes low, strange sounds. He tries again to turn the calf and finally manages to pull the calf but the calf is already dead and he drops the calf to the barn floor and he may or may not be crying. Anger or frustration, what is it? He runs his forearm across his face. The calf is wet and slick and lifeless. *Why can't I get anything right?* The vet calls in the morning. Says he is sorry. He had missed the call. Did things turn out alright?

"I don't know why you're so attached to this place," Elise said. "Your entire life ahead of you."

Not anymore, he thinks. *Not getting any younger.* He takes the calf out and puts it in the pickup bed. The cow lows all morning. Turns around, searching. Like she has lost some part of herself. He gets it, he tells her. *Things happen and there's no way of knowing.*

"Maybe we could have stopped it," his father said to Marg soon after their mother died. She had not wanted to go in when she first started noticing things. Like hands were pressed over her eyes. Except it happened when her eyes were wide open. *Like a bunch of kids standing around, she said.* Maybe they could have stopped it.

She used to stand out and watch the sun splitting down into the canyon. "Say one of us got sick," she used to say. "We could lose everything." *Well.*

The cost of staying here on the land, Paul thinks now. *No help. Alone and we never had any kind of escape. Couldn't go anywhere. Although it didn't seem to matter much.*

The rain stops suddenly one day and he goes out and tags the last calf and marks the calf and cow pair down in the book and sits in the cab smoking and looking at the cattle and the eerie purple sky. Near the rock fence then a dark shape shifts. A kind of loping thing. He straightens. Squints. Not a coyote or badger or anything. *Like a kid out there. What the hell?* The cottonwoods shift behind it. And it looks to be digging beneath the rock fence. And is gone.

Too tired, he thinks. *You're too tired and you're losing it just like everyone else.*

There are times, he confesses to Gretchen, when he feels like pebbles are rattling around in his head. And he thinks maybe he has a few screws loose. And Gretchen winks and pats his hand. "Join the club, mister," she says.

He watches the rock fence. There is nothing. The newest calf totters beneath its mother and butts her and steadies itself. Righted into the world. The cattle seem content. And yet he feels a scurrying up the nape of his neck. *I swear it, Paul, Kitty said. I swear it.* And Kitty was crying or close to it and she said she hated him for not believing her.

He closes the pickup door and starts the engine and drives slowly through the ruts and toward the old house. The windows like a face there, groaning into the earth.

≈ Part Two ≈

40. Creatures of the Deep

The townhouse is vacuous. Larger and emptier than it has ever seemed. The vaulted ceilings, beige walls. *They forgot the ocean was there or maybe they never cared.* The people drift through the lit rooms. Oblivious to what they already have. The ocean right there. *Although what does it matter?*

At Muriel's Lucy looks through the enormous book: Creatures of the Deep. The shadows return. *What I always knew to be true.* "A glitch in the brain," Jason had said. "And sometimes we need help." *I'm done needing help*, she thinks. *Anyway, wouldn't make a difference. I'm already here.*

Lucy names the shells and marine life and Muriel helps her to pronounce the names. The things way down deep. The anglerfish. Lucy flips through the gigantic book. *Five years old.* "You don't have to be pretty when you're in the dark," Muriel tells her. "You can be yourself, completely. Fangs, bulbous head, you name it." Lucy moves her hands across the photographs, diagrams. *Something different.*

At the shore they watch the seagulls catch crabs. "Lucy should be more involved," Jason said one evening. A "You should sign her up for ballet or gymnastics. Find something that interests her."

"The ocean interests her," Kit says.

They get by, the two of them. She brings Lucy to the gatherings. She has learned to exist amongst them. To nod and babble and make small talk. At night she feels him slipping away. Like some figment of her imagination that never quite added up. *How did I get here?* It doesn't matter, she considers. She spends the days on the shore. With Muriel. Collecting and forgetting all that. *And I can play the part.*

She smiles at him.

"You're right," she concedes. *You've got to try. Make an effort. Let him know you're trying.*

"She'll be in school soon enough," he says. "She'll have to learn to be around other kids."

They enrolled Lucy in a private school for the fall. The best reviews. You have to do your utmost, they tell her. The world is full of sharks. *Only a few months and Lucy will be thrown into that world.*

Now Lucy chases the gulls, flapping her arms. The water pulls the crabs back and the gulls wait and then rush toward the water and tear the crabs apart.

Kit brought Lucy down to the shore from the very beginning. Set her out, small and vulnerable, on the beach blanket. And Lucy would bat her hands at the wide expanse. Excited. She always stopped crying out there. As soon as she was outside.

≈ ≈ ≈

At home the salt is on everything. On the railings and beneath the cars and on their shoes. Under the kitchen counter, on the door jamb she finds it. She does not say anything to Jason. *It's getting in. You can't avoid it. It will come around. There is more to everything.*

"Lucy will start ballet next week," she tells Jason. "I thought you'd be happy to hear that." *Do your part.* Kit drifts into the other room, onto the balcony, down to the shore.

For years she had only floated along, she tells Muriel. Until Lucy came shrieking into the world and everything broke open.

The radiator clicks in the old house. Lucy is drawing an anglerfish. She likes, Lucy says, their *vile* mouths. "Where does she pick this stuff up?" Muriel asks, winking. She feels now, Kit says, like things are getting through. Through the windows and floorboards.

"Some people," Muriel says, filling the kettle, the charcoal on her wrists and hands, "the ancient Celts I think, talked about thin places. Like holes or passages. Maybe the universe is trying to tell you something." Muriel takes down a few cups and blows out the dust and settles onto the wicker chair.

Kit feels, she tells Muriel now, like she is slipping. "Like I'm losing my grip. And I can't sleep and it's like there's this hollowing and I'm inside it and I don't know what's what anymore or who I am and maybe it has something to do with Lucy but it's like everything is collapsing around me and I can't grab hold and no one is who I thought they were and I'm not who I thought I was and I'm not sure what happened because everything was going so well or I thought it was but now I don't know. Things are getting through."

She tossed the rest of the medication, she tells Muriel. And she quit seeing Nancy. Unbeknownst to Jason. "Anyway, what does she know about anything? And it's just this constant stupor and you don't care about anything or feel anything and I can't stand it anymore. I can't think straight with it. I mean, I begin to doubt what I know to be true."

Muriel rubs the charcoal onto her jeans.

"So, wake up. Simple enough," she says, glancing at Kit.

Muriel turns back to her shadowed drawing. A finned thing with teeth. Almost abstract. Kit does not ask her what it is. She feels she should somehow just know, intuitively. *Simple enough.* Lucy laughs and throws the paper bits she has ripped. Muriel gives her more. "Look, confetti," she says, sprinkling the torn pieces around Lucy. And Lucy laughs.

Kitty needs some kind of help, Paul said, months after you disappeared. He stabbed a fried potato. Cleaned his plate with a slice of bread and then carried his plate to the sink and washed it and then dried it. The cattle were like static clings in the window. *Nothing made any sense but did it ever? He never believed me. But how could he?*

And we heard the ground rearranging. Roots jarred out suddenly, tripping them. That first winter the starlings came down and the air was different and they passed the burning bush on their way home. And she never heard it. *You have to listen, you said.* He swore to her he had heard it. He pricked his finger and then hers and they were blood brothers. *And Carrie patched his jeans and the house was freezing until Paul brought the wood and she never said anything about it. Back when we used to help each other out.*

"Everyone was just making ends meet back then," she tells Muriel now.

"Yes," Muriel says, as if recalling the same thing.

≈ ≈ ≈

"I feel like I'm forgetting something. And there's Lucy. I don't want to miss her. I don't want to feel nothing. I'm done with feeling nothing."

"Right. You block out the hard stuff, you block out everything," Muriel says.

Muriel pours tea and opens windows and lights candles which immediately blow out. And the curtains blow in, like angels standing around.

The sketches move on the walls.

The angels billow.

The angel nearest the window nods.

"We should get going," Kit says. She watches Lucy in the corner, drawing. She does not want to tear her away. *However.* "There's a thing. He said Lucy could meet a few kids. That would probably be good. I mean. Otherwise, she may turn out like me."

"Yes," Muriel says. "Hanging out with crazy old ladies." She winks again and stands. Gets the door. "Send them my best."

"You'll meet new people," she tells Lucy. She will be starting school soon, she reminds her. *The water runs through everything and it is never really gone but the same water passes through again and again. Was what you always said. Maybe Jesus drank this water. Maybe we all come around again.*

Kit feels cloudy. Far away. As if a truth is on the periphery. *There are thin places, Muriel said. Where things get through. I'm remembering. What am I remembering?*

≈ ≈ ≈

Later, at the gathering, she wonders what Muriel is working on. *Blobfish, squid?* She refills her glass. Wanders around the room. *Like they say. Loneliest around other people.* The sea salt coats things. The chairs, wide screen. The people mingle, completely unaware. Here and there the salt falls in big clumps. Crabs scuttle. They walk right through.

Tonight, Jason introduces Kit to Vanessa. She is new, he says. Right out of college and sharp as a tack. Vanessa swirls her chardonnay. She is flawless. Lips like cherries. Skin like snow. "I'd be lost without Jason," she confides. Kit does not know what to say. He pours another glass and another and Stephanie brings up the issue regarding the new diagnostic and they discuss, the three of them, without Kit, whatever that is and the ocean is silent behind them through the huge window and Lucy sits in the bay window and her feet are bare. The other kids scan their tablets. Tap their screens. Pale as ghosts.

And the sun never shines here and so what to expect? Vitamin D deficiency maybe. Lucy is tucked up beneath the curtain and there are her muddy feet and ankles and she does not want to talk to anyone and he will ask why. Later, he will ask why. *Didn't you have fun? Did you meet any new kids? What were they playing? That looked fun. You should play with them. You should at least try.* And Lucy will go bounding to her room. And he will sigh and collapse with his device. *And so on and so on and they don't even see them now.* The starfish are caught up in the dish drain. Vanessa pours another glass. *Entire mountain ranges beneath the ocean and we never see them. Continental shelf. An abrupt drop into the depth. Anglerfish. And the sea creatures were here before anything. Before anything even crept onto land. Ages and ages.* Muriel drew anglerfish, isopods, viperfish, giant squid, goblin sharks, dragonfish. The things we abhor, she said. *Reckonings*, she called them.

Vanessa opens another bottle. She is clearly drunk but it only seems to make her more attractive. At ease. *Some people are so comfortable in their own skin and what would that be like?* The way he looks at her. *Obvious enough.* Kit feels she is standing outside of herself. *Eels, stingrays.* The light in the room is too bright. It makes her dizzy. *The things we abhor.* The sea debris is everywhere and they do not see it. Gnarled rope, soda rings, bunched plastic bags twisted with kelp and fishing twine. They knock right through it in their nice shoes. *Hagfish.* Jason leads Vanessa around the room. He is helping her to find the ropes. *Hold the ropes? I don't remember.* The refuse washes up against the countertops. They are ankle deep and they do not see. A message in a bottle. A pirate's knife. A selkie skin. *Water goes around and around you said and this could be the same water Jesus drank maybe and isn't that something?* Jason comes around. Says she should maybe switch to water. Gently removes her wine glass. Replaces it. *And we don't know Kitty you said because everything goes around and around again and we don't see it and we don't know it's there. They could have been here for thousands of years. Only no one looks.* Lucy has a tailfin. Flapping it there. Kit wants to laugh. *Rockfish, codfish. Old cod.*

Vanessa laughs and grabs Jason's arm. *Carrie had pictures of those Greek figures. National Geographic. What happened to their hands? Probably they were too thin, frail. Aphrodite, Dionysus, Jason.* And they pour the wine and Dionysus shrugs and his hands are her hands and her hands are his hands. Kit holds the empty glass, smoldering. She feels as though she has touched nettles. *You did first and then I did.* She pours more wine regardless until the warmth courses through her and things no longer matter. *Trivial, silly. Wontons, tarts.* She fills a heaping plate. *Not one bite. They'll never let you leave.* She sidles to the corner. And Lucy there beneath the curtain. The glass stings. *Jellyfish.* Vanessa is youthful, extroverted. *She's like Aphrodite and I'm getting older and you can't get it back.* Her pretty face. Askance. *Someone should paint her.* And Lucy pulls the curtain around. *We should go.* The wine bottles are empty. And it is time to go. She wants to tell him. She does not want to tell him. *How long before this breaks apart like glass?* She only stands there. The empty plate. Considers a refill. *What do they care? And I'm getting older now and when I wake up things hurt and her skin is like snow and her lips like cherries or blood on snow and you don't have to be pretty in the dark.* And maybe they got the giant squid mixed up with the kraken and maybe it never hurt anyone really or never meant to but only wanted to be left alone. The shells break beneath her feet and she trips over a buoy and the salt starts on the walls and the wine is burgundy and there is nothing left. Her head splits. *Woodchopper. Even so. And he split the wood and the woodcutter did and the nettles burned there and Paul brought her the kindling and never said nothing and the nettles burned and he touched them first and then I did.* She feels them now. The stinging. She searches for a focal point. A shabby chic sign on the kitchen wall: Mermaids live here! She feels a chill creeping up beside her. *Everything is here and nothing has ever been gone.*

He laughs with Vanessa. And maybe it is the wine or maybe she never knew him the same way ever since Lucy. *Maybe I never did.* She was so quiet, he told her that first week. Too quiet, she said. On the contrary, he said. It was a nice change. And not long after, too soon. *Why don't we make things permanent?* And then Lucy, maybe three years old. She could make wolves, she told him. And she flew the shadow-hands across the wall. And she growled and loped. She needed to be involved, he said. Meet some other kids. *I didn't try hard enough and now she doesn't know how to be with anyone.*

She finds Lucy beneath the curtain. "Hello in there," she says. Lucy waves one hand. Her hand covered in wet sand. *Look around.*

"I need to go home," she tells him. "I think maybe I'm catching a cold. Things feel funny."

He taps her lightly on the shoulder and says his goodbyes. He seems disappointed.

He walks home with them and he is somewhere else entirely. And she does not want to know what he is thinking. *Because if he tells then everything will be lost.* The street is wet and the ocean is far away beneath the townhouses. A fragment only. A forgotten piece. He does not put a hand on her. And he does not say anything. The road tilts and falls away. Sloped.

Hours later Lucy stands in the living room, the ceiling fan whirling overhead, her hair knotted up. She has seen someone in her room, she says. A short, squatty person. Or maybe a dog. Hard to say. The ocean pushes through the open bedroom window. Passages. Five years like nothing. *Time, it speeds up.* She tucks Lucy in. "Only a dream," she says. *You can wake yourself up, you know.* The shadows twist on the floor and up along the wall. Bowing. *The way time passes. Snip, snap.*

"I don't want to miss her," she told Muriel when Lucy was only a baby. "I don't want to miss anything." Lucy grounded her. Pulled her down to earth.

41. Beachcombers

Saturday morning and Lucy points out the sea stars, clutching stone. The crabs. The tide is out. Along the beach there are caves and outside the caves Lucy draws in the wet sand. The sky is pearly. Lucy wanders into the cave and Kit calls her back again and takes her cold, wet hand. They walk farther down the beach, until the townhouses mostly vanish in the fog. *A figment of the imagination.*

They first find John slanted on the horizon. *Another figment.* He is snow-haired, stooped. A big coat, torn at the sleeves, stained. He hands Lucy a perfect sand dollar. "You have to get out early," he says, "to find the best ones. You know, before the masses." He surveys the empty beach, his blue eyes sparkling. *Cliché*, Kit thinks. *Like an old poet.* The gulls come squawking now and Lucy runs toward them, flapping her arms and screeching. They rise and land a few yards away, undeterred. "Such tenacity," he says, laughing. He has taken to sleeping in the abandoned Jesuit church down the shore, he tells Kit. Prior to that, he slept beneath the overpass. Now he could at least build a fire on the sand. He invites them to the church for a bite to eat. *Anytime.* To come along and visit.

Later Lucy sorts her shells and stones on the kitchen table. *Isn't that bad luck? Someone said?* And Lucy runs to her bedroom and leans out the window, calling to God knows what. She returns to the empty room. Could they go see John? She wants to see him. Go in the church. "Maybe tomorrow," Kit tells her. She had seen him, Lucy says, bobbing way back in the water. And he came out and he was slow at first and then grew larger. "Okay, then," Kit tells her. "Time for bed."

42. Swings

The other kids are together on the cement slab and Lucy is alone on the playground. The swings hang motionless and Lucy runs toward the swings and flies on her belly and touches her hands to the ground. Lucy can see their legs leaving. The cars collect alongside the chain link and the chain link casts diamonds on the ground. The ground sways beneath her. She stops abruptly, digging her toes into the gravel. *Right now,* Lucy thinks, *I'm spinning and the earth is spinning and I'm spinning too only I don't feel like it unless I pay attention.* The car engines and conversation evntually die out and the world goes almost silent. Other than the squeaking chain. She squints until things get fuzzy and the downy bits swim. And she envisions herself, tiny, fixed like a magnet to the earth. Going around and around. The swing creaks. Then the car door slams and there is her mother's familiar voice. They need to hurry up. *Ballet.*

The room is solid gray. The instructor, Jessica, lifts her long arms. "Up, up," she says. The girls follow. Jessica adjusts Lucy's ankles, arms. "Too low," she says. "Higher, higher, chest open. Open." The girl next to Lucy soars across the room with her willowy legs. The other girls pose in the wall mirror. Focused. Somber. There are no windows. Only high, gray walls and mirrors and blue floor padding. "Focus," Jessica reminds Lucy, touching her lightly on the shoulder. Jessica holds a hand at her heart and legs out a big breath and then lifts one small, Cinderella foot above her head. Effortlessly. Lucy tugs at the material on her belly. *We won't have time to go down tonight.* Jessica goes to the closet for the hoops. The girls gather around. Lucy wants to cry. She hates the hoops. *There won't be time and we'll have to go somewhere and it'll be too late.* She wants to go down to the shore and feel the cold aching on her bare feet and the tiny things biting and the sinking sand. Jessica tosses the hoops around the room and the girls spring from one hoop to another. "Lily pads!" Jessica shouts. Lucy follows. She can vaguely see her mother through the plexiglass. Lucy waves at her and her mother waves back and smiles. The other girls wander toward the dressing room in a cluster and Lucy follows. "You want to quit," her mother says on the way home.

"Yes."

"Okay. You're done." She laughs.

Lucy laughs too.

Outside the sun has already gone down. *Another time.* There is somewhere they need to be.

43. Salt

"Come on," Muriel says.

Come on, Kitty. Don't be a chicken shit.

And your eyes were clay marbles and we cut our hands and now we were blood brothers yes.

Lucy would be back from school in a few hours. "Now is the time, the warmest day in ages," Muriel says.

"I don't know."

The water always scared her, she tells Muriel. The feeling she would just sink, and keep sinking. Like a stone. That the physical world would not work for her. She had not gone swimming since she was a kid, she tells Muriel. *We were kids and the river carried us and they came loping but no.*

"Come on."

Muriel takes her hand.

"You're okay. I promise you're okay," she says. And Kit dips down and feels the ocean surging up around her. *I was always scared after that and they said to stay away and we should've listened.* Freezing cold. The ocean overtakes her. Over and over. She pulls up. "Totally fine, see?" Muriel says. *Her face is gray like the charcoal and what shall we draw next? What do you think, Lucy?* Kit can taste the salt on her lips. Her heart knocking. "Bongo drum," she quips, holding her chest. Muriel laughs. "You did it," she says. "Told you it would be okay."

≈ ≈ ≈

"It wasn't the river," she told the girls. "He didn't drown."

She threw in her jelly shoe.

The river never cared, never answered.

≈ ≈ ≈

Muriel wrings out her hair on the sand. The cold runs through Kit's bones. "Tea time," Muriel says. And they head toward the blue house, wringing out their hair and shirts. The cold quakes in her blood. So cold out there you could drown or the undercurrents pull you out. Sneaker waves. Unless. Unless there was more you happened to see.

44. Dog Days

Midsummer and he had eyes like oil spots and Carrie held the back of the kitchen chair and her hands were small and her knuckles red. "You'd like to go with me, Pat, wouldn't you? The rest of the summer? Me and you. We'll fish." *And her hands were holding so tight and her knuckles red.* "Teach you to fish. Learn some things. Maybe get some weight on you." *His eyes like oil spots and she just stood there holding.* Rob looked around the room. Smirked. A temple or shrine she had taped up there. Her hands held tight and her mouth was a flat line and she looked ready to pounce. "Quite a place you've got here," he said. And Kit could not tell if he was joking or not. He peered around then like he was thinking hard and he looked to be chewing on something. *And you were shaking and the window was open and the curtains were wings and you didn't want to go you never wanted to go you said.* He shook Patrick's shoulder hard and grinned his black teeth and said he would be back after he settled a few things around town. And Kit followed Patrick to his bedroom and he looked through his things like she was not even there and his hands were shaking and he was picking things up and putting them down again. *What you collected.* He lifted his head. Turned toward her. "Come on, Kitty," he said. And his hands were still shaking. *And you had to step around him. And the way the oil spots tracked. Like they were hit with light.* He had gone and the pickup had gone and Carrie stood by the chair still and had one hand on her face and they ran through the yard and Carrie her face was blotchy. *And he was always chewing and I heard it snap. Didn't I hear it snap? And then in the yard he spit and I saw a bone but I never and the light heaved everywhere and I invented things because I didn't know what else.* The day widened and panned out and he drove away and the dust settled and he was gone. Anyway, he was gone.

The heat buzzed in the field. The sun was straight above and Queenie followed them down toward the irrigation ditch. The dog days. *When even the dogs go mad.* The tractor pulled the baler across the field. They ran alongside the irrigation ditch with Queenie and the grasshoppers clicked and hit their skin. The baler crossed the field and released the bales and the sun was heavy. *This was when you found the quartz.* Along the rock fence. The trees were absolutely still and the blackish spots between the trees retreated and the swallows swarmed suddenly above the cottonwoods. Patrick looked up. "A flight of swallows," he said. *A kettle of hawks, a parliament of owls, a tide of magpies, a batter of quail, a murder of crows.* He turned the quartz in his hand. Then held it to the sky. *Someone must have lost it there.* He ran into the trees then and she followed. *And it was like we were being watched but then your mind plays tricks. A feeling you get. Someone running alongside you. A weird certainty.* The trees rattled overhead and the sunlight dropped through the trees and dotted the ground and their faces and he was ahead of her and they came down the river and he rolled the quartz in his hand and then set it on the bank and took off his shirt and waded into the shallow parts in his jean shorts and moved his boney arms in the water and she followed him in and the water billowed out her pink shirt and shorts. The shallow part. It was late summer. *Safer.* His shoulder blades cut the summer air. The river hardly felt cold. She tried to catch the minnows. They eluded her and then disappeared entirely. He dunked beneath the water and for an instant was gone and then shot up again in a different place and she felt a quaking in her chest. *Undercurrents,* they said. *Could sweep you away for miles.*

And the dark spots murmured in the trees and the dark spots were not empty spots. Trinkets and treasures, Marg used to say. They'd hide. *And we saw them and then they were only the dark spots and maybe we only created them because we needed to.* He came up in the middle of the river. The river was so low during midsummer. They could see the stones beneath the water. *Like a joke, the way the water disappeared over the summer.* The stones were rounded and she reached for the largest stone that rose from the riverbed. She dog-paddled toward him and momentarily sank beneath and came up with the silt in her mouth and in her eyes and she felt at the bottom with her hands and crawled along and in her hands the rocks grazed and cut and she could hear him humming or singing and the minnows were quickened there.

They stepped onto the shore and the silt was in her mouth. Between her teeth. And his ribs showed and she could see the knobs of his spine and his white hands and he seemed wraithlike or feral and he sang *one for sorrow two for gold* and she saw the magpie then. Patrick looked at Kit and winked and she crouched beside him and the magpie looked at him with his dark beetle eyes.

"They'd be pretty if they weren't so pervasive," she heard someone say once, years later.

And we found the silty mud there and we sank into it and the mud was sparkling with fool's gold and we washed the silt and mud from our hands and it stayed glittering on our skin and the water was so low. She, Kit, felt the quaking inside her again. A creature wanting out. *The unfurling.* Some property of the quartz had maybe affected him. They walked home along the bank. The sun hammered down. She was already warming. And Patrick looked crooked and thin ahead of her there and his head was bent down a little, like a tiny old man.

45. Stick Insects

The school counselor has a tank of stick insects. They are so easy, she says. Low maintenance. She hardly has to do a thing. She lets Lucy hold a stick insect while she discusses Lucy's *situation*, as she refers to it. She is worried about her, she tells Lucy. She wonders why she does not engage with her classmates. The stick insect moves slowly up Lucy's arm. Lucy sits motionless. Afraid that she will injure it. She looks at the counselor. *She could pick me up in her big palm*, Lucy thought. *Get a good look*. "I can see you're thinking," the counselor says. "I wish you would share your thoughts, Lucy. You're such a creative girl."

The counselor takes back the stick insect and releases it into the tank. It clings partway to the side, thrashing. The counselor squirts disinfectant on Lucy's palms and rubs them with her big, warm hands. Her fingers are covered in gold and silver rings and the rings pinch her red skin tightly and her fingernails are painted a blackish-purple. *Like bruises.*

The counselor leans forward with her sandflea eyes. "You're so quiet," she says. The big clouds pass the window. Ships, horses. Sometimes near the ocean Lucy can only hear the water moving and the ocean gets so big that everything else seems to be swept away in it. And does she like ballet? To feel like she is flying? "It doesn't feel like that," Lucy says. "And I'm not going back."

The counselor says that is unfortunate. She leans back and pretends to smile. She would like to understand what makes Lucy happy, she says. And how she can help. She hopes Lucy understands that she is a friend.

≈ ≈ ≈

After school her father sits in the kitchen and the light is like water on the walls. She asks him if he wants to go down to the shore in the morning with her. To catch the ocean. He has to work, he tells her.

"It's Saturday," she says.

"Even so," he says.

She has not seen him for weeks.

"And you never go," she says.

He taps the screen.

"What you do is dig a hole in the sand," she says. "And it fills right up and then you have to make it deeper and it fills up again and keeps filling and pretty soon you get a hole deep enough and the water doesn't fill up as fast and then it doesn't fill at all and then you've won."

He glances at her and back at his spreadsheets. She stands near him, twisting her hair. And then she goes into her room and shines the flashlight at the window. The ghost-fishermen rise upward, dragging seaweed. She sees them, like dark slits in the sky. They do not recognize this place. They drift around, disoriented. She sings them the sea shanty John taught her. And they sway there awhile, bowed in sad recognition.

46. Shore

When Lucy turns seven her mother makes an angel food cake and they take it down to the shore to share with John and Muriel. "Seven," John says. "The age of reason." Muriel laughs very loudly for some reason. The percolator is charred, blackened. John unties it from his backpack with fisherman's twine. Sets it on the fire to boil. They slice enormous, sticky wedges. John builds fires on the beach nearly every day and no one seems to notice or care. Muriel again offers John a room in her house but he does not want it. He is happy sleeping in the church, he says. No one has said boo.

"Hardly anyone comes down here anymore," Muriel says. "Maybe they forgot about it."

"Perhaps they have," John says.

Lucy props the black stones in circles. Sorts the shells. Takes out her sketch pad. He pours them coffee from a tin kettle. "You've got to look at the shape," Lucy says. "Look at the shape and not think about what you're drawing."

"As with everything," John says.

47. Tablet

Jason returns the following week.

He scans the surface of his tablet. "Are you finding what you're looking for?" she asks.

He flattens one hand on the table and looks at her.

"Stephanie said you were hanging around some beachcomber guy."

Something reels inside her.

"He lives down there."

"Where?"

"He finds places."

"God, Katherine."

He turns back to his tablet. "Anyway, the homeowner's association is looking into it. Stephanie is on the board now. She says he gives her a bad feeling."

"He's harmless."

"Really, Katherine. I wish you would make more of an effort."

I don't remember him being so pale.

He does not seem to notice the splintered shadow on the wall. *Listening in.* Lucy hurries into her bedroom. Her padded steps. Quick, impish. Lucy will be upset. What did they mean about John? she will ask. What are they doing? *Him in his nice creased shirt when we first met and his smartwatch and he broke another crab leg and swished it around in the butter there and the candles burned and his hands were so soft.* She looks at him looking at his tablet.

≈ ≈ ≈

And they had walked down to where the seafoam left a ragged line in the water and he did not come down to the shore very often, he said. She must be good for him. Getting him out in nature and so on. She looked at the black water and she saw them stick their heads out, nodding. *And with Jason there were no abstractions.* It was like turning on a light and suddenly she could see clearly. Maybe it would work, she had thought. And she would not be such a social pariah.

An outlier, odd duck.

She looks at him and she suddenly wants to laugh. A weighted thing rolls around inside her. *What he thinks matters.* Jason taps his tablet. *Absurdity.*

She did nothing while the other parents scrolled and posted pictures. Lucy stood in the big mirror, one hand on her belly, sucking in, eyes wet and even from across the room Kit could see it in her face.

"She's done with ballet," Kit says now.

He looks up. "Why?"

"She doesn't like it," Kit says.

"She's just a little kid," he says. "She can't know what's best for her. We can't expect Lucy to decide these things."

"She wants to be near the water," she tells him. "Outside."

"For Christ's sake, Katherine," he says. "I only want her to fit in. Most girls her age have friends. Who are her friends? I'm not sure she has any. There's something," he says, "maybe off with her. And we need to nip it in the bud. She needs to spend more time around other kids."

He stands to go. He has a leadership meeting with Vanessa, he says. *Plug up his ears, Muriel said. Tie him to a mast.* He arranges his electronics. *And it's up to you to make this work.* Jason brushes his sleeve a little. *Kelp bits. Oblivious.* Lucy has elaborate collections along her windowsill and she does not think he has ever noticed.

"I see things that aren't there," Kit told Marg.

The cherries spilled.

"Don't be so quick to assume," Marg said.

We belonged there. And it scared us but we knew it. We knew better than we knew anything. And we trusted it. Time-tested.

"It's a gift," Muriel told her when she disclosed everything.

"One heck of a gift," Kit said. Muriel laughed hard and drew a rounded shape.

48. Jellyfish

The jellyfish are lit with backlights. They drift upwards, ethereal. Then cascade downward, pushing water. The other kids are already in the foyer, waiting to go. Lucy watches the jellyfish. She has only seen them on the beach, washed up on the shore. Nothing like this. Here they are dreamlike, mesmerizing. Across the tank a face emerges then. A boy about her age, murky through the glass and water. "They sting," he says. He slaps the glass and comes around to Lucy's side. He slaps the glass again.

"Stop it," she says, almost whispering. *You're so quiet no one hears you.* The jellyfish glide serenely upward. He presses his palms against the tank. A woman with a very round face comes by and presses his shoulder.

"Time to say goodbye, Braxton," the woman says. "We've got to go."

"You could smash one to bits," he says, glowering at the jellyfish there. "And they wouldn't even know. They don't feel anything." He slaps the tank again and follows the woman out. The jellyfish smolder. Lucy watches them and then goes out to the other kids. She feels removed. She blinks into the brightness. Outside the foyer the sea lions are so loud she cannot hear anything else. She followed the kids to the bus and sat alone and leaned against the window and she heard them laughing and someone yanked her hair and she sunk down and pressed her hands on the seat and closed her eyes and pictured the jellyfish floating.

49. Quiet

"We only want to get her centered," the school counselor tells Kit. "She's so quiet. Withdrawn."

Lucy sits with her hands jammed in her raincoat. *No wonder,* Kit thinks. The counselor adjusts a paisley shawl. "She's just so reserved," she says. She turns toward Lucy. A blue construction paper star falls from the bulletin board. "I know it's not an easy solution," she tells Kit. "I do want to assure you there are plenty of parents in your situation. This particular medication has been a gamechanger for them. Gets them back into a routine. They can engage with the world."

Kit reaches for Lucy's hand and Lucy's hand is small and hot. *Down by the sand, she said, I saw them going in. One after another and they were black and fast and moving and they had dark eyes and they were watching. And we don't belong here. We don't belong anywhere around here.* The counselor looks at Lucy. Her wide mouth crackles. "You have to time to think about it," she tells Kit. "Talk it over with your co-parent. And Lucy, you're always welcome in my office. If you ever want to talk. Hang out. I'm always here for you." Lucy's hand, small and hot. *Burning. We cut through the brush and beneath there were footprints. Everyplace has them. It's just a matter of paying attention.*

They walk down the bleached corridor. *A gamechanger.* Lucy squeezes her hand and the door opens automatically and they walk out into the silvery air.

50. Moss

They drive through the green hills and the leaves are enormous like kites or umbrellas and Lucy thinks maybe she can use one as a shelter or some kind of hideaway. Through the trees Lucy can see the mossy stones, like green children napping on the forest floor. They lift their heads a little. Everything is sopping wet. The road is drenched. Wipers going fast. The road narrows, winding. They drive in the opposite direction of home. They pass a sign: Entering Tsunami Zone. A blue wave. *Just in case you have to run for it.* The road dips abruptly, then rises. Her mother parks at a restaurant along the highway. Above the shore. There is no one else around. The building is weathered, shingled. The shingles are feathered upward and covered in thick clumps of moss. Hardly visible from the road. Inside the restaurant there are crab shells all over the floor. Her mother orders Dungeness crab and ginger ale and a bread basket. They settle into a corner near a foggy window. The man behind the counter has a reddish complexion and enormous arms. He brings Lucy a coloring sheet and a jar of crayons. He has pink fingernails and wears a gold bracelet with a name engraved on it. He returns shortly with the crab. The crab, Lucy knows, dunked into boiling water. *Alive, then not.* The shells are all over the floor. He crunches right through them in his large, black shoes. He sets the crab on the table. Then returns again with bread and melted butter. His cheeks are like apples. He crunches back to the kitchen. Lucy can hear him humming some sea shanty and moving things around. She tears at the crab legs and swirls the meat in the thick butter and sucks on the legs. "What did she want?" Lucy wants to know. "She wanted me to have something. What did she want me to have?" Her mother breaks a crab leg and prods out the meat.

"She thinks you're too quiet," her mother says. "That maybe you're unhappy. That maybe you'd be happier if you were around more people. Said more."

Lucy sniffs and dips another bit of meat.

"They always want to know what I'm thinking," Lucy tells her. "I don't know what they want. I don't understand what's wrong with me."

"There's nothing the matter with you, Lucy. They want to know what you're thinking. It makes them uneasy when you're so quiet. They think you're keeping secrets from them."

She tears the leg.

"And maybe you are, huh? Because you can *see*. That's all. You can really see. And it scares them. That they can't remember or don't know how."

She rips the bread and slathers the warm butter on and hands a slice to Lucy. "There's nothing the matter with you, Lucy. You're perfectly fine."

Lucy can see the waiter now through the lit portion of the kitchen, preparing food with his paddle hands. *Maybe he lives here*, she thinks. Her mother sips the ginger ale. Looks at the smudged ocean in the window. *Who is he cooking for when no one else is around?* The waiter disappears somewhere but still she can hear him singing. It has stopped raining outside. The ocean is right there through the dirty window. There are plastic starfish on the walls. Fishing nets, glass balls. A painting of a ship in a storm, about to capsize. *Splinters*, Lucy thinks. A carved mermaid, three or four feet high, holds a menu. She winks at Lucy. No one else comes inside. The other tables are dusty.

The waiter has gone away somewhere. Her mother leaves cash on the table and they go out into the wet air. Lucy likes to breathe it in. To fill her lungs. "Refreshing," she says, closing her eyes, throwing out her hands, and smiling up at the sky. Her mother laughs beside her.

They walk down through the trees and to the shore beneath the restaurant. The trees are thicker here. There are no houses. *The mossy rocks moved, didn't they?* The rain still drips from the trees. On the wet sand and past the trees they walk barefoot and Lucy sinks her heels into the sand and above them the trees are so thick she can hardly see between them. The sand is freezing and the cold wanders up her legs and into her core. The restaurant is gone somewhere. There are bits of ocean refuse and a biting chill and Lucy's entire body aches with it and she does not want to ever leave. Maybe they can be sailors or pirates. And her mother agrees. They could sail away.

On the drive home the car rises upward, above the greenest part and out of the tsunami zone. "Guess we're safe now," her mother says. Soon enough Lucy can see the monotonous buildings. The littered shoreline. And her mother's face has gone flat in the rearview mirror. They pass the buildings. Flower baskets.

≈ ≈ ≈

Tonight, her father comes home. He has not been home for days. He closes the windows and locks the doors and they go with him to the party and the woman talking with her father has sparkling white teeth and a painted red mouth. *Like Snow White*, Lucy thinks. *She's pretty*. The kids sprawl across the carpet with their tablets, directing cartoon images across vivid landscapes. The ceiling fan flickers overhead, cutting the stagnant air. Lucy sits in the bay window, as she usually does. The townhouses are all the same and so she always has a place to be. The same place, but different. Expected.

The newest townhouse is closer to the ocean. She can hear it now, even with the windows closed. At home she had pushed the screen out of her bedroom window so she could lean out and hear the ocean. At night the curtains billow into the room like sudden angels and she sleeps with the salt smell in the air and the taste on her lips and she thinks of the way the sand sank beneath her heels and the waves that looked like mermaids or the kraken. *What lies beneath. You never can be too sure*, John says. *A selkie or mermaid. You just never know*. Occasionally she waves from her window or from the shore.

Now the living room light is a halo around her. She adjusts the halo in the window reflection. The people at the party are like the images they show in her classroom on the smart wall. The avatars on the smart wall are blurred at times, but they can always speak. They break apart when the smart wall closes down. There, not there. *Ho-hum*. All that bores her. The other kids are always fascinated, wanting to touch the screen and watch them bend, but Lucy turns away every time and tries to find the spot of sky in the window that is not blocked by buildings. Sometimes she even finds a bird. And then she thinks of soaring. And what that would be like. Hanging on the air like that. Letting it take you wherever. And then she is reprimanded and sent to see the lady with the big mouth and stick insects. A shrinking violet, the big-mouthed woman calls Lucy. She just wants her to be okay. To feel included. What does she know, her mother said, on their way out. And they hurried toward the car. *And the moss and the sticky ocean and the way the sand sinks down and down and the way the sun catches there on the water.*

Lucy puts her forehead against the glass and pulls the curtain around her. Beneath the curtain it is cool and dark and the ocean is right there. They're all made of star stuff, Muriel told her. *Crab shells and stars and fish scales and bugs and apple cores.* She closes her eyes and careens downward into the tumultuous abyss, alone.

Lucy pushes the curtain back and goes to the kitchen for olives. Her father holds a glass of wine and Snow White chirrups near him and her teeth are opals and her mouth is smeary red, like it was drawn on with crayon. *Razzle dazzle. Pink fizz.* Lucy scowls at her without meaning to. She often scowls without meaning to. A habit she has. "A little bird told me you turned seven," Snow White tells her. She asks if she had a party. "We had cake," Lucy says. She grips her hands there. She does not mean to grip her hands. It just happens. "We always have cake. Angel food. Down on the shore with John and Muriel we had it." *Seven, the age of reason,* John said. His face like smashed roses and his hands were like that too. Almost purple. Her father had called and left a message from wherever else on her birthday. He had tried to get her to video chat with him. Her mother said she did not know how. And Lucy had shrugged and gone back outside. And now Snow White's face is dried up like plaster of Paris with bits of shells and sticks and junk stuck all over it. Lucy looks at her father and his lips are pressed like playdoh. *Ho-hum.*

She needs to talk to someone, was what he said. And she found the quiet corners and rested there in the nooks and crannies. Like a crab. Scuttling, sideways, always hurrying toward the dark. *Smile, Lucy. Smile. Jesus. It's like she's at a funeral, he said.* She was not supposed to hear.

Lucy stares at Snow White. *She's not pretty,* Lucy decides now. *She's not anything.* From far away she looks like one of those paintings made up of dots. Close up, smeary crayon.

She turns and crosses the room without saying anything and pulls the curtain up around her again. She hears him apologizing. She feels like crying and she does not know why. She forgot the olives. *And there are mountains beneath the ocean, maybe.* She pulls the curtain tightly around her. *Just stay here and she'll come find you when it's time and she won't care what they said.* She presses her forehead against the cool class. She thinks of the jellyfish. The way they pushed upward and dropped down again, unrattled by knocking hands.

51. Holy

Sundays they go down to the church to sit with John. The church is like an upturned boat. Exposed, wooden rafters. A blue Virgin Mary is painted above the entrance, standing above the ocean with her arms out a little, as if she has dropped something she cannot recover. There are faded places where the stations of the cross once were. *And the things we thought we needed we've stopped needing and no one comes down here anymore.* John is reading the Gnostic Gospels. He sets the book down beside him on the pew. Puffy with moisture. "They never want you to know," he says. "Because, otherwise it may be too simple. And they don't want anything to be simple. Let me paraphrase," he says, turning towards Kit in the hard pew. "Turn a stone, it reads. And you'll find me there."

There is a yellow light within. It haloes everything. Lucy darts between the pews. John turns back and sighs and opens a can of sardines. *Loaves and fishes.* His wool blanket is folded neatly beside him. The stained-glass fractures across his face and worn shirt. He smells like the ocean. "I have yet to see anyone down here," he says. "Unless we missed one another in passing. Us holy ones." His teeth flicker gold. Lucy sits beside him, out of breath. He offers her a sardine, cracker. She eats it without flinching. Her hair is knotted up from the wind. *Lucy draws things toward her,* Kit thinks. *Things that matter. Light and dark and water and eccentrics.*

"Maybe we're the last ones on earth," Kit says. John says he thinks that sounds about right. He coughs into a red bandana and then folds the bandana neatly and returns it to his shirt pocket. *Plaid. The woodcutter. You would have to go. Say you were asked. And he can't get past here, you said. He tried and the trees won't let him. Anything is possible, perhaps.*

John clears his throat and snaps the pocket closed. The altar flickers with light. He had these revelations, he tells Kit. And no one wanted to hear about them. He realized, little by little, quite early in life, that he was losing himself. Literally. He had the distinct suspicion that he was leaving little bits of himself around. And then he met this physicist and the physicist told him that was exactly what he was doing. Leaving little bits around. "Peculiar, huh?"

Lucy sings to herself. She kneels at the altar, arranging the tiny black stones. They watch her without saying anything more.

52. Drones

"I don't know how I ended up back here," Gretchen says. "It wasn't anything I'd planned on. And now that trophy home right on top of my mom's place. It's never, ever good enough for them. They want more and more and you can't have everything. There's not enough to go around. There just isn't."

"True," Paul says.

Earlier they had flown the drone overhead, she tells him. She has no idea what they were doing. It buzzed there, killing the stillness. She only stood there in the yard with her coffee.

"They're never satiated. They think they deserve it. They hate their lives. They think moving here is the answer. They'll never get it. A few maybe. But most will never get it."

She dries a glass.

"It's ego," she says. "You know that."

The drone there and the buzzing and flying overhead and then the drone stopped directly overhead and hovered. And she could not figure it out.

"That huge house. They carved out the side of the mountain. They carved out the damn *mountain*. You can see the road clear from the highway."

"Yeah. I saw that."

"That mountain is scarred now," she says. "Permanently."

"Nothing is sacred," he says.

"Like some behemoth came and ripped the side of it out with one hand. That's what it looks like. It looks like shit. They piss all over everything and they'll say they've earned it. Everyone is so entitled. I'm sick of people."

Now it's just me and Marg and she's one hundred years old and I'm closing in on fifty.

"We won't be around forever," he says.

"Thank God," she says.

He smirks and peels his beer label.

53. Flotsam

They should try. At least they should try. *Where on earth would we go?* Lucy presses the colors. She is drawing waves. Variations of blue. She presses the blue harder and harder. Creates shadows. "Just a little while," Kit tells her. Lucy deepens the blue. She does not want to go, she says. There will be snacks anyway, Kit tells her. Lucy adds scales, rocks. She sighs and stands and the window behind her gleams.

The newest house has an identical layout. *Like I'm going in circles. Always arriving in the same place*, Kit thinks. They take her and Lucy's coats. Jason is already there. Straight from work and he would meet them, he said. He waves limply now from across the room. *I don't want to be here. And he's hoping we would opt out, maybe.* Stephanie finally stopped by. Told her she needed to make more of an effort. "If it all falls apart then where will you be?" she had asked.

The other kids are absorbed in their tablets. Lucy sighs and retreats to the bay window. *Don't blame you one bit, kiddo.* She wishes she could do the same. Jason is turned toward Vanessa. Engrossed. They are nearly touching. *I've already lost.* You can't just opt out, Stephanie told her. You have to work at it. You have to invest, she said. Vanessa is swanky, gregarious. She traveled throughout Europe in college, she had told Kit. To get it out of her system. You know how it is. *Actually, no.* She is thirty now, she said. And has already done so much more than she ever would have imagined.

Lucy pulls the curtain around her. *A creature of habit.* A group of them cluster near the faux fireplace. *Fake everything. Contrived. They don't care.* Stephanie breaks away and finds Kit and hugs her. Then leads Kit around the room and introduces her to the newest addition to Stone Harbor. The faces meld. "We're so happy to be here," the woman says. "The view. My God. We just lucked out. It was the perfect time for us." Kit drifts away, glass in hand. Pretends to admire the wine cabinet. "Bali," Stephanie barks a few moments later, elbowing the man beside her. She is already drunk. "You know how resorts are."

Vanessa teeters with Jason at the kitchen island. *Snow White*, Lucy calls her. Lucy is hidden beneath the curtain. *We should not have come.*

She knows now they should not have come. She was not even trying, Stephanie said. *It's not a commitment. It never was. He never said. Happenstance. Spontaneity. He never said he was in it for the long haul.*

Lucy draws the curtain completely around her until only one foot is showing. Kit takes the corner table. *Somewhere to nod off,* she thinks. A cake, bottles of opened wine. She pours another glass and sits alone. Maybe no one will notice her. And she can just sit alone until it is time to go. He wanted Lucy to get out, he told her. Meet other kids. Maybe she didn't want that for Lucy, but he did, he said. *Why am I here? Why not go right now? They'd chase you down. Stephanie would.* The wine tastes fuzzy.

The river was so fast and we threw rocks and the water was even faster and we couldn't see and we swam back and forth and we were not supposed to be down there. And she could see him. And he was dissolving. And the trees were taller and closer and Queenie dug in the rocks and barked. *At what? Canis Major. We found. Look, Kitty. The dog in the sky. Like Queenie.* And Carrie eventually went to stay with her brother and they never heard from her again. Kit saw her for the last time at Safeway and she was stocking ice cream and when she saw Kit she stood in her black apron and the door was wide open and the glass was fogging over and her face was twisted up somehow and outside it was gray and starting to rain and it was November again. *And her looking at me like I reminded her and she did not want to be reminded and she did not want to have to live without.* She said hello *and she held me very close and I could feel her heart beating. St. Anthony, please come round. He's lost and can't be found.* And Paul stood there behind her, waiting. Asked her how she was doing. *A stupid thing to ask but you never know what to say.* And she turned back to the ice cream and her face crackling like that and she and Paul left and she could still feel her hands on her back.

"They never found his body," she told Muriel. "She never had a wake for him."

Her head seethes. Jason is moving his hands around expressively and talking fast. *And who knows what he's talking about and his hands like white marble.* And they nod and sip and laugh around him. Say cheers and clink their glasses.

≈ ≈ ≈

"And where will you go, my dear?" Muriel had asked. "Say things don't work out as planned."

The sliding door bangs open. Muriel charges through in her gaudy yellow raincoat. They turn toward her and back. Shoulders tighten. Muriel shakes out a yellow sleeve. Then empties her enormous pockets. Bottle caps, plastic rings, pop tabs, wads of plastic. They scatter across the floor. The new woman only watches and she looks like she will be sick. "Heathens," Muriel exclaims now. She received an invitation, she announces. From the homeowner's association. High pressure sales, she figures. They glance at her, apprehensively. *My God, they're scared of her.*

Muriel sits across from Kit at the corner table, her hip hitting the side. The new woman is picking up the garbage and a few of the others are helping her.

Muriel pat's Kit's arm. "Why so forlorn?" she asks. "Heavens, you're at a *party*."

Stephanie hobbles over and she is already three sheets to the wind and she balances deftly on a heel and says she is so glad Muriel could make it and she would be more than happy to take her around, make the rounds, so she could get to know the community here, and so Muriel obliges and she goes with Stephanie from one group to another arm in arm. *And you've got to be joking.* They watch Muriel, nonplussed. She is barelegged and barefooted and they seem not to notice or to care or maybe they do not want to draw attention. *They must really want that house.*

"And how could you pass up something like that," Stephanie had said. "Does she have rocks in her head?" And she poured another. And another. Forgot Kit was even there until Kit finally went home with Stephanie passed out on the wraparound sofa. *Blot it out, make it go away, whatever it is you thought you were going to have.*

Muriel returns to the corner table. Pours a glass of merlot. "Classy," she says, reading the label. She is still in the enormous raincoat, dripping water. She leans back. Assesses the room. Jason is red from the wine. *They're already drunk and why'd we come?* Lucy sticks another foot out from beneath the curtain. Vanessa laughs with her head tossed back and pokes Jason on the shoulder and he turns toward the wall and she cannot see his face anymore but can sense his demeanor. Loosened, smitten.

"I feel like I'm drowning," she tells Muriel.

"And why wouldn't you feel that way?" Muriel asks. "Just look around you. Fools."

Muriel swirls her glass, the enormous yellow sleeve hitting the bottles. Vanessa howls and Muriel knocks the table with her knee and the table wobbles and the bottle and cake platter rattle and Muriel's knee is bare and she maybe does not have anything on beneath the raincoat. The wall shifts behind her, like water. Kit feels the sand fleas biting. *She brought them with her.* Muriel empties the bottle of merlot. Adds shiraz. "God, I'm thirsty," Muriel says. *Sand fleas.* Kit slaps her own ankles. Muriel glances at her and smirks. *She knows.* "They can't block it out," Muriel had told her. "It will keep getting through. Mother nature always finds a way." *And Steph said who wouldn't want that? It's just a decrepit old house, she said. Place is moldy and cold. It's like she's just stubborn.*

"Thought they'd convince me by inviting me here. Go figure."

She's stood the test of time. She's been here always. Over and over again.

"Maybe Jesus swam in this water," he said.

Your thin hands and mine.

Muriel is puffy and red and ugly. Kit has never seen her drink until now. "You bet your ass you're drowning," she says now. "We're all drowning." She swirls the glass and the red wine spills onto the white tablecloth and bleeds into a red shrub. *The burning bush.* She swirls the glass again and time slows. She pulls the wrinkled invitation out of her raincoat. Smoothes it on the table. "Housewarming, etcetera, etcetera," Muriel says. And Stephanie said her house, Muriel's, was colder than hell. "No one would want to live in a place like that," she told Kit. "And the woman doesn't even close the windows. They don't even lock. Someone could walk right in. She said what did she care. She said Jesus wouldn't lock his door. She's crazy. I don't know why you go over there. We've tried to reason with her to no avail. We just want the best for Stone Harbor. Did you hear what they offered her? And she couldn't care less. Remarkable." For a moment she had seemed impressed. Then she snorted and passed out on the sofa.

Muriel leans forward now and slices a segment of cake and eats the cake with her hands and licks her fingers. Her fingers are gray with the charcoal. Her nails are cracked and torn. "They can't leave anything alone," she says. "They'll bulldoze right through it fast as they can," she says. "They can't leave one single thing alone. This was my father's place."

They float by now. Good clothes, wine.

Are you never satiated?

"I don't want what they want," Muriel says now. She pours more wine. "It's my father's house. There are traces of him. They don't get that. They'll never get that. Lost souls, lost sheep."

"Things change," Stephanie had told her. And she knew change was hard. But she could look forward, she said. To the future. She could have a new house. They guessed the lot would sell for quite a bit, she said. And Muriel slammed the door on her. And still, they asked her back. Got to keep trying, the developer told them. They needed to include her, be diplomatic. He dealt with this kind of thing all the time. People cling, he said. They need a motive. They need a sense of purpose. "Can't you reason with her?" Stephanie asked Kit, days ago. "She's your friend. Maybe she'll listen to you."

The candles burning, going out. The wide-open windows. The sketches fluttering on the walls. The charcoal fish, whales, and stones. Around her, she thinks now, *I'm finally awake.*

"There are ghosts in that house," Muriel says now. "And not everyone is so fortunate." She scans the room. Her yellow raincoat is mud-splattered, torn. *She's got nothing on maybe.* And Kit suddenly wants to laugh. "They don't see what's right in front of them," Muriel says. "That's no way to live." She rises now, bumping the cake platter. She is wind-torn, ruddy. "You think you know what you want and you think you have everything and then you come banging on my door and telling me what I want," she shouts. "When you don't even know what it is *you* want. I know what I want and I know what I'm about."

They stare at her. Flummoxed. At the splattered yellow raincoat. Her bare legs. "Well, I've had my fun," she says. "Thanks for the cake. Although you can stop inviting me. I'm not going anywhere. And I hate parties."

Muriel crosses the room and throws open the sliding door and goes out, slamming the door behind her. There are wet prints across the beige carpet. Lucy throws open the curtain.

This is how, Muriel told Lucy. Shades, tints, anglerfish, never pretty in the dark. Everything makes sense when you get close enough to it.

"Some people just can't deal with change," Stephanie says now. She shrugs and the new woman concurs. Kit glances at Jason and he is looking right at her and his face is empty. Kit stands and her legs feel enormous. She feels like she has grown too large. Like Alice in that tiny room. The wine and cake and table seem ridiculously small.

Comical. She tries not to laugh. The room warms and she feels so hot and the laughter creeps upward. *She didn't know what to wear, she said. Went for a swim and just donned this. Her dirty coat.*

Kit trembles on her big legs. *I'm too big for this place*, she thinks. *This whole thing. This way of being.* They had emptied several bottles. She maybe will be sick. She wants to laugh and be sick also. Her head roars. The cake is smashed. Like someone punched it. Lucy stands looking at the cake now. She wants to go home, she says. Or to Muriel's. She is tired, she says. Kit cuts a few more slices of the cake and wraps them in a linen napkin. *They'll never miss it.* She senses them watching her but she does not care. *My tree trunk legs. My neck elongating. Drink this, not that. Not one little bite. Or you'll never.* She finds their coats and they pass him on the way out and he still has nothing to say. *They have tied me to her*, she thinks. *And I'm happy to be tied to her.* She feels the laughter rising again. "May I take your coat?" she asked. *What's her name? New lady. The look on her face. When she realized. When she. Stephanie. Can't you reason with her?* She feels it bubbling up. *I'm about to lose it all over their nice, new carpet.* She has never felt like this. Like she could shoot through the roof. Larger than anything. *What caused it? What made it become? I don't care. Why don't I care anymore? Maybe I'll care tomorrow. I won't care tomorrow. Or ever. What they thought. What they must think. What they'll say after we go. Doesn't matter. None of it matters. Never did.*

On the walk home Lucy takes her hand and her hand is warm and sticky. They follow the shoreline. They take off their shoes and walk in the charcoal air and feel the sand fleas biting. They share the cake on the walk home. The rain has stopped. They pass Muriel's but all the lights are out. They will check on her tomorrow, she tells Lucy, bring her cake.

54. Quarry

Three in the morning and Lucy is asleep in her bedroom and the curtains are like ghosts there. The windows are open and Kit can hear the ocean. At some point Lucy pushed her screen out. Kit had collected it out of the rocks. *The window wide open and it's a wonder she didn't fall.*

The murky sky is out the window now and the moon is smudged. The front door clicks and Jason is home. In the kitchen he rests one gray hand on the burnished granite. *A fish belly.*

At first it was easy to be around him. His measured steps, skepticism. The way he rationalized things. *What you thought you saw you never saw, he said. No sense in losing sleep over it.* There were few abstractions. *Everything will be figured out eventually, he said. An explanation for everything.* And he has never known that terror, Kit realizes. That seizes you in the middle of the night and you have to zoom out until you realize you're only a speck of dust and don't really matter. *The most real you can get.*

She can see it now. He has never known anything like that terror. And this realization startles her. Her limbs feel thick and swollen. *It arrests you and you can't stop it.* The wine, maybe. She has never been able to drink it. *But that was hours ago and now here you are.* Jason turns on the lights. *Snow blindness. And we didn't know which way we were headed.* His eyes are divots in rock. She holds her head and there is the slamming. *And Lucy's window wide open and I didn't notice. She could have fallen out.* And the seashell her mother held. *Quiet, Kitty, and you'll hear the ocean. And someday we'll go.* The burnished granite now and his hand like a fish belly and the divots hold the water. *And she got thinner and thinner so fast and they hardly knew what to do. And someone carved out that granite from some quarry and sent it out here. Natural materials, sustainability, they'll tout. The things they try and sell you. Everything we need or think we the world owes us. The best views. And you have to be quiet, she said, to hear the ocean. And the ocean is yourself. The ocean is yourself, calling you back.*

The room is too bright. Jason clasps the countertop. *His soft hands.* She cannot see him clearly. She never has. *And maybe someone died in that quarry getting us that pretty slab and the ocean right there and listen and her long hands and the minnows we caught and what we lost and they never see it and her window wide open my God and I didn't see it and Lucy could've fell and they're always talking and saying nothing at all and the wine makes me sick and I've never been able to drink it and I don't know how to be with him or with anyone.*

"You need to get some help," he says now. "You're not thinking clearly, Katherine." And that artist lady was beyond comprehension. Maybe she had spent too much time with her and it had warped her thinking. He had tried to make this work.

The roaring will not cease in her head. *The pounding and then your blue jacket tiger shirt clay marbles and you were running.* He looks past her. *Fish belly. Divots.* "I tried," he says. "But I can't anymore. I'm sorry, Katherine. I'm just out of ideas." She does not have anything to add. *In my head.* She feels him looking at her. Assessing. "I'm sorry, Katherine. I think it's best I let you sort things out here. You can take as long as you need. Stay here as long as you need."

Lucy's sea glass is on the table. The only superfluous thing in the room. *Other than myself.* Lucy found the glass days ago. Came shrieking down the beach. "A piece of the sky," she said.

She can stay as long as she needs, he reiterates. *I don't need charity.* While she figures things out. They can manage the particulars later. With Lucy and everything. *What's good for the goose is good for.* For now, he will stay with Vanessa. She has an extra room. He does not look at her when he says this. He will catch up with Lucy another day. He does not want to wake or upset her. He is sorry, he says again. He is sorry it turned out this way but things being what they are. Maybe they are from opposite sides of the tracks, he jokes. He tries to smile but then looks away again. He did not want to go down this road, he says. Yet life is short. And here we are.

He answers the buzzer. Vanessa is down on the asphalt. Kit can see her there in the lights. The sky is sopping wet. She goes to Lucy's room. She can see them there. The car plummets beneath the black hill and is gone. With him in it. *There goes your father.* She does not say.

She can hear Lucy breathing. Can see her now in the dim obscurity. She is smiling and holding one hand open, as if waiting a talisman to be placed into it. Quartz, maybe. Good luck charm. *A piece of the sky.*

Kit wakes an hour or so later, head swimming. The room slowly comes into focus. *Sea glass.* She does not know what she ever wanted or expected from him or from anyone. The room darkens with the cloud-shadows passing by. The rain has stopped. Lucy emerges from her bedroom in her polka-dot raincoat, holding her yellow plastic bucket. Her hood is up and her expression disaffected and the clouds pass again and darken her momentarily and lighten her again and she wants to go down and check the tidepools, she says. They had planned on that today. "Remember? The tide will be at its lowest right away," she says. "We have to hurry."

55. Thresholds

They spend the entire day on the beach. They have a picnic lunch with Muriel and John. Cream cheese sandwiches and apples and moon pies. Coffee. *What am I forgetting?* Lucy goes into the cave and Kit can hardly see her there and then she emerges in her lavender kitten shirt *and maybe we don't belong anywhere.*

John sips his coffee. Muriel is building castles with Lucy.

"What happens to us?" she asks John.

"What do you mean?"

"The way we become. We lose ourselves."

Lucy jumps up and down, the waves taking out her castle.

"Oh, cynicism, I suppose. People become lemmings, running off cliffs. They forget what they're about. Can't see past themselves. Need a tribe. All that." The kelp bits are on his coat. He needs to go lie down, he says. He wanders toward the church.

Lucy stands on the horizon, in the wet sand, and the horizon dissolves and the sun falls in an ever-widening arch and Lucy is on the sand and light. The ocean shimmers behind her and the sun is massive going down and Lucy is slanted there on the horizon. She stands on the brink with the sun flashing red and the world tilted jarringly on its axis. The horizon is washed out like watercolor and rarely is the sun this red and Lucy stands on a barely perceptible edge. *You can't hold anyone*, Kit thinks. *Or anything. She's not yours and nothing and no one belongs to you.* The sun is fast going down. Lucy arranges the black stones on the wet sand. *This is all you've got.* Muriel sits beside her. Knees up like a kid.

"You know where you belong," Muriel tells her.

"Not here."

There was never any other place.

"You know what you know."

"They found me out there, waiting for him. I'd go out when the sun was going down thinking that was when I'd be most likely to see him. And I thought maybe at least he'd give me some kind of sign. Then the years went by and I thought they must have been right."

Muriel looks at her, almost sharply.

≈ ≈ ≈

Later they see John from the balcony. He rises and goes under again. Kit checks the temperature. Forty-six degrees. Lucy jumps up and down, waving. *There's something the matter with me and she's got it too.*

≈ ≈ ≈

The curtains billow and Lucy kicks the covers away. She is burning up. A fever. They're crawling up the walls, she tells Kit. Kit touches Lucy's forehead, face. *Her window open and I should have seen it coming.* "They're crawling up the walls and there's a fire in the room."

"It's the sun," she tells Lucy. "Just the sun going down and things seem scary but you're safe in your room and everything is okay." Lucy twists the covers and sits up and falls back again and her face is enflamed like she has absorbed that red sun. Kit holds her hot hand and the red sun drips down the walls. *And we set sail the bark boats and he was faster and then only this morning with Lucy in the dark cave.* Kit called her back and there were footprints down toward the water and the gulls carried on like they were spreading gossip. "They were John's," Lucy said.

"What were?"

"The footprints," she said. And he was going to leave soon, he told her. They were starting to notice him around there. *And the son of man has nowhere to lay his head.*

Run, Kitty.

The trees closed in.

Lucy reaches for her and her hand is blistering. *Or is it mine?* The room rocks. A boat, a bark boat. Sail away. Lucy tightens her grip. "Please stay," she says.

"I'm right here."

The red wall.

There is a fire and they cannot put it out.

"The room is on fire," Lucy says.

"It's only the sun."

And my own mother, only a dream. A fever. You'll be okay, Kitty. Cold hands. And she said she saw them, scattering into the trees.

And years later there was Patrick and he was in the trees as if he was waiting for her. *The dark we had and we could hardly see a thing but we knew exactly where and who we were.* Lucy in the tide foam. Messages, black stones, topsy-turvy. *I saw him in the water there.*

They came out of the trees. They came out of the trees and they had hollow eyes and silty faces and they had muddy hands and there were things growing out of their hands. Like starry moss or chokecherries. He gripped hard her hand and his hand was hot with the terror of it. *Or was it mine?*

They wanted to know if there was any mental illness in her family. Anything she remembered. *The red wall.* In her past, they wondered. *Their hands like twigs and mud and I never said.* The school counselor wrote a prescription for Lucy in case she changed her mind and Lucy was already walking down the hall. Away from them.

And those kids threw rocks at Marg's house and Marg never mentioned it. Maybe she never noticed. *The red wall. And things have a way of returning. Said the nurse when our mother died. Said John.* The yellow roses and Marg in her tiny kitchen and he went faster through the cottonwoods and she could no longer see him there and the clouds moved faster and the sky was rounded and strange and they shifted. "We saw them there!" he shouted. *Marg turned and she knew. And the red sky and the trees were torn and I couldn't hear you anymore and the sky came down and everything was flipped.*

The heat swells. The red nearly vanquished. Lucy wakes and grabs her arm.

"Stay."

"I'm right here."

"Please stay."

"I'm not going anywhere."

"The sky broke."

"I know. It's okay. We can fix it."

"Okay."

She touches Lucy's forehead. The townhouse lights come on. The red light is gone.

They had to go. There was a gathering. And Lucy screamed and refused to leave the sand. And the townhouse lights coming on and she could no longer see. The ocean was so loud. Kept getting in. Insisting. *Our minds play tricks on us.*

And the mountains were like die-cuts. Queenie was far out in the field and he threw stones and they swam and they were not supposed to swim and he found the quartz. *Where from?* Sometimes, Marg told them, they hid things. *And maybe he hid them too. Because in some ways he was like them.* Or maybe she did not see the road right there and the pickup in the road and maybe she only wanted it to be that way. Or maybe Marg had told too many stories, like she said. Filled their heads with nonsense. The cigarette smoke and the opened windows and the woodcutter going. *Always leave your windows open.* Passages. And they were not malicious, Marg insisted. *Although the potential was there.* And they were not scared of them. It was not like that. *We wanted to go back. Him, especially. It was like we had revealed some ancient truth that was only available to us.* She glimpsed, at times, his form. There by the rock fence or in the crooked path. *Later I thought I'd imagined it but I had seen you or thought I had.*

Lucy rolls the sea glass in one hand. Lucy needed to be outside, Kit told Jason that first month. It was the only thing that calmed her. The crying, screaming, colic. Kit would bundle her in the star-covered bunting and take her down to the shore and show her the tide foam and the crying would cease. A few years passed and there was the private school. A chance to excel, whatever that meant. One moment Lucy was placed howling on her chest and the next they were discussing milestones. *Opportunities.* And Lucy only wanted to be near the water. To hear the water hit the sand.

No one sees. There are hallowed places, holy places, layered. They're all around us and everyone brushes past. Forgets. Goes right by, unheeding. There are creatures that saunter and lope and hold secrets. And this doesn't matter, all this. All this striving and pretending. Real life, this life they think is life, is more dangerous than anything the forest can manifest. Because it removes you from yourself. And you forget. You become dried out, wrung out, and everything becomes pointless and muted. We have to go back. Lucy, we have to go home.

And Lucy, in the gloaming now. Lucy's pale hands. "We need sunlight," she tells Lucy now. "We'll drive south. See the mesas. We can sleep out in the desert. See lizards and stuff. What do you think?"

Lucy turns the piece of sky over in one white hand.

"Okay," she says. She does not ask about him. She seems to already know.

≈ ≈ ≈

Kit calls Paul. There is a certain dimension behind him. The landline, Kit figures. "It all fell apart," she tells him. "We need someplace to go. Lucy and me."

A break. A still point.

"You don't need to ask," Paul says. "You know that, Kitty. The door is always open. Whatever you need."

56. Path

Paul saw her walking toward the house at an angle, one hand on her head. There was that hard August light. The swallows shattered past. They were good or bad luck. He could not remember how it went. Afterward his father turned his hat over and over again. *Everything came down so red. Say one of us got sick, she used to say.* Her hands were like wasp paper when he touched them and Kit had that picture she drew, cherry trees or birds, and she said oh Kitty, that's lovely. *And the swallows and their wings were like bat wings and everything seemed wrong.* She used to watch the sun going down into the canyon. At first it lit the perimeter and then the dark crawled up the sides of the barn and house. God was in the canyon, she used to tell him. She had seen her there. *An old woman, picking huckleberries. And all this is yours, she said. Yours and Kitty's. Lucky kids.* And then he could hardly see her for the sun shooting through the room. Through the water glass, vase. Where the bear-grass had wilted there. He could taste the dry air. An insatiable thirst then. He went to the kitchen and drank and drank the cold water. He wanted nothing else. Like the waterfall water. They should not have but they dipped in their hands and drank. *So cold.* And it was like time had stopped. Left them there, like ghosts, Kitty once said. And the swallows came from somewhere. So many the sky practically darkened with them. His father stood on the porch and turned his hat in his hands. And Kit was asleep and they never said a thing. She wasn't afraid, their mother said. Things just happen. A decade later and the smoke caught up with their father. *Us here, like ghosts.*

Now Paul wakes with the prowling. *I've got to cut back the drinking.* Gretchen had wanted to follow him home last night. And he had slipped away before she noticed and had ended up at home. And he saw the cougar in his sleep. Or on the verge of sleeping. It slunk past the window. Low, muscular. *You don't even know it's watching you.* He woke soaked, thirsty. *That mountain water could have made us sick and maybe would have but we drank it anyway. Straight out of the falls and colder than ice.* They brought home the bear-grass. And soon after she started in with the hallucinations. Then she was gone. *Don't worry about me, Paul. Be good.*

He sits up now. Holds his head. The light through the bedroom window like needles. *Now Kitty is coming home. With this kid.*

He wanders out to the kitchen and starts the percolator. *When the hell did everything start scaring me?* He opens the front door to let in the dog and the dog wanders past and sighs and drops to the kitchen floor. *God, I need to sleep.* At times he thinks he sees dark figures moving past. Stooped and laughing. *God, more than anything I need to sleep or quit drinking or get out into the world and stop it with the hermit shit. How old is this kid?* Shortly after Kit moved away, she had started the medication, she said. And for quite some time it helped, apparently. To squelch the ghosts, as she put it. Some guy then. A hasty marriage. A house by the ocean. *Never did sound like Kitty.* All the houses were new houses, she said, and everything smelled like fresh paint. They were married at the courthouse. *You don't need to come, Paul, she said. I know how you are. Laughing like that didn't sound like her.* The new house was entirely bereft of magical beings, she joked. There was a rock fence there, too, she said, only it was built out of some kind of plastic material so when you leaned against it, it began to topple. Phony, she said. Like most of the people around here. She thought this was funny too. *We're all phonies, Paul.* He rarely heard from her after that. Supposed she was doing fine. She called once after having Lucy. She rarely called again afterward. *Kitty's fine,* he figured. *Getting along alright. Let her live her life.* She had made the most of things. *We do what we can.*

At times, now, he feels as if someone is brushing past him. He pushes the thought aside. *Maybe we're all batshit crazy when you get down to it.*

And Kitty. After Patrick disappeared that summer, she swore she'd seen it happen. "The trees," she said. "Or the places between trees." He had told her to stop. Or they would stick her out on that place on the flats they saw on their way out to see the geysers. And the wind out there going like mad and the trees like they were about to rip straight out of the earth. *Why did I say that to her? How did I think that would help? The way she looked at me.* The apple doesn't fall far from the tree, they said about Kit. Like mother, like daughter. *Just stories, Paul. I didn't mean to scare you.*

And Marg turned to pin a pillowcase on the laundry line and she seemed strange, vaporous and unfamiliar, in the blinding sun. She never said anything.

≈ ≈ ≈

It has been days now since he has seen anyone. He stops to check on Marg with the tractor running in the dirt road. Lately she does not always seem to recognize him. She pours coffee and slices cake, pretending to know who he is. Looking for hints. Asks him where he is going or how long he will be staying. "Forever," he says.

"That's nice," she says, searching his face.

"I'm not going anywhere, Marg," he tells her. "Where would I go?" She laughs. "I'm only teasing," she says. She knows him again. In her behavior there is something deliberate. As if she is trying to prove herself.

Pie taps on the door. Wanting in. "Bold bird," she says, shuffling toward the door.

"Sundowning, they call it," that realtor, Vicki, told him. "They get worse and worse and she shouldn't be alone."

57. Sand

Lucy is asleep on the couch and the sky is an ominous gray and Muriel sits cross-legged on the living room floor. "You'll figure it out," Muriel says. "Same as anyone." She had tried to blot things out, Kit tells Muriel. She thought maybe she could stay here. Where everything was ordered. The houses and streets. *Like a pattern you only had to follow.* "And even that I couldn't do," Kit says. *And him in his creased shirts and glossy shoes. And the clear glass. Thought I could walk right through it.* "I should thank Vanessa," Kit tells Muriel. "Weren't for her, I'd have maybe stuck around here."

Kit looks at Lucy asleep on the couch. Early evening and her wiped out from the sand and sea. Jason has been gone for several days. *Nary a word.*

"Regardless," Muriel says now. She looks suddenly very tired. "At least you have Lucy," she says.

Muriel kisses them both on the forehead and goes out the back door. *And John with his blotched face. The toll things take.* There was nothing he needed, John said. He no longer drank. God and the ocean had cured him of it. The sparrows don't worry, he said. Why should he? She supposed he had some sort of plan. *And the wet prints he left wherever he went and we saw him out there but we didn't. Fever dreams.*

≈ ≈ ≈

The glass shatters. Turns back to sand. Kit holds Lucy's hand and they rush down the stairwell and to the empty parking lot and Lucy pulls a thread from her sweater and the thread is like a dream and it unravels upward, like helium. *They say we're running out of helium.* Lucy's hand is surprisingly strong and warm. The townhouses collapse behind them. Real as anything. *What I think I saw I never.* Lucy is portioned out in the rearview. They sit for hours in traffic and finally the traffic lessens with everyone going to work, to their normal lives. And they turn southeast, toward the desert.

"Where are we going?" Lucy asks.

"First, the desert. We'll find you some sun. Then back up north. To see Marg and my brother."

"You have a brother?"

"I told you that."

"I don't remember. How come I've never met him?"

"You will now."

"Who does he live with?"

"Nobody."

"Why is he alone?"

"He likes to be alone."

"Then shouldn't we stay somewhere else?"

"We don't count."

"Why don't we?"

"Because it's the same with us."

The blue sky becomes limitless. *You forget.* And Lucy in the backseat, her profile tipped against the sky. *His eyes were like divots there and Vanessa with her opal teeth and red mouth and you can only do what you can do.* The road opens ahead of them, like a yawn. Lucy draws in her notebook. Cacti, hawks, red rock. She hums. *What's she humming?* What did she think this would be? He did not dream in color, Jason told her once. What, then? Black and white, he said. Sepia, sometimes. *He dreamed in sepia.* This should have been a sign. Of banality, if nothing else.

She looks at Lucy in the rearview. Focused. He would be okay with one kid, he said. Couldn't be that hard. *What's one kid?* And then Lucy came shrieking into the world and everything cracked open. And the way he had looked at her, Kit, like she had hoodwinked him. *We can handle one kid.* And already she could see the twinge of regret.

They pass another state line. She is okay now. Capable. They have made it this far. She has not done anything out of whack. *The crazy lady can cope,* she thinks.

"The apple doesn't fall far from the tree," they said.

Thought I didn't hear.

It's in our genes maybe, Paul said. Broken inside us and now and then it rises up. A monster out of the bushes. Shut up about it, Kitty, he said. It's bad enough as is.

They built a fort from irrigation tarps. *And through those torn holes we saw them running through and through and you caught up my hand and I felt your breath on my skin and your heart was my heart and we were the same.*

Lucy names the clouds. Cumulus, stratus. Writes them down in her notebook.

"I hear music that isn't there," Lucy says. "Far away sounding." Kit meets her gaze in the rearview. "That's okay, Lucy. I wouldn't worry about it. We don't need to worry about those things anymore. We're going home." The horizon seems to float ahead. A mirage. *I should stop and rest.* The road is black. *What's she humming?*

The shadows waned. *What did you think this was going to be?* And then. *I'm sorry, Katherine. I never meant it that way.*

They stop in a small town in Wyoming. A little river. Cottonwoods. Hardly anything else would grow in a place like this one. *The winters and I can't even tell you.* The town is a splash of green amongst gold.

Kit had tried to adapt at the townhouse. She copied the setup from a lifestyle magazine. How else? Everything spacious and untouched. *And you knew it wouldn't hold, didn't you? You had already seen past. You can't unsee it. We ate their bread, drank their wine.*

The woman at the motel pours them coffee in ceramic mugs. The walls are teal and the curtains are faded and the woman says hardly anyone stops by anymore. *But what can you do.* Lucy looks out the smeared lobby window at the mesa. The woman says she has some toys from the grandkids and maybe Lucy would be interested. "That would be nice," Kit says. The woman brings them out from beneath the counter. A plastic barn and silo. Fat, plastic figurines. She sets them on the coffee table. "There you go, honey."

A border collie strolls out from the office and greets Lucy and Lucy kneels down and they look out the window together. "Look at that," the woman says. "Like old friends." She opens and closes the red barn door. "Used to moo," she says. "Don't think it works anymore." Her hands are knobby and red. She stands, slowly, hands on knees. Lucy turns to her and smiles and the woman smiles back. The dog sniffs the plastic barn and then curls up on the floor. Lucy sips the coffee and scratches behind the dog's ears and moves the figurines around, out of kindness. The woman brings out a key, polishes it on one wide hip, and hands it to Kit. The front door is wide open. The cottonwoods shake. *Listen.*

Sunrise and the woman waves from the front door. They are her only guests. *Come back in a million years and she may still be here. Offering silos and collies and golden keys. Impervious to change. Same as we were.*

58. Home

They stand in the road. Her and the kid. To see Lucy sparks a recollection. "Spitting image of you, Kitty," Paul says. The cottonwoods rattle overhead. Lucy skips between the leaf-shadows on the dirty road.

In the kitchen Paul sets out coffee and cookies. He didn't know what to get, he says.

"It's lovely," Lucy says. She stands there in the kitchen in her sandals and pink pony dress and Paul feels a clanging inside him. *An old soul*, Marg used to call Kit. And he recognizes the same thing in Lucy now. Like she knows more than she is letting on. Kit pours the coffee. Lucy adds creamer and opens a sandwich cookie, swinging her legs. She looks past them at the window.

"She drinks coffee?" Paul asks Kit.

"She drinks it, yes."

"She's seven?"

"Almost eight," Lucy interjects.

"Right. And you drink coffee."

"Her father didn't like it," Kit says. "But he was never around to enforce it one way or another. I guess she got used to it."

"John was always drinking it," Lucy says.

"Who's that?"

"John lived in the church. But not anymore. He went back to wherever he came from."

"Okay," Paul says.

Lucy swings her legs.

Spitting image.

They are quiet. The walls in the room shift, rearranging.

The rusted pickup.

Why didn't you say nothing to her?

"Then the kid goes missing," Gretchen said. And Kitty at the kitchen table. She looked right through them at the window. He pulled out a chair and sat beside her and the way she kept tapping her hands unsettled him and the curtains were all dirty and why didn't they notice things like this or fix anything up ever and maybe they should wash the curtains, he thought, but then who cared anyway and they were just stories, he told her. She needed to not mix things up, he said. What was real and what was pretend. "They're looking for him," he said. "They're doing what they can." And maybe he went with his dad, he said, and didn't tell anyone and will turn up here soon enough. Maybe they're up in the woods somewhere. Kids lose track of time. *People lose track.* And she did not say anything but the light was on her hands and her face was dark. *Apple doesn't fall far from the tree.* They questioned Rob when they finally located him. And there were the cars gathered that day and days after and then the hard, cold snow. They went to see Carrie. Stood there in her drafty kitchen with the can of coffee because they had not known what else to do.

Carrie had felt him pulling at her sleeve, she told them. It kept happening. She couldn't sleep, she said. Some days she could hardly move. She heard him running through the house. Woke up and it was only her. In the dark. Her eyes were dark and sunken and it bothered him to look at her. And then she sat down suddenly, as if she had been pushed. They sat with her. Just sat there, not saying anything. And Paul holding the can of coffee. As if that would be enough. Remedy things. A magic elixir. *Coffee.* She did not look like she had been eating. There was not enough of her to go around, he thought. She was so thin. It was obvious she was not eating. "Is someone with Kitty now?" she asked. She was visibly shaking. "She's with Marg," he managed. Carrie nodded. Twisted her sleeve. "Marg has these ideas about things," she said. "I don't know."

They dragged the river. They put his face everywhere until one day they didn't. Paul drove Kit to school. And the river flooded and the land thawed and they never found him. *The water was so cold and could knock you flat out they said, like a hammer to the head. Scared the hell out of us but I guess that was the point.* "Those dark things we saw," Kit said one day on the drive to school. She was looking out the window. Always looking as if expecting an answer to come forth. Reveal itself. And if they found him, he thought, he'll already be. Bones, debris. *I need to get it together.*

Then Kit moved to the coast. To clear her head, she said. Started on the medication. *Now she's back here and it's like she never left. Other than this kid to prove she'd been anywhere. Spitting image.*

And she, their mother, had divulged what she had seen. There they were, running near the trees. Sun coming up and like they were running from it. Like they didn't want to be caught in the light. They didn't want the sun to catch them. It was comical, she told him. *Apple doesn't fall far.*

Kit sips her coffee now and Lucy is out the screen door. "That kid," she says, beaming. "She has to be outside. Like she belongs to it." *What's she implying?*

59. Attic

Lucy puts her things in the upstairs bedroom. Kit has to tilt her head to go inside. The cottonwoods are right outside the window. "This was my room," she tells Lucy. "Now you can have it. If you want." The cottonwoods right there, the narrow bed, wall mirror, wooden dresser. *I was hardly ever in here. We practically lived outside.*

Lucy sits on the brass bed, creaking. Kit opens the window. The leaves rattle. *Listen.* Flooding back. *The water's too high and you kids shouldn't be down there. We swam beneath and something changed.*

Lucy sprawls across the bed, closes her eyes. "I can see the leaf-shadows," she says. "Darker places."

And Patrick had no idea he was even around or who he was until he showed up one day wanting God knows what and they crouched against the bedroom door with Rob ranting. *His eyes like steelies when he finally prized it open, you told me. That's what he looked like. When he got inside the room. And it was already dark out but there were the stars you said and they were going and blurring there and they blurred for hours.*

Outside Paul leans on the porch railing. Lucy is across the yard with the dog. Paul peels the chipped paint from the railing. He should have painted it, he says. Time just gets away.

The church, the woods, a sanctuary. Nothing can touch you.

"We can get after it," Kit says. "Fix things up around here."

They had the ocean and the crashing waves and the white sand and smooth, black stones and green gardens and rhododendrons big as your head and they never noticed any of it or cared one way or the other. No one sees.

He grinds the paint between his fingers.

Lucy runs with the dog through the yard.

"That dog looks like Queenie," Kit says, sitting on the top step.

"That is Queenie," he says.

You think you forget a place and it's like I was here yesterday.

Lucy starts toward the trees and Paul calls her back and tells her to stay out of there. *I shouldn't have let you kids run around down there.* Lucy throws a stick and Queenie chases it. *Wouldn't have mattered.*

Paul sits beside her, bunching up his long legs. Lights a cigarette. The house is eerily silent behind them, as if it is eavesdropping. Kit looks at her brother watching the canyon. Lucy is hopping up and down in the yard.

"Are you glad you stayed here?" Kit asks him.

"Wasn't really an option," he says.

"It's ridiculous out there," she says. "Everyone competing for the top rung. Trying to claim some kind of golden apple. God knows what for."

"And you?"

"I didn't make it to the top rung. I made coffee."

"Well," he says. "People need coffee. You might have saved them."

"Missed opportunity," she says.

He flicks the ash.

"Maybe we'll stay here," she says. "Help out."

Paul is quiet, considering.

"That'd be good, Kitty."

He taps the cigarette into the empty flowerbed. *They took Queenie or she went with them and it was weeks before she returned.* Queenie yawns. Lucy settles beside the dog, weaving grass. "That dog looks just like Queenie," Kit says.

He looks at the dog and Lucy and puffs. "I already told you. They're all Queenie. She keeps returning. I just said." He looks sideways at Kit.

She considers Queenie.

"I suppose you're right. Huh."

By now you should realize, Marg said.

When will you ever?

"The river is flooding," Paul tells her now. "Lucy shouldn't be around it. But you already know that."

"Yeah," Kit says. "I already know that."

60. Tricks

In the attic room they can see the stars beginning. *I saw you running into some other place and why'd you leave me alone?* Kit asks Lucy if she wants the hall light on. She likes the dark, Lucy tells her. *A closed fist.* Kit can barely see Lucy in the darkening room. Queenie settles on the floor beside the bed. Kit covers Lucy with a quilt. "The lamp is right there," she tells Lucy. "Or you can just holler and I'll come right up. Say you get to feeling lonesome. It can be like that in a new place."

"This isn't a new place," Lucy says. She is rounded with the quilt and blankets. With the hall shadow on her she looks bigger than anything. *I know right where I am.* "I don't want the light," Lucy reiterates. Kit clicks the light into blackness. *The dark we had.*

They are selling lots near the river, Paul told her. They have it up for sale, right next to Marg's." They were trying to convince Marg and Paul both. "High pressure sales," he said, wryly. *This was my father's house, Muriel said. Muriel and her canary coat. Graphite cliffs, outrage. Stephanie said she had a chip on her shoulder. More like she had it figured out.* Kit feels her way downstairs.

And Paul. He looked as though he had not slept for weeks. Paul alone all this time and the faded back porch and everything falling apart. *And I just left him here*, Kit thinks. Although any other world would have swallowed him up and spit him out the same way it had her. The grass is always greener, so they say. He felt like an anachronism, he told her. And it wouldn't matter where he went or who he went with or what happened. He would always feel that way. Wrong time, wrong place. *Off-kilter.* She knew exactly what he meant.

Downstairs the windows are all open. The trees clatter. The cottonwoods, she told Lucy. The stories. You have to listen, she said. And Lucy did. She paid attention. And it was like they had never left and suddenly she was wide awake. *I already know this place.* The clock ticked in the kitchen. Where had she been all this time? Checked out, with blinders. Time does not pass. Only rearranges. She had tried to acclimate. She bought the clothes and the gadgets and she scanned when they scanned and blotted it out the same way they did. With prescriptions and wine and shopping. *And Muriel dove into the water and John too and it was freezing cold and they're selkies, Lucy said, and why wouldn't she think this? They dove right in. And Lucy digging out the holes and chasing the gulls down and why didn't we come back sooner?* Lucy never asked about Jason. She only packed her bags and waited by the door. And she left all the gadgets he had bought for her. The blinking things. She brought only her pencils and paper and the stuffed seal. As if she had been preparing for this very thing. Was just waiting for the cue. An old soul, they used to tell Kit's father. *So serious.* And Lucy too. *And we were in the trees and Patrick found the moon shining there and we lobbed it back up and it stuck fast and this could be the same water Jesus was baptized in by John and John ate locusts and John ate sardines and the cold water and we hardly felt the aching. Freezing cold and you finally know you're alive.* They hated originality, Muriel said. And Kit had tried to live alongside them. Tried and failed. And Lucy only a few months old and she only wanted to be near the water. She would have tantrums otherwise. The wind never bothered her. It was as if some magnetic force pulled her toward it. The crux of things. And the collections Lucy had. Shells, black stones, driftwood, sand dollars. And she and Patrick had entire shoeboxes full of collections. Bird bones and pinecones and teeth. *Where on earth from?* And she first saw Patrick near the dented-up mailboxes and he ran down the dirt road and she followed him and the sun fell in scraps through the trees and later they dragged the river and they never found him and they never would and she knew they never would because she had seen it happen. Nabbed, gone, taken. No, he went. He wanted to go. The school was concerned. She had seen things that were not possible. *Fact-finders.* Maybe it ran in their blood, Paul figured. Some genetic abnormality. *They all said it was your father or that you'd drowned.* And Rob in the dirt road with his wolf hands and the yellow pickup running and the trees closing up. Closing him out. *And you and Carrie backed against the door you said and he knocked so hard it rang up through the floor and inside you and he was three sheets ten sheets what was he and they pressed against the door and she told you to be quiet just stay quiet and it was too late already and the stars were already blurring and the room was dark so he couldn't see could only feel and get out of here if he comes around, she told you, you said, you have to get out if he comes around again and still you felt the fists inside you they were so heavy.* And then the trees closed in around him. *Because he wanted.* He had told her.

He can't find me in there, you said.

And Paul stood there in the attic room. They wanted to know what she had seen, he said. What she remembered. And his hands were knotting around. "Leave the windows open," Marg always said. And the boxed attic room and the low ceiling. And her mother. The room was so small. That room was small, too. And the leaves moved soundlessly on the walls. "Only a fever," she said. "You can wake yourself, Kitty." It wasn't true, she would think, years later. She could not simply wake up. Or maybe she did not want to. And they ran along the bank and they threw the stones and found the stones and floated the bark boats and the river flooded and went nearly dry and they were told to watch out. The undercurrents. Could sweep you away. Farther and farther. And you don't see them but they're there. And the geese landed on the bank and they snuck up and scared the geese and the geese flew away and Kit saw their dark shapes then between the trees and their mud hands and eyes. *And I didn't ask you if you had seen them because I didn't need to.* Tricks. *And that last morning.* She could hardly distinguish the objects in the room. *Always in your head, Jason used to say.* And Marg was in the yard and they pitted cherries and her mother had the bandana over her hair and her arms were browned from the sun and the beads on her like dew and it was late afternoon and she got up and it was August and the sun was orange and hot and she stood and held her head. And everything like it was burning. *August, drying up.* And they had caught the minnows only weeks prior. Waded out into the shallow parts and it was so hot that day and her head in her hands and she laughed. *The Milky Way. Your mother in the stars. And now they say hardly anyone can see the stars. Our own galaxy. What with the light pollution.* And she, Kit, had seen him pulled into the trees. You become a tree or stone, Marg said, and someone could pass right by you and not even know you're there and then time goes on and one day you wake or are awakened and you go looking for the people you once knew and they are all long dead and buried. And you're caught up somewhere in between. And the only way out is to trick them. Walk backwards with your eyes closed. Turn your clothes inside out. Topsy-turvy. *Unless you want to stay there. Unless you don't want to come back. A sanctuary.*

"I don't know who I am anymore," she told Jason after Lucy was born. And he did not reply. *Nothing to say to nobody.* And now. *I know exactly who I am. You saw what you saw, Marg said.* Her eyes sparked and she cut another slice. *You saw what you saw. I know exactly who I am.* And there was the absolute quiet like every sound withheld and then the same place they knew so well was suddenly foreign. The knot in a tree. The swell of water. Pronounced, exact. And that first time it happened they walked slowly backwards and they found their way out and things had altered. They could see where the ground was trampled down, like an animal path.

And we ate the bread and you were first, you were always first. Go ahead, Kitty. And I loved you.

The clock now. Lucy, upstairs. The things she says. Funny. The things she sees and hears. Uncanny, familiar. *And we walked backwards and the trees were caught in the gleaming and the sky came rushing down like water and everything was reversed.* Eclipsed. *We could not come back from it. It had changed us.*

Then the news that night. His fifth-grade picture. The striped polo shirt with the tiny embroidered tiger. Leaping, *ad-infinitum*. The background like water. His hair combed down for the picture. The picture etched in her mind. Months later and she still could not sleep. The river was so high that spring and they thought they would maybe find him after the water dropped. *Remains.* The silt in his eyes and hands. What it would have been. And the window was opened and she could hear the aquifers beneath the ground, like secrets. *We're mostly water.* And he carved the bark boat and his knee was up on the fence and he spit out the alfalfa he was chewing and handed her the bark boat and Marg sliced the cake and her sweater was pilled with stars. *And they don't see the stars anymore and maybe he wanted to go.*

And Jason has not called. She had not expected him to. Why would he?

"Acute anxiety," Nancy said. Whatever the hell that meant. Another prescription. And Muriel into the rocks and gone. A few days later and the waning winter light. *Later I thought maybe it was an anomaly in the soil or water. Arsenic? Lead? Our own mother. No, it was deeper. Memory. A door opened, waking up.*

The clock ticks. Kit checks on Lucy. The room is dark and she can see the leaves through the window and she can hear Lucy breathing and her breath is like falling beneath. She closes the door, slightly.

61. Cake

When Kit first knocks, Marg rises like she is rising up out of the floorboards. A ghost. Her hair is downy and white as milkweed fluff. She looks at Lucy. "Well, would you look at her," she says. "Come on in. I'll make coffee." She ushers them inside. The house is dark as a cave as it always has been. As if no time has passed. *Nothing has changed.*

Marg pours coffee and slices cake. Rich, chocolate, glazed. "Paul said you were on your way," she says. Lucy takes a bite. The swallows swoop past the window. *Good luck.* There are nests in the eaves. They dart past. Again and again, chopping shadow. "That woman keeps coming by," Marg says. "She's real bold. Pushy. I don't know where she comes from. Gives me papers with these old birds on them. Thinks I'd like to be there with them. Playing checkers with strangers till I die. She asks me what would I do if someone breaks in here. Says I should lock my doors. I told her I don't care if they shoot me so long as they shoot me dead." Marg looks at Lucy now. "And now *you're* here," she says. *He was in the trees and we both were and the crabapples bobbing in the water and Marg made jelly and we slathered the jelly and the early morning came and we showed up here and we never knocked and if she cared she didn't let on and the bread she made and the earthy coffee and the sawyer's stories.* The maahinen, the sawyer said. Watching out over things. At times he was difficult to understand, Marg said, with his heavy accent. Perhaps she had misheard. The stories, it seemed, were all he had. The creatures underground. People used to go missing, he told her. He recognized it here. The density of trees. *What escapes you.*

A change of scenery, Kit had told her brother. The west coast. The city, maybe. Something completely different. *As if that would be enough.*

She had told too many stories, Marg said, the winter after Patrick disappeared. The sawyer's stories; her own. The woodcutter chopped. They were only stories, she told Kit. And Patrick's blue jacket, the white piping. And him waving for her to come on. *And the swallows came down then too and we ran beneath them and they were everywhere and they were above us and around. Then the creatures beneath the earth. Their wispy murmurings we heard and the snatching fingers and the sound like far away laughter or the laughter like it was inside my own head and what they took.* Then. Carrie and him pressed against the door. The stars, he said, were all blurry. And the pounding would never stop unless. *I bet he'd kill us even if he didn't mean to. He couldn't stop it, you said. He couldn't stop being mad. She didn't recognize him, Carrie said. You think you know someone.*

The smoke circles throughout the kitchen. Lucy chews and watches the swallows out the window, absentmindedly. Marg waves the smoke away and cuts Lucy another slice. "Have as much as you want," she says. "Look at you. Thin as a rail." *The swallows came down all at once and we could hear them around us and you rolled the quartz around in your hand. Then stared at the dark spots and something had changed in you. He kept coming around, you said. Making things worse. Carrie was looking at leaving, you said. Away from all this. And the trees seemed to bow or wave and you just stared at them, turning and turning the quartz.* The way Patrick looked at her then, turned and looked at her, like he was trying to remember something he had long forgotten that he meant to say. He left the quartz on the rock fence. It didn't belong to him, he told Kit.

Now Pie comes to the window, tapping. Marg opens the window, wide. She has never had a screen that Kit can remember. Pie stands on the windowsill. "What do you want?" Marg asks him. Pie tilts his head. *One beetle eye.* He hops a little and waits. Lucy laughs. "Have you two met?" Marg asks Lucy, turning. Marg opens her hand to him.

Outside Lucy runs into the field and the sun is already warming and Kit hollers at her to come back to be careful and Marg smokes on the front porch. "Oh, let her go," Marg says. "It's inevitable." Her black eyes cut. As lucid as ever, Kit will report to Paul. Maybe more so. *Something inside us only we forget.* Kit looks at Marg and Marg's hands are trembling and Kit feels something wrench inside her. Pie is out there on the post. He follows Lucy, in steady bursts. Marg peers at her then with those mud-eyes and Kit can see her own reflection in them. *For God's sake.* Kit catches up with Lucy and takes her hand and Lucy yanks her hand away and runs. "I'm okay," Lucy shouts, turning back. Her face is red and strange. *Because she has to find it too.* "They're not going to do anything," she tells her mother. "They've always been here."

"It's the river," Kit says. "I don't want you near the river."

Pie hops near Lucy, giving a look of admonishment.

Honestly.

"They're watching out," Lucy says.

The way they pulled us toward, the way they gave meaning to things around. Only you couldn't pinpoint it. They just made sense. They're not malevolent. They only want you to take care of things.

Which we always.

No one knew how to help you, Paul said.

Then there was Marg. The cake. The opened windows. Always open, even in the winter. *Or at least that's how I remember it.* And he ate sandwiches she made for him and drank the whole milk and took home extras for Carrie too and he had just shown up one day. Waiting at the bus stop. He sat with her. At first without saying anything. *And his gray eyes, thin hands.*

"Funny how things work that way," her father told Marg. "With Kitty needing someone around her own age." Things being what they were. And Marg smoked into the yellow roses and gazed softly at them both. "Yes, funny," she said. And Marg sent Patrick home with jars of raspberry jam, sweet rolls, cake.

Kit follows Lucy through the trees. Quickens her step. When she turns back Marg is in the yard, seemingly talking to no one. Kit stands with Lucy by the rock fence, on the outskirts.

Pie is with Lucy, like a guardian. "You're a weird bird," Lucy tells him. He opens his beak a little, as if laughing.

"That water would sweep you away so fast," she tells Lucy.

The water, the trees.

Lucy walks ahead of her, her face reddening.

"I'm not stupid," she says.

62. Ice

The ice came through. There were lines in the rock. All of time, history, recorded in stone. *The center of the universe is wherever you are.*

Early morning and a different kind of light. His head spins. Funhouse mirror, tilt-a-whirl. Paul fills the percolator, fries a few eggs. His head reels. The kitchen is sunny. The percolator rattles. He pours coffee. The door slashes open and Lucy emerges, Queenie trailing. *Shadow-self, shadow-work.* He read somewhere. *Where?*

Something was the matter with her, they told Kit. They wanted to give her something, some kind of drug. *A little kid like that. Jesus. The center of the universe and you never believe me, Paul.*

63. Corners

She thought maybe if she got far enough away things might start to make sense. She would see things as they really were. Then it was the opposite. Things clouded over. *And Jason and the boutiques and medication and the rhododendrons and no one noticed them and no one cared and no one went down to the water anymore.* She played the part anyway. And then Lucy came along. And it was as if someone had opened all the curtains, turned on the lights, like some insanely drunk and honest person, telling it like it was. An airing of dust and grievances.

The last few days. Corners. She could not get the sand out of the folds, Lucy said. And the sun was burning everything up. It was rarely red like that. And the footprints ran down toward the water and Lucy said she had seen someone swimming out there. A selkie. Those are only stories, Lucy, she told her. *Maybe they came along with him, the sawyer said. And he never noticed. Followed him here.* And Lucy squinted up at her and then ran down toward the rock cave and was inside and did not want to come out. Kit could see her there, just vaguely. *Element and matter and what are we anyway?*

≈ ≈ ≈

"They're just stories," Paul said. "Be careful what you say to people. You can't just go saying things like that. You have to be part of the world."

≈ ≈ ≈

"Whatever's wrong with me I gave it to her," she tells Paul now.

"You didn't give her anything, Kit."

Lucy flips over a stone.

Lift a stone, I am here.

The Gnostic Gospels, John.

They've missed it, John said. They miss everything. What a shame.

They found him there, apparently. Gave him a few days to collect his things and make accommodations. He found this funny, he said. *Accommodations.* The church was not a motel, they said. *The son of man has nowhere to lay his head.* John folded the wool blanket and tied the percolator to his pack and said his goodbyes. There was a shelter outside the city, they said. They would be happy to buy him a bus ticket. He shook his head and went out the door. Said he would be fine. Would walk up the shore until he found what he was looking for.

≈ ≈ ≈

Now Lucy runs toward the river and Kit has to chase after her and pull her back and get down on her level and look her right in the eye and hold her shoulders maybe too hard and the water is starting up the bank and the fallen branches thrash in the water and she stands with Lucy on the muddy bank and they can hear the river pulling things down with it. All the runoff and the mountain snowmelt and year after year it floods and then it dries out and then hardly moves at all and the earth dries up and everything else along with it. "That water isn't funny," she tells Lucy. *That river's not a joke.* And she holds her hand too tightly and Lucy yanks free and runs the opposite direction across the field. She knows, she shouts back over her shoulder. She knows this already. She is furious and biting. *One of us.*

And time after time Kit wakes with the terror of Lucy having fallen in the water or down some cliff face and pulled down so quickly that she cannot even see her and she is gone and she tries to get to her, across the water or ice or chasm, and she cannot and she is already gone and she is already pulled down deep.

In the yard Queenie paws at the ground. A swath of grass bends against the barbed wire fence and Lucy is hiding something in there. A stash. *And we got caught up on the fence. Our jackets, hearts. Nothing disappears, only changes. Or maybe it doesn't even change.*

Paul takes the shovel to change water. He looks worn through. "What do you have in there?" he asks Lucy. She brings out a wasp's nest and a round stone and something shining. "You find all that? Good for you."

He crosses the yard, the shovel over his shoulder, his shadow dragging out beside him.

64. Stars

It is so dark at night that Lucy cannot always remember where she is. The wall is angled above her. Right there so she can almost touch it. She initially thought she was in her bedroom at the townhouse. Then things materialized. The bedpost and branches. The dark closes in around her. It has a form, a texture. She could make an imprint of it. A rubbing with paper and crayons. A black crayon. *It's different here*, she thinks. She does not ever want to go back. *It's so dark here.* She goes to the window and listens to the trees. *They take you and they don't let you leave. If you take one little bite or forget to leave your window open. You could stay with them forever.*

Her father has not called. Maybe he never existed. Maybe she invented him. *Maybe he closed the windows and now if we go back, he won't be there. I don't want to go back.*

The counselor was concerned, she told Lucy's mother. She frowned at Lucy when she said it. The counselor wore heels, a bone-colored dress. Directed Lucy in and out of the bleached hall. A week later her father called, his face flickering on the screen. He was out east somewhere. The school had called. They said Lucy was not there. He wanted to know what was going on. She was taking a break, her mother told him. She was here, with her. Maybe they would homeschool, she told him. His face glowed blue on the screen. She wasn't getting anything out of it, she told him. She needed *room*. His voice warbled and broke apart and he fizzled out and her mother closed the tablet. That was that, her mother said. And she pressed her lips as if she would laugh.

Lucy searches out the darkness now and finds the shape of Queenie in the dark. She curls beside her on the floor. Feels her warmth. Her beating heart. She smells like the river, mud. Good. The stars move and shine and Lucy touches the dark fur and the stars shine again. The window is open and the leaves shake out there and Lucy hears them. *Come on, come on.* She senses Queenie raise her head a little. She can hear them too.

At the ocean house the glass shattered and turned back to sand. She had seen it. She had seen John too, in the water, his satiny black head bobbing there. And she waved and waved. Jumped up and down. And her mother held her hand and they hurried down the stairwell with the sand collapsing behind them and it was like they were running down dunes and the glass disintegrated and they drove farther and farther and she only had a fever, her mother said. And she woke her up and the following day they packed her bag. Was all. "Things get distorted," she told Lucy. "See, the house is still here."

"Quite the imagination," the counselor had told her mother.

"Yes, she does have," her mother said. The counselor recommended, then, a prescription. She worried about Lucy, she said. Her mother stared at the counselor. Held Lucy's hand. *And mommy, her eyes burned.* And they drove out to the Tsunami zone. And later Muriel let her look through all the colors. And when she came home the colors were all over her hands and she tried to place them in the world. Where they would go. She read guide books, fables. They found creatures in the tidepools, clutching stone. Clinging. She quit going to school entirely. John told them the stories. The fire burned. They went to one last party. "We should try," she said. Something had seemed urgent.

And here she runs fast toward the cottonwoods. She likes the way the leaves clatter, spilling secrets. And the river runs black as ink. And the river never answers when it should, her mother says. Ask and it never answers. And Marg tells her stories. She shouldn't, she says to Lucy. And yet.

65. Fuzz

Marg has no idea what day it is. *Why'd I come out here? And why am I standing out here like a fool?* The girl is in the front yard now so that must have something to do with it. The girl is waving the swallows down and the swallows are swirling away and kids always see things but then they forget. Which is unfortunate. She gave the girl cake, that's right, and the girl dipped the cake in her coffee and the girl was always going. Having to move. She asked for more stories and Marg obliged. Because, what else? *She looks like Kitty at that age*, Marg thinks. And the yard now is hard and rocky and looks burnt. The trees and fields. Probably something the matter with her eyes, she thinks. *Like fuzz*, she thinks. Sometimes she sees things and she cannot tell what they are. Partly she does not know where she is but can cannot tell them that. She sits in her porch chair. The girl is gone somewhere in the long grass. Kitty is with her. *Isn't she?* Marg puffs her cigarette and watches the trees and leans back in the chair. *Anyway, nothing bad will come to any of them.* She tries to remember. Things twist and turn and sometimes she does not know who she is or where she is but it always comes back. Nothing to worry about.

66. Catkins

Lucy runs along the irrigation ditch and then wades back and forth across the murky water and the land is sunlit and Queenie follows. And quickly Lucy is gone in the brush and Kit finds her there and Lucy is crouched with the dog and they are trying to catch something in the water, the two of them. *Hurry, Kitty. His quickened steps.* Lucy stands in the tall grass. *No time has passed.*

At the house they have coffee and there is the broken kitchen cupboard. *How long since anyone painted anything?* Paul sits on the entryway bench, as if composing himself. He is so tired, he says. Why is he always so tired? Another day, same thing. "It's like something is just off-balance," he says. She stands there with her coffee.

"Some religions," she says, "think everything is an illusion. That we're only dreaming ourselves."

"Doesn't sound too far-fetched," Paul says. He stands and opens the front door, the sunlight engulfing him. Lucy wants to go back out. She needs to collect catkins, she tells Kit. Offerings.

67. Old Country

It was too loud in the grange hall and Marg wanted to leave and the moon was so full that she could see about everything along the bank and through the trees. She found him down by the water's edge and he looked at first like he was standing on the water. It was like he had materialized there. He tipped his hat. Then stepped up onto the bank. "Thought I was alone," he said.

"Thought I was."

"You're not," he said.

"You're not either."

He had a heavy accent. She came nearer and he was very real. She could smell his tobacco. And she could see him grinning there in the moonlight. "Too much hullaballoo," she said. This made him laugh. He asked her to repeat what she had said. He leaned forward slightly, absolutely still, as she repeated it, and then he laughed again. Only harder. He had never heard this word before, he said. His own words were broken. She had to really pay attention in order to understand. Had to lean close enough she could feel his warm breath. He lived here, he told her. Near here, he meant. He waved an arm upward somewhere. Within walking distance. He, too, had left the party. The hullaballoo. Too many people, he told her. And he didn't dance. He offered her a rolled cigarette and she accepted and he lit the cigarette for her and they watched the river together. She could hear the water and see the smoke trailing. They hardly said anything but only stood there together. Then he walked her to the edge of town, where she lived with her mother. Said maybe he would see her another time. Another day? No dancing? You think so? Would that be good? She said yes. That would be fine. And the way he kept nodding. And he returned early the following morning with a bunch of lilacs. The sun hardly up yet. There was something vaguely familiar in his conduct. She felt as though she had always known him.

He knew the woods like the back of his hand, he told her. There were times, however, when he felt the landscape around him slipping away and then it was like he was inside something globular and dark.

Others said they felt that way too, sometimes. After they had been drinking, usually. He felt it frequently, he told her. Without liquor. There were stories he had heard growing up, he said. In the old country. This sort of thing was familiar to him. They want to go finding it out, he said. Proving things. Good luck.

They married months later. She moved to his farm with him. He had land there. Shorthorn cattle, a few hogs. The river ran alongside. He had seen things in the trees, he told her one night. They were lying in bed, fingers laced. His hand gripped hers and his hand was like wood. He turned toward her and lay facing her. Maybe you get to know a place too well, he supposed. Maybe it gets inside you. Holds you together, and you shelter it. You are responsible for it, or it for you. Yes, she agreed. He squeezed her hand. Yes. And everything in the dark room was real and everything was right where it belonged. The wind outside shook the cottonwoods.

And then one night it happened and they were swimming and she could not tell the difference between the water and the bank it was so dark and he grasped her hand and there were these lights then in the trees like tiny fires and then like animal eyes and they climbed up onto the bank and took their clothes and hurried naked through the dark trees. *Him fumbling with his overalls and shirt and shaking like a leaf there on the outside of the trees where I could see their eyes and him shaking and he tried to hide it.* She ran through the trees in her slip and carrying her clothes and barefoot and she did not even feel the ground beneath.

They came home and they were scratched up and he lit the fire and he looked past her at the door and then said something loudly, pointedly, in his other language that she did not understand and he did not relay to her. Like an incantation. There were things you could do, he told her. She thought he was joking but he did not laugh. Yes, things you could do, he repeated. *Measures taken.* In the old country, he said, they would inside-out their clothes. Leave windows open and doors unlocked. They were here first, he said. He seemed determined. He sat down on the edge of the chair in his shirt and suspenders, his pants torn and muddy at the bottoms. They were here first, he told her. It's knowing that. And he opened the window and the window was open ever since. You had to abide by their rules, from her understanding. Which simply meant, quite reasonably, not making a mess of things.

Once, they almost had a child. He apologized. As if he had caused it. As if it had been some fault of his own and not just the way of things. You luck out or you don't. Something had not worked right. Something inside her would not hold a child, she figured. She had felt a kind of blooming there and she tried to slow it but then she could do nothing and the sun sank down beneath the horizon and he was sorry, he said. And that was when they first came inside. After he had gone to bed. And they looked to be carrying things. And they sat down in the corners, quietly, until they became like the shadows themselves. And they had been there ever since, coming and going. Keeping her company.

68. Twigs

Kit waits for Lucy at the bus stop. The same dirt road; rural mailboxes. Most of the mailboxes are empty now. The bus lurches to a stop. The driver is an indistinct shape. Lucy had gotten on that first day without hesitation. Only a few weeks left of school. *Nothing fazes her*, Kit thinks. *Nothing has ever fazed her. And why should it?*

Lucy holds a heart-shaped stone she found on the playground. *Lift a stone.* A splinter starts in the sky. *Worlds away, time lapse.* Lucy's hand is warm. *Where else would we have gone?* Lucy drops Kit's hand and runs down the dirt road, the sky widening ahead of her, her pink sequined backpack bouncing past the red willow. Yellow and green now. *I see you still have nothing to say.*

It was like an eclipse, Kit told them. Nothing was in the right direction. The light was all wrong. Everything rearranged. Just like an eclipse only it wasn't. Afterwards there was an awareness that had not been there before. The things kids will invent, they said.

Lucy climbs the barbed wire fence, snagging. *Our hearts.* She yanks her backpack free and runs toward the house.

I think Lucy should talk to someone, Jason said. A professional. The things she concocts. We shouldn't be encouraging it. I feel like you're encouraging it.

Lucy flashes across the yard. *What we thought we saw and the light rearranged and their hands and something like hooves they had and I don't know what's what. We swore on it. Swear on it, Kitty. And we both were shaking so hard.*

Outside the house Lucy gathers bits from around the yard. Leaves, twigs, berries, pebbles. Offerings, she calls them. She arranges them on the porch. She spends hours. Methodically. There are worse things, Kit considers.

The porch darkens. *I held your hand and your hand was hot in mine and shaking and you were up ahead and I should have gone after you but you were already gone.* Lucy arranges the assortment on the porch. Then steps back, admiring her work. Rubs her hands together. "This should be sufficient," she says. She goes inside then, the screen door banging behind her. *And Lucy, three or four years old. She fell asleep inside the shells and he had not been home for weeks. At times he looked surprised when she came into the room. As though her very existence had left him dumbfounded.*

She fills the percolator. Why bother going to bed? *Apple doesn't fall far from the tree, they said. Psycho, headcase.* Chanted those girls. And she felt it like thorns. *We were sucked down into the water and I went swimming with you and we were closer and closer and we knew it was there and you've got to shut up about it, Kitty, Paul told me.* And those girls with their zebra cake. Like Stephanie and the nymph woman. Pink hands. Roses. Stephanie and the women laughed and poured. *Like those girls with their denim and zebra cake.* And Paul shifted the pickup into gear and those girls stood there on the cement and the pickup lurched and his hands were red. "Why are they looking at us like that? Kit? They're just staring." *He was probably murdered, she said.*

Kit stands and pours a cup. Paul is not back yet. *Where to?* The past slips through like water. Takes everything with it. *I can't remember right.* A hat, face, tiger. She stares at the coffee. Her reflection. *Homunculus. I'm drowning.* She had seen him, later, in the black trees. *No, I never. I'm inventing things.*

I made excuses for you, Jason said. Why you couldn't come.

They were back, Marg said. Wrecking the house. Turning over bowls and clambering up walls so she has to clean up after them and putting their feet up on things and never making any sense. Which is just as well. The light changes so fast. Inverts. Upside down, sideways. He gripped her hand and still she felt him shaking.

You can't be thinking nothing, Jason said. And past him the enormous window glimmered.

She checks on Lucy upstairs and pulls up the quilt. The cottonwoods talk out the opened window. *What we heard.* She returns to the kitchen. Pours another cup. *I've quit sleeping and maybe I'll never sleep again.*

She walks out into the yard. Having sensed. Near the barbed-wire fence they are like enormous ink blotches. Like between dreaming and awake. They move a little, as if about to run, and then stop. And wait. They shift a little, reorienting. She can see their bent limbs. *Hats?* They appear to bow. They vacillate there in the field and then saunter away. The wild loam smell hangs in the air. *Remember? You held my hand and your hand was burning or was it mine?*

She leaves the door open, unlocked. Opens the windows wider. *It's an agreement we have, I said.*

Paul comes in the front door and passes by her without saying anything, like a disparaged ghost. He is drunk. Anything to make it better, the women said. Wine, concoctions, you name it. And the way it ached inside. Something to conceal it. *Make it all go away.* Queenie emerges from a kitchen shadow and stands there behind him. "Loyal, that dog," he mumbles. "Wonder why." He pours a cup. She does not ask if he has seen them too. She knows what he would say.

69. Muskrat

"Oh, here she is."

"Lucy."

"That's right."

Marg leaned down and her hands were not hands. Her eyes were dark and darkening, like where the water pooled in the shaded places.

"Just like your mother. And you're how old now?"

"Seven."

"The age of reason."

"That's what John said."

She stood.

Her hands were tree bark.

"Seven," she repeated.

And then the muskrat Lucy saw there. In that ditch water.

"Look, Lucy," her mother said. "He's going back to the bank. That must be where he lives."

She woke.

Where am I?

The dark room. Ebony. Black.

A tomb. A heart.

She was drenched.

Sopping.

She could hear the blood in her head.

Her teeth and they were sharp and she was in the mud.

A muskrat, Marg's tree hands.

Seven angels, John said. What was it? "The age of reason. When things start making sense." He laughed and the waves broke. And Marg's bone-teeth and the mud.

"Nothing ever makes sense," her mother said to him.

"Precisely."

And he laughed again.

"I'm worried about her," she overheard her father say that last week. "She always wants to be alone. Says she wants to be alone. You should bring her. She can meet some other kids. Make some friends."

"You never wanted this," her mother said.

He did not reply.

He turned on the hall light. Saw her standing there. His face changed.

The tree knocks on the window.

And the woman with her clicking feet. She was new here, she said. So blessed, she said. The woman gave Lucy a pink vitamin water and the water tasted like syrup. *Wouldn't you like a bite, Lucy?*

Not one bite.

When she looks downstairs, she can see her uncle there and he is bowed over the kitchen table and it looks like he is playing heads up, seven up. His figure cuts out the space around. Lucy pulls back into the darkness. And she can see the stars in the window, blinking.

70. Heels

Marg wanders out to find something but she cannot remember what it is she is looking for and the sky is like paint touched with water. She tosses Pie stale bread, cake. She does not remember how she got here. *That boy, what was his name?* Earlier he had walked along the rock fence. *How did I get here?* Pie hops toward her. "I don't know what's what," she says to Pie. The cottonwoods shudder there. She has misplaced something maybe, she tells Pie. She cannot remember what. Something she was supposed to do out here. *What am I looking for?*

The girl comes by later that morning. She is elfin, peculiar. Too thin and rather homely, which endears Marg to her. The girl calls to Pie. Marg gives her cake to toss and the girl laughs and laughs. *Maybe it was her I saw out there.* Pie eats the cake and then studies them with his scheming eyes. The girl is filling a bag with cottonwood catkins. They are falling everywhere, she tells Marg. She holds a few up in her hands and they catch the sun and look like snow. Marg puffs her cigarette and Pie settles on the fencepost. *And why wouldn't she be? And where are the others? That boy?* The feeling swells inside her again. *Sundowning, the ice-woman calls it. You can't say nothing to them.* Fact is sometimes she remembers quite clearly. There are just those times where things momentarily blur, become foggy. Time, decades rearrange. And it gets confusing. And she has to be still. Things will return. They always do.

The ice woman drives up in her big, red car and parks the car in the dirt road and staggers across the yard. *Speak of the devil.* Her high heels sink into the earth. Why is she wearing heels? Lucy stares at her. Then turns and runs toward the trees. *Good sense*, Marg thinks.

Inside the ice woman peers down at the empty bowls on the floor. "Cats?" she asks Marg. Marg looks at the floor, assessing. She had left the empty bowls for Lucy to fill.

"Something like that," Marg says.

The ice woman shrugs.

"They've been ripping out my signs," the ice woman says now.

"Who?"

"I don't know. Some kids, probably."

Marg looks at the wall.

"You're laughing," the ice woman says.

"I'm not."

"Maybe I'm jinxed, they told me. Maybe something's out to get me." Her face turns red, in patches.

"Perhaps," Marg says. "Who can tell."

The ice woman shifts, her plastic jacket squeaking.

"You're getting up there," she tells Marg now. "You don't expect Paul to take care of you, do you? He's got enough on his plate."

"I'm perfectly fine."

The ice woman snorts. "And I'm the queen of England," she says.

Marg ignores her and adds sugar. They scoff at the ice woman from the bleary corners, with their seedy eyes. They seem to be mocking her. The ice woman sips the coffee and dots her lip with the cloth napkin and they leap around her. Marg draws out another cigarette from the carton and the ice woman studies her. "You shouldn't be out here all alone," she says. "And smoking like that. It'll make things worse."

"Perhaps."

The ice woman adjusts her collar. "The estates, Marg. Right along the river. You wouldn't have to do a thing. They cook all your meals. You'd have a great view. Right along the river."

The smallest one knocks one of the empty bowls. The bowl spins across the floor and the ice woman jumps. Marg blows a smoke ring. "Cats," Marg says. "Like ghosts. You hardly know they're there until they want something."

The ice woman looks around the room. The room darkens with clouds. The cottonwoods outside shake. The smallest one brushes something from his leg and crawls out the open window. *People don't see what's right in front of them. What day is it?*

The ice woman seems agitated. The woodcutter chimes in the next room. Four o'clock. The ice woman stands and pushes back her chair and Marg follows her to the front door. The sky leaps. She thanks Marg for the coffee and hopes she will reconsider. Pie is on the front porch, waiting for a handout. Marg holds the door. "Just something to think about," the ice woman says. "You've earned it. And with land prices being what they are right now."

"It's already going to Paul."

She feels the ice woman watching her, stiffly.

"You're not in the place to make this kind of decision," the ice woman manages. "Your condition."

"Nonsense," Marg says. "Pie will see you out."

She watches the ice woman climb into the big, red car and knock the mud from her heels and drive away. Quickly and never to return. Marg brushes her hands on her hips and returns into the dark house, Pie following. They think they have it under their control. "They don't even ask. No manners," she tells Pie. "As if they own the world." Pie's black eyes shine. He follows her into the kitchen. "What do you want now? Come on, come on, let's have coffee."

71. Swallows

Lucy leans on the porch railing, rotating the kaleidoscope. She had found it in the attic room. *Hidden, maybe.* The kaleidoscope broke the world into mirrored, fractured, perfectly identical prisms. Geraniums, trees, the infinite black dog. *The way we saw everything back then.* Now Lucy sets the kaleidoscope on the porch railing and they walk together out into the hayfield. She wants to go into the trees, Lucy tells her.

Paul stops the tractor in the field. He climbs down and walks around the tractor and crouches down and then stands looking first at the tractor and then at the sky. He climbs into the cab, halfway out, turns the engine off and crosses the field, head down. *Something always broken*, Kit thinks. *Can't get ahead, he used to say. Something always needing fixed.*

The swallows swoop and lift, Lucy watching. She never fit in at the private school. They were concerned, they said. *Something always needing fixed.* Queenie follows Lucy. And the water so high this time of year. *I'm walking on water, you said. Like Jesus did. Look, Kitty. Anything is possible.*

The cottonwoods drop their seeds everywhere now and the seeds turn everything blurry. Kit cannot see clearly. The trees seem to shift a little there.

72. Dusk

Marg falls asleep. When she wakes the windows are all open and she can hear the sky. *They come and they go and they come and they go and I never know where.* On her best days she knows what is what. Exactly who she is and who she is not and in what form she is existing. *I think you're still here, and then I remember.* The hat he wore and the hat still on the hook and the checkered shirt still hanging and the way he would ramble in that other language and she would not always know what he was saying but it had not mattered. They had an understanding. The way they saw things. And him down by the river that night. *Just wanted some quiet.* And so had she. And he tapped his hat and walked along the bank with her and he belonged out there. He rarely understood what they were trying to tell him. And out in the woods, or with her, it no longer mattered. They hardly had to say a thing. *I knew what you meant.*

She breaks the ash outside. *I start thinking I'm nineteen again. Wake up and there's this old lady looking back at me.* She empties the cake crumbs from her pocket for Pie and goes back inside and the sun already setting. Pie follows. *Sundowning, she says.* She has been sundowning, she tells Pie, all her life, apparently.

Inside they are nestled in the corners. Like they are napping. Funny things. She steps around them. They were here first, like he said. A part of things. *People just don't look.* What are they? She cannot remember what he called them. They had a name. It was a foreign name. They tracked in mud again. She lights another cigarette. She does not bother sweeping. Never has. The room darkens and eventually they traipse back into the trees. She sees their light out there for a little while and then only the dark.

73. Silt

Paul has to order the tractor part. A week, maybe two. *Figures*, he thinks. On his way home he stops for a drink, the sun aching through the windshield. *One, maybe two and then straight home. And now Kitty's back. Thought she'd escaped this place, everything. Guess not. You go anywhere*, he thinks now, *and the past follows you. Pulls up a chair.*

The dusted afternoon light is a band across the barroom. *A week, maybe two*. He can never get ahead. Vicki is always stopping by now. This last time she was visibly upset. Her face all red and patchy. She, Marg, should have assistance. She should not be living on her own. And by the way, she told Pau, Marg could make a fortune. *You both could, she said. A fortune.*

He stood there in the road as she drove away. The geese all flew down. They still wanted to be here.

≈ ≈ ≈

Gretchen pours him a drink. "I'm afraid I'm enabling you," she says. And she means it. The way she holds firm. The dusted light is oat-colored. The sun lowering.

"I suppose maybe you are," he says.

She winces.

She found another job, Gretchen tells him. An administrative thing. He may have a new bartender.

"Anyway," she tells Paul, "I took the liberty of making a few calls for you. About those things you found." She braces the gold rim of the bar, like she is on some sort of carnival ride. "Couldn't get a hold of anyone. Kept going to voicemail. That was a week or so ago. I haven't heard back. I'll keep trying."

His insides bristle. "It's okay," he says. "They won't call back."

She is quiet, momentarily.

"You know more than you let on, Paul. Even if you don't admit it to yourself."

They were in the trees and they were running and I saw they were there, crouched in the corners but that was a dream I must have had.

He rotates his glass.

Maybe.

Paul woke at night over the years. Having turned a stone, a face. *They were right there. Him and Kitty.* A hand, out of the river, the rock fence, the mountain shale. A hand, bone, teeth. They used to go high in the mountains until the air changed, cooled. And they reached the alpine. *Losing my mind*, he thinks now. The drink warms him. He is alone too much, he tells Gretchen. *Alone too much and you go crazy.* The light in the window weakens and is sucked up slowly. The shadows begin. *Those bones were not his bones and maybe not even human.* Pilfered, Gretchen figures.

Carrie could not have been that much older than Paul was, looking back on it. There were those magazine pictures taped to the wall. A bare lightbulb. *They had nothing. We didn't have much but they had nothing.* She was glad Patrick had a friend like Kitty, she had said. *Neighbors like you.*

He draws his knuckles through the wet ring on the bar. Gretchen touches his shoulder. Two weeks for a part, he tells her. Until then. Maybe he can weld something. Piece something together. She sits beside him. *Gretchen, at the grange.* She had braids. Sweet kid, perky. No one could shut her up. "It's like I'm tethered here," he says now. *Rooted.* He waits for her to laugh and when she does not, he is quiet. She presses his hand.

"Kit's back," he says.

"That's what I hear."

Your crackpot sister, they said. He braces the bar and sees the floor angle beneath as if it would slide away. *What did they want her to say? He's not coming back, I told her.* And she crumbled the granite in her hand. The mountain breaking open in her hand and the eons slipping past. Someone had to be realistic, Paul told their father. *You, of all people, should have known better*, he thinks now. He had gone with them to drag the river, he tells Gretchen. Every ripple of water a body, a delusion. A branch, the sun on the water. Made you sick inside, momentarily. You felt it in your guts, your knees. Until you realized it wasn't. Every movement, change of light, terrified him. He had not wanted to be there when they did find him. He did not want to be the one who did. Weeks passed. Nothing came of it. He told Kit not to say a thing. They would never believe her. They'd lock her away somewhere, he told her. That mental hospital they had driven past. *But that was a thousand years ago.*

Gretchen is propped on her elbows, watching him.

"Kit thought she saw him disappear," he says. "We never could reason with Kit after that."

Gretchen straightens.

"I don't know, Paul," Gretchen says, rubbing her fingers together. "Everyone's got some story. When you dig down real deep. Glowing orbs, ghosts, you name it. I've heard them. I know you have too. There's nothing the matter with Kitty that isn't true for pretty much everyone."

"The way they talked about it. Like it was a television drama and not someone's kid."

"Small towns," Gretchen says.

Kitty looked right at them and they hadn't noticed her there and all the blood pooled in her face and she was hot with rage. And the blood in his own head pounded too but it was out of what she might say or do. *We left them there with their eggs and bacon and Kitty with her face red like that.*

He stares at the empty glass. He is burning up inside. A *furnace.* Maybe he really could weld the broken piece.

"Kit swore she saw something," he says now. "Something in the trees. That they both did."

Gretchen pauses. She looks tired.

"I don't know why you're such a skeptic, Paul. You have every reason not to be."

He is suddenly parched.

Me and her drank right out of the falls.

"Sometimes you have to go with your gut," she says.

Don't act like you've never seen nothing.

The wall slides away. The water has spilled. When did she give him water? He tries to right himself and cannot. Things are off-center.

"We were going to get married," she says now. "Remember? You and me."

And it comes back to him then. A fire in the woods. They were kids. They were all there and they were drinking and she asked him would he walk through the fire and they did and the flames leapt around them and they walked right through it, or thought they had, felt like they had, unsinged, and she was laughing, and a fight broke out and he was pulled into it and soon after she was gone. She had driven away with someone else. "We crossed the fire," he says now. He braces the bar and the floor angles beneath him as if it would slide away and she looks like she will break down.

"Everything just goes so fast," she says, looking hard at him.

He cannot steady himself and he slides down the bar hand over hand over hand. She will give him a ride, she says. He is fine, he says. Right as rain. Her face goes dark. She adjusts his collar. "You think no one's got your back, Paul," she says. The floor opens and closes again. He finds traction.

Right as rain.

The exit sign is blurry. He feels his way toward it the same way he had passed through the spinning tunnel at the county fair when he was a kid. Slowly, methodically.

Outside he crosses the parking lot to his pickup. Checks his pocket for his keys but they are gone. He leans awkwardly against the pickup bed. Checks the ignition, under the seat. Searches the gravel beneath. Looks back at the bar. *She took my keys.* He can walk home. *Only a few miles.*

Above him the sky is immense. The stars like nail heads. He starts into the trees. *We walked through fire.* Through the trees he can hear the river flooding. He pushes through the undergrowth.

The riverbank is drenched. The trees jolt and he slips his way along the muddy bank. The moon is a ram's horn through the trees. Paul stoops above the crashing river. *Maybe I'll jump in.* How fast would it be? He cannot hear anything but the roar. It is inside him. *Has always been and you can't get away from it.* He would not have to do a thing but let the water carry him down. *You're drunk.* The river shakes an entire fallen cottonwood, pulling it downward. *I could dive in right now and say to hell with everything.* The bank is muddy. Slick. They would never find him.

Vicki shook his hand and her hand burned cold. Some kids swiped her signs, she told Paul. She had seen their tracks. *Looked weird*, she told him, *like a bunch of goats.* Probably the rain they just had.

Don't act like you've never seen nothing. They protect the land, and the people on it, Marg said.

Do they?

Can't you tell?

He can already taste the silt. Has tasted it for years. *The way it settles between things.* The cottonwood in the river thrashes hard and fast, like it is being pulled by some underwear deity. *I'm so tired.* He had considered it. Had heard of someone who tied his car battery to his feet and jumped into a lake. Simple. A quick break for it. And there were times, winters gone by, he could almost taste the acidity of metal. *But who would take care of anything?*

The bank is sopping wet and the entire damn tree is caught up in the river and bouncing there almost comically in the black water and he wants to laugh but cannot somehow and he is losing it same as Kitty and same as his mother and same as everyone. *Him in the rocks and Marg and Lucy.* The tree thrashes. *They can build their trophy homes along the river and go on their fancy fishing trips and come here to escape from the lives they thought they wanted, but the river won't stop.* The current throbs inside him like he is already drowned. *I've failed at everything.* The water is on the bank. Closer.

Saw them swimming and I yelled at them both.

And Marg breaking the ash. *Don't act like you've never seen nothing.*

The riverbed and all the rocks we stacked and they come up again every year and I do it all over again and now the water and you're drunk and you can't get it together. You're not thinking right.

A snapping then and Queenie emerges. Queenie is wet and wild-looking and she briefly greets him and then passes into some dark depression he cannot define. He calls to her but she does not return. *You think no one's got your back?* The tree thrashes.

The bones in the mud. Smooth as marble. He is shaking. *Wasn't what we thought it was, they said.* They never called back. *Something they know and won't say. Can't trust anyone.* In the river now he can see it. *A bone, driftwood.* Lit. *You've got to be kidding.*

He slips, then, suddenly, down the slick black bank and the water hits him hard and fast and he goes quickly under and then rises and grabs for the bank and the mud is slick and he claws and thrashes at the water and the water is like a hammer to the head. The river pulls him down. And then a branch. The cottonwood, caught up, buoying. A knot. He reaches for it and it snaps and hits him hard in the jaw and he falls into the deep cold fury again and he feels the water threading him along. *A knot.* The current pulls him along. *Tricked you.* Through and through and through. He tastes the silt now and it is sweeter than stone and he reaches for an anchor but there is nothing and then the paddling above. The heavy, enormous black feet and swell of body, feet, fur, belly. Above him. The black mouth comes down and the black mouth is the night and is larger and larger and the black mouth comes down around him. The water and silt are in his lungs. Silt, sand, bones. Against the current she pulls him. *Good dogs have soft mouths, black mouths. A good dog has.* Queenie drags him out of the water and she is bigger than anything and she wags and they are there and they are saying something maybe and it sounds like nonsense, nonsense, and the silt is in his lungs and it settles there between his bones and will always be and they are patting Queenie and they have crooked hands and yellow eyes and they are tossing something to Queenie and then they are leaving him on the bank and dispersing into the trees.

He crawls up onto the bank and rolls over and lays prostrate on the wet, black earth. He tries to find them, but they are already gone. Queenie stands there. Soaked and panting. Happy. And he is drunk, he decides. Way far gone. *You start to see things.*

Years ago, his father had taught him to weld. He lit the fire and he said you don't look right at it. You never look right at it. There are some things, he said, you don't look at head-on. Paul could see the flame reflected in the welding helmet where his father's face did not show and the metal connected with the liquid metal and it looked warped but it was stronger than before. *You can fix anything.*

The stars are holes punched in black tarp. *Their crooked hands.* He had seen them. *I'm drunk.*

Queenie sits beside him in the dark. A sentinel. She looks toward the brush where they had gone.

The earth is rounded, whole, and solid beneath him. *You didn't drown.* The ground is wet. He shivers. He cannot stop. *Don't act like you've never seen nothing.* He contemplates the sky. *Kitty was just a kid and they were outside.* She was already dying then and they knew it and still she had the bear-grass and he ground the stars in his fist and he found Kitty outside and the roots were pushing up through the ground. *They were in the trees, she said. She had seen them in the trees. He wanted to go, she said. He wanted to go with them and so they opened up the trees. For him. I'm drunk.*

We called Queenie in but she didn't come. She returned weeks later, fat and happy. She kept leaving and returning.

Their crooked hands.

≈ ≈ ≈

The dawn reveals branches first and then entire trees. The sun illuminates the cottonwood seeds. Shining. The river is so loud Paul can hardly hear anything beyond it. The water seeps up onto the bank. Queenie is gone. His clothes are damp and he is chilled. *Nothing's right.* He cannot remember quite what had happened. The grass is mashed up beneath him. The river laps upward, still roaring. His shoes are out there in the brush, like they had been tossed there. His head pounds. He gathers his shoes and stands, slouched. *The water and the light in the water and Queenie and I can't think.* The field is a vibrant green through the trees. Startling. He squints at it and he can hear the water behind him. The handline is covered in dew. The sky is honeyed. He stumbles, putting on his shoes. The place he had slept was like an animal had been there. There is a smoothed path down toward the river. Slashes in the mud and what looks like hoofprints. *God.* Something ripples inside him. He coughs. The river shakes the tree. *God, I've lost it.* He removes a cigarette, unsnapping his shirt pocket. Soaked. He pushes the wet carton back into his pocket and looks around. He must have walked several miles. *Isn't it enough to see the sun coming up every morning? What is it you want?* He looks at the sunny, blazing field, the river flooding behind him. He puts the wet cigarette in his mouth. *Anyway, I don't need a thing.* The field blazes. *The center of the universe is wherever you are.* Queenie appears suddenly. An obscure blur from out of the brush. She looks to be covered in some kind of sleet or snow. *Cottonwood seeds.* He reaches down and pats her and brushes the seeds away. Feels at his shirt pocket. Returns the wet cigarette. He feels grounded. Queenie turns her head away from him, toward the trees.

74. Pie

The magpie swoops down.

Black eye, beady eye.

And the image of myself in her eye.

Homunculus.

"You have something to say, Pie?"

He drops the quartz.

An offering.

He tilts his head.

"Pie. Come on. Out with it."

Shining, black.

They steal things, pluck out eyes, those kids told Patrick. They threw the stones and he tried to stop them.

"They do no such thing," Marg told him.

75. Cottonwoods

Lucy sees the cottonwoods like they are waving at her. The early morning light blazes through the small bedroom window. The same light hits her eyes when she first opens the door. The sun races across the fields and the swallows come in a swarm and the sound is full, animated. Lucy snags her sweater on the barbed wire fence. She yanks free and runs toward the cottonwoods. The cottonwood seeds shine. The dark spaces between the trees are like creatures about to awaken. *Giants, trolls,* Lucy thinks. She finds the path. The trees above her rattle. Telling stories. *I heard them.* She passes the rock fence down to the path leading into the trees. The trees come alive. *Listen, Lucy. Hear them?* There's more to things, her mother said. *Listen, listen.* She turns briefly back in the direction of the farm. The old house is lit with the morning sun. The barn. Everything is bright. The cottonwood seeds cover the ground and hold in midair and catch up in the trees and shrubs. Floating, like warm snow.

Lucy runs fast into the trees. The seeds drift past and everything deepens. She can hear the trees whispering but she cannot translate them. There is a layering. She sees the river flooding through the trees and the water runs up onto the path and the path is muddy, the river raging. There is a tree caught up in the river and it bounces there in the current. Lucy runs alongside the river. *I heard them.* The seeds are caught up in the brush and they float silver and she can hardly see through them. She runs faster until she hardly feels her feet touch the ground and it is like someone is running alongside her and she is so fast. She is becoming like the river or the air. The cottonwood seeds blur her vision and she is lighter than anything and then suddenly everything looks exactly the same.

She stops. The trees hush. Every sound is vanquished. And it is as if she is looking through the kaleidoscope. Each image rearranged and copied again and again. She does not know where she is. How to get back. Her insides quake. She turns around. *Everything is the same. North, east, west, south.* She can only hear her own breath. The absolute quiet. A *trick*, she thinks. *I don't know where I am or how to get back.* Her heart bangs. Her own breath. *I don't know where I am and they said don't come down here not with the water so high and now everything is the same and I don't know.* She can see the water moving faster and faster and the water does not make a sound. Nothing. She knocks her own ears, like they are water-logged. Everything is muted. *A trick.*

She does now know where she is and the brush alongside her shakes but makes no sound and a dark form darts quickly past and she cannot track it and she can see the water moving but the water is all around her, the molecules of water, and it is like she has entered the kaleidoscope. An image. *Only trees and water and the water cut up. Like paper cut up. I don't know where I am.* The trees shake and make no sound. The trees grow taller and taller until they sweep the cerulean. *You've never seen any blue like this blue, Lucy. Just wait, she said.* The sound is gone. She is crying and she cannot find the light and the light is wrong and the river is cut up construction paper and something is dancing around her. *Cavorting. What does this mean?* She does not even know what this means. Various words and phrases enter her mind and leave and she does not know what they mean. *Someone else's words.* The light is the wrong light. Like evening light. The cottonwood seeds cover the ground. Iridescent. The path is gone. *Erased.* Lucy draws her sleeve across her face and her face is wet and she can only hear her own breath. The path is smudged out, like charcoal on paper. *This is how you tint, shade. See where the shadows are? Find the shadows, Lucy.* Where the light doesn't hit, Muriel said. *The shadows are what bring the drawing to life, Lucy. Otherwise, it would be flat.* Lucy sits down in the path. Head in hands. Feels them scampering around.

The cottonwoods are colossal and she can hardly see the blue sky through them now and everything is rumpled up and wrong like night coming on already and she pulls her sweater over her head and stands and turns the sweater inside out. *What Marg says.* The seeds gather on her pink undershirt and she pulls them away and puts the sweater on backwards, inside out and then walks slowly backwards. Hands out like she will hit a wall. *Marg said you have to trick them and go backwards and there's no sense crying about it.* The seeds catch up the light. She senses figures beside her, hurrying past. She can sense them there, blurry. *Don't look right at them.* The light shifts. The seeds drift like snow. She walks backwards, catching her feet on stones and roots and they move right alongside her and something brushes past and she feels it there like feathers or fur and the silent stones roll beneath her feet. *Which way?* The knots on the trees blink. A *man.* And his hands are curled around in the bark and the air is thick, viscous. The knots on the trees are eyes. *They're telling me the way to go. The way out.* She can see the rock fence through the trees now, like it is angled in the sky. Like it is being pulled upward at an edge. A hazy line. A gray portion. Sudden. *It's like having the flu, a fever.* "Thank you," she says. Out loud, bowing a little. They move around her. They have muddy limbs and funny hands. She looks, closer. Right at them. And they are like beneath a stone or the stars far off. *Once you see you can't unsee.*

There is a man standing on the outskirts of the trees. That same man. Looking in the direction of the house. By the milkweed there. No, only the sudden light. Trick of light, shadow. *Doesn't matter, yes or no. Go home.*

Lucy runs, the world opening around her. The rock fence hovers in the field and the sound comes crashing back like water. Like laughter. *Their muddy hands and faces like tangled roots.* Lucy pauses in the open field. She touches the rock fence. Sturdy, real. The cottonwood seeds are gathered beneath the rock fence. Thick and luminous. *They are centuries old, she said. I could have stayed there. Gone with them. They would have let me stay.* And they are the trees and the ground and the water and they are and always have been.

The sky above is domed.

76. Nooks

The living room fills with eastern morning light. The light so bright Kit can hardly see anything else. *The sun doesn't rise, only looks like it, you said. And the sun caught up on your skin and you looked to be radiating it somehow. Getting older, losing my sight. Time goes so fast. Time is a joke.* The light fills every nook and cranny. Brighter than anything.

They tore the bunkhouse down, years later. Carried the pieces away or burned them. Left the foundation. Rock and mortar. The hollyhocks still grow there. *Nothing disappears, only changes.* The clay marbles they found. Like some truth contained that was impossible to impart. *You did not know how to exist here maybe.*

Kit came home that night. Dark so early then. And, the trees. *I was so sick and no one knew what to do for me. You've got to talk to them, Kitty, or they'll never leave you alone, was what Paul said. You've got to. Come on. And the way they turned and looked, but never straight at me, always avoiding me, like they were looking at the sun. No one knew what to say to me, I guess.* She had to get out of here, she finally told Paul.

I'm alone. No, there's Lucy upstairs. Still sleeping. The light and she can hardly see for it. She forgot how sunny it could be. The cottonwoods clatter outside.

The cottonwoods tell stories, Marg used to say. No one listens anymore. How did it go? The way Marg told it. He had gone out to fell a tree and when he cut the tree the tree bled and a man stepped out. He had become the tree or somehow been inside it. He was disoriented, grimy. A slash on his arm. He did not seem to notice the cut on his arm but was very stoved up from being in the tree for so long. They did not know what to do and frankly he scared them, so they left him alone. And after gathering their wits, you know, they returned to find him. Help him out. He had staggered home. Or where his home had been. No one was there and things looked different. He sat there in the weeds. The roof was capsized, the house filled with nettles. They've all gone, someone said, when he asked about them. *Everyone he ever had known.* All the people he had known were dead. They had no idea what to do so they just left him there, sitting in the weeds, staring at the dilapidated house. Figured they would at least give him time to think. The following day, when they returned, he was gone.

Kit sits up, head in hands.

Yes, losing my sight, mind, everything.

I can't think straight.

She and Marg went out to the path the following morning and tried to find his footprints or where they might have been and they brought a pitcher of water and they poured the water in the path where maybe he had gone. Because that was supposed to help. And the helicopters hammered overhead. "Worth a try," Marg said. They hurried back to the house without running into any of them. She did not know what to do without him. *Sometimes it's a blessing, she said. Going with them. A shelter or hideout.*

The screen door taps now and there is the hard, blue sound of the sky and he is standing there. Just standing there. His face holds some kind of resonance and she knows it is him. He regards her slowly, like someone just now making sense of things. Or having just woken. Graying temples, worn. *Liminal space,* she thinks. My *God.* Thresholds. She stands. There is a thin veil.

And here he is.

"Kitty? Nothing's the same."

I can't stand. Can't feel my legs. I can't tell what's around me. Can't tell anything apart. They were there and now you are.

He had only just gone, he says. He looks at his hands. He had gone beneath and beneath and beneath. He cannot say how. He steps into the sunny room. *Going blind, nuts,* Kit thinks. Patrick turns his hands over and over. Studies them.

Everything is holy.

"You must have noticed," she says. "Your hands."

He rubs his hands together.

Like tree bark, knotted.

Kit sees now there are bits of things stuck to him. Pieces of willow catkin and cottonwood seed. Pine needles and clumps of mud. Patrick turns his hands over and over. She stares at him.

What on earth to say?

"Coffee? I was just heating the kettle," she says.

Because, what else?

He follows her into the kitchen.

His face is in the dark now, out of the sun. It is like here, mostly, he tells her. Only different. You get used to it. He cannot explain it. He cannot explain much of anything, nor does he feel the need to. Flipped upside down, topsy-turvy. Time is not what you think. *After we ate the bread. And you at mass and your face lit. I no longer live but Christ lives. True presence. We are rarely present.*

Patrick had seen the yellow pickup days prior and so he ran into the trees and crouched down and the trees closed his father out. And Patrick could sense the knotted marl depth and substance and could smell the dark humus, water, stone. *Say you were asked.* Days later, he was gone. And the soil and furrow and gnarled white roots, beetles, spores, what have you. It was a sanctuary, he tells her, like the church. A sort of in-between. Liminal space.

She pours the coffee. Sits across from him. Holds the cup.

Familiarity.

"You're different," she says.

Pieces of lichen crumble on the table. *Tree knots, his knuckles.* She is not sure he can hold the cup. His hands are peeling, sappy. *My God.*

The same clay-marble eyes.

I'd know you anywhere.

"I waited for you," she says.

He looks at the window.

His hands are not hands.

And, yet.

Silver temples, crows' feet. Same as my own.

Things fold over, he tells her, and there is an impenetrable silence and you think you are dead but then a drumming starts in your ears and it is like listening to a seashell or being underwater. "Remember when we swam underwater? Like that." Stifled and distant-sounding and it would make some people crazy, and probably had. But to him it had made sense. Because who understands the universe better than a kid?

"And now you're here," she says.

"I've been here all along. More or less."

"The hell you have. What you put us through."

Make haste.

He looks at her.

"They tore down your house," she tells him.

"And her?"

"She went north somewhere. It nearly killed her."

He blinks.

Detritus, sleep.

"I waited and waited," Kit says. "It made me crazy. I tried to tamp it down and it kept rising up. I had to come back here. This is the only place I can exist."

He turns his hands, studying them. Looks up at her.

"We swam out there, Kitty. Remember? You and me. The bank was so black. It was like looking at the night sky. The bits of granite and mica, like stars. Upside down."

"That was a long time ago."

"Not really."

He seems boyish, soft. *Other than the crumbling bark, the earth.* He has not touched his coffee. *Can't.*

She does not know what else to say.

Chokecherry hands, woody.

His teeth are wood or seeds.

"I didn't know how long." he says.

How fast time goes.

"Is there anyone else here?" he asks.

"Paul. He's out. And Lucy."

"Lucy," he says, straightening a little. "I thought she was you."

He turns his hands. Over and over.

"She found me," he says.

Out of the tree.

He knots his hands.

This kind of thing isn't real. Our minds play tricks on us.

"Lucy," she says, standing.

Jesus.

Kit rushes up the steps and there is Lucy's window, wide open. Her bed, empty. The blankets on the floor. The curtains flutter. *Where?*

Downstairs she stops, briefly, in the kitchen. He is standing, bent a little. "I can't stay," he says.

"Of course not."

He looks at the window and his face is in the light and not in the light. He is beneath or through or past. *None of this is happening.*

≈ ≈ ≈

The swallows quicken past. A cloud, torrent. *Lucy.* The ground is resplendent with cottonwood fluff. As if it had fallen all at once, in one go. *It wasn't like this yesterday.* The ground is almost white with it. She calls for Lucy and there is no response. Through the trees the river flashes. She hurries through the trees with the sunlight flickering down and stops at the riverbank and shouts again and the river pulses and thunders and grabs and something like electricity shoots right to her gut. *I shouldn't have brought her here. I never should have.* The river roars. *Anything but her.*

And at the townhouse Lucy pushed out the window screen so the ocean was right there. She always wanted to be close to it. *The crux of things.* Along the beach there were those caves and Lucy was in the gloaming and she never responded when Kit called her back. Spellbound. And the tide crashed on the rocks and sometimes she, Lucy, was like a stranger. *The ocean is a fact. The river. You still have to.* And the screen down in the rocks. *She maybe was leaning there. As if she were being pulled. Say you were asked. Lucy. Say you.* And you could get too close to the ocean, the trees. And those things could sweep you away. *Anything could sweep you away.* "There's something wrong with her," Jason said. "The things she does." And his expression, hard as concrete. "If you don't make an appointment, I will."

Kit stands on the riverbank. The river is distorted, bulging. Vertigo. There are times she feels like the space around her is twisted up. Ask the river to find him, the story said. *The girl threw in her shoe and the river answered and they found him there and they brought him out and their hands were not hands and their eyes were not eyes.* "Your head is in the sand, Katherine," he said. "You're not being rational."

Say you were asked.

The river roars. The swallows shatter across the water and through the trees and in the direction of Marg's house. *Not the birds but the shadows of the birds.* Time stops. A thin veil. The river stops. Moves and halts at the same time. *Something that's deep inside us maybe and we don't know it's there until it comes charging out.* Kit turns back toward the open field. Lucy is running along the rock fence. On her way home.

They all had it. Because they had lived here long enough that what was hidden in the landscape had revealed itself to them. And after they had witnessed this, like some seismic event, they could not return to their former selves.

She sees Patrick now, faraway in the trees. A *figment, a reality*. He stops and waves and she waves back. *Time is a joke*. Patrick melds into the trees, into the dark.

"We have things to do," her father had said, leaving the church, all those years ago. "We need to get home."

≈ ≈ ≈

The door is open. As it always has been. Always open. *You kids don't need to knock, don't be silly. You come right on in.* The dust is in a column of early morning light. There is Lucy, the floor seeming to rise beneath her. The roots are expanding beneath the house. The trees around seem closer. Lucy is covered in cottonwood seeds. Kit stares at her. *Like she's lit from within. Same way you were.* Kit cannot speak. A stone caught in her throat. *River stone, heart stone, quartz. What we found there.* The percolator is going now and Lucy with her mussel shell eyes says it does not matter because it all goes around again. Lucy's face shines. *Like Moses down from the mountain.*

Marg emerges out of the darkness. "Well, now," Marg says. Beneath Lucy is the same rag rug. The end trailing, unfinished. *Something or someone I forgot.* Kit sits down. *So tired.* Marg pours them coffee and lights a cigarette and smokes, tapping the ashes on the windowsill. She does not need to ask. *She already knows.*

77. Crossings

Lucy would wonder now and then. Years later, the world being what it was. She knew they would never believe her and consequently she would never bother telling them. *Keep quiet about it, Lucy. Their eyes like mud and their funny hands. Centuries, eons. Older than dirt.* She could have gone with them, if she had wanted to. Could have. *That bread and light they held in their mouths.*

But this is neither here nor there.

Acknowledgments

A world of thanks to Christine and Danilo at Baobab Press for their insight and expertise, and for taking a chance on this weird little book. I am grateful to Deirdre McNamer, for her generosity. Always, with much love—Dave, Tess, Claire, Mom, Dad, Andy, Alan, Lesley, Kevin, and Jennifer. And to the land, my constant muse.

Photo by Sara K. Ashline

Joan Maki was raised on a fourth-generation farm in western Montana. She holds an MFA in Creative Writing from The University of Montana in Missoula. She has an affinity for open spaces, dark nights, back roads, and forests. She lives in western Montana with her family. *Undercurrents* is her first novel.

ADVANCE PRAISE FOR

A SENSE OF THINGS BEYOND

"A deeply emotional, haunting story about the secrets buried during wartime and the heartbreaking lessons that follow, *A Sense of Things Beyond* explores how to face the past once more, how to bring those secrets into the light, then how to live again."
—**GENEVIEVE GRAHAM**, bestselling author of ***Bluebird*** and ***The Secret Keeper***

"In *A Sense of Things Beyond*, Belliveau challenges us to look beyond 'glorious victory' to the true cost of war, the moments between breaths that shaped Rose and Frederick during the First World War, and the recognition that those who were not on the front lines felt as if their experiences were less notable. This is a quiet story and yet tough and tensile, driven by endearing characters who will capture your heart with both their softness and strength and keep you turning the pages long into the night."
—**DONNA JONES ALWARD**, author of ***When the World Fell Silent***

"In this poignant novel, Renée Belliveau challenges us to have compassion for our enemy. To reconsider how the vanquished are punished. And above all, to question the rhetoric that glosses over the carnage that is war. This is a story that is tender, hopeful, and eminently eye-opening."
—**CHRISTINE HIGDON**, author of ***Gin, Turpentine, Pennyroyal, Rue***

"Belliveau's compelling and poignant *A Sense of Things Beyond* takes aim at the hypocrisy of the Imperial war machine and highlights the oft overlooked efforts of women who laboured under horrific battlefield conditions only to return to a life that sought to erase their efforts. Shifting in timelines from bucolic beachcombing in Nova Scotia to festering, overcrowded field hospitals, to an alien detention camp in Berlin, Belliveau's characters deftly exist in a kind of half-life, burdened by the secrets they hold, searching for a balm for hidden wounds. Redemptive, profound, and gorgeously crafted."
—**STEPHENS GERARD MALONE**, author of ***Jumbo*** and ***The History of Rain***

"Renée Belliveau illuminates the dark corners of history to reveal lesser known perspectives from the First World War. In the aftermath of all those awful battles, whose stories get remembered, and whose fade into oblivion? Can some type of deeper healing come from remembering the forgotten, and recognizing that war is never glorious? In questioning the myths we've been told about this transformative period, *A Sense of Things Beyond* tackles hard topics, but also unfolds as a tender love story about two people grappling with war's intangible wounds."
–**KRISTEN DEN HARTOG**, author of ***The Roosting Box: Rebuilding the Body After the First World War***

PRAISE FOR
THE SOUND OF FIRE

A Quill & Quire Best Book of the Year (2021)
Shortlisted for the ReLit Award for Fiction (2022)

"Belliveau has created an immersive sensory experience, using vivid snapshots of the many lives affected by a devastating fire. But against this backdrop of death and destruction, there is an enduring gentleness…A heart-wrenching and gripping story, incredibly told."
–**NICOLE LUNDRIGAN**, author of ***The Widow Tree***

"Both riveting and tender, *The Sound of Fire* is an unexpected page-turner rich with historical detail and an interconnected cast of vibrant characters. Belliveau's clean yet emotive prose paints a captivating portrait of a tragic fire in a small community told from multiple perspectives, including, most strikingly, from the fire itself."
–**DEBORAH HEMMING**, author of ***Throw Down Your Shadows***

"Using a kind of personalized-archive technique to piece vivid shards of historical and imagined detail into an intricate mosaic, and told from the dozens of individual perspectives of those whose lives were changed by the events, *The Sound of Fire* sets a very local tragedy against the larger contexts of the still-lively memories of one world war and the ongoing carnage of another."
–**MARK BLAGRAVE**, author of ***Lay Figures***